YURI VII

OLEG SAPPHIRE

THE HUNTER'S
CODE

The adventure begins!
Yuri Vinokuroff

BOOK THREE

PUBLISHED BY MAGIC DOME BOOKS

The Hunter's Code
Book # 3
Copyright © Yuri Vinokuroff, Oleg Sapphire 2024
Cover Art © Vladimir Manyukhin
English translation copyright © Alix Merlin Williamson 2024
Published by Magic Dome Books, 2024
All Rights Reserved
ISBN: 978-80-7693-430-6

ALL BOOKS
BY THE AUTHORS:

The Hunter's Code
by Oleg Sapphire and Yuri Vinokuroff

An Ideal World for a Sociopath
a LitRPG series by Oleg Sapphire

War Eternal
a LitRPG series by Yuri Vinokuroff

I Will Be Emperor
a Space Adventure Progression Fantasy Series
by Yuri Vinokuroff

The Healer's Way
A LitRPG Series by Oleg Sapphire & Alexey Kovtunov

TABLE OF CONTENTS:

CHAPTER 1

"MAY I COME IN, Sir?"

"Ah... Galaxius. Do come in! What brings you here?"

"I need your help, Sir."

"Is that so?" The head of the Monster Slayer Center, Duke Vasily Petrovich Khrulyov, tore himself from the papers before him and raised his head. "Judging by the reports I've received, help is the last thing you need. Is Galaxius himself truly asking for aid?"

"Everyone needs help sometimes, Sir."

"True enough," the old Slayer chuckled. "Would you like some tea?"

"Sure."

To my surprise, he didn't call in his secretary, but stood up himself, walked over to the big samovar, picked up a large cup and filled it with

1

aromatic tea.

Then he smiled mysteriously. "Honey?" he asked.

"Please." I nodded again.

"I'm afraid my honey isn't from Azure Bees, although it isn't bad either." Mischief flashed in the old class-two Slayer's eyes.

That caught me off guard.

"Someone snitched, huh?"

"Snitched? Oh, no, not at all." He placed a large cup before me, and a jar of transparent honey beside it. "Reported. It was a response team, after all. They are obliged to report such incidents."

I shrugged. "They nearly killed me."

At that, the old man laughed.

"Somehow that seems unlikely to me. But yes, you acted by the book. Only, Count Fyodorov has been whining ever since that you took his gear away."

"I can give it back if necessary. Though there is one problem... My apartment was blown up. If the firemen find the sword, I'll give it back."

The old man's smile dropped.

"Yes, I heard of your misfortune. My sympathies."

"Thanks," I nodded. "Actually, that's why I'm here."

The old man sat back in his chair and looked at me with interest.

"I need to live in the Center for a little while."

Clear intrigue flickered in the old man's eyes.

"How long is a little while?"

"Just until I solve certain..." I faltered. "...difficulties."

The old man drummed his fingers on the table, his gaze fixed on me, apparently thinking something over.

"You do understand that we aren't running a hotel here, yes?"

"I do, but I'm willing to pay..."

"And I don't need your money," the Slayer interrupted me.

"So it's a no?" I frowned.

"I didn't say that. You are young and brash, but still a Slayer. Your reputation speaks for itself, and your potential..." The old man scratched his gray head. "Well, I can't even predict it myself, to be frank. That hasn't happened for a long time. Normally, I can see right through all you types. Will you tell me how you closed those Rifts?"

I leaned back and crossed my arms.

"Sorry, no can do. If that's a condition of my staying here, then I'll have to get gone."

"Oh, relax," the Center chief said, waving a hand. "Just an old man's curiosity. As for your stay here, you'll have to work it off."

"How, exactly?" I pricked up my ears.

"I will assign several Rifts to you. You will have to close them."

He saw me tense up.

"Don't worry, I'm not planning to make a slave of you. Just two or three problematic Rifts. On one condition — that you take others along with you.

A group of Slayers that I select."

Thinking about it, I already had to close them all the time anyway, so why not go with them, so they could see that I was just doing the same job they were? After all, if I always went alone, then they'd invent stories about some great Gift that I was hiding. Instead, I could beat up some monsters side by side with them, and at the same time get a boost to my karma. It wouldn't look right for me to agree too fast, though.

"Can't I just do them alone?" I asked, keeping the scowl on my face. "I'd find that a lot simpler. I'm used to only having to look after my own ass."

"No. This one is a condition of your stay. I consider it entirely reasonable. You can take it or leave it."

I nodded. I'd have to try hard to make sure I didn't get found out. But the old man was right — it was a reasonable condition.

"Fine then, I agree. But I need a few days first for a business trip. In the meantime, there's a girl that needs to stay here, and I'd like you to keep an eye on her."

"Not a problem. We'll watch her like a hawk. Her room service check will be waiting for you when you get back. Ha-ha..." The old man smiled at his own joke.

"Thank you, Sir!"

I stood up and offered him my hand. Groaning, the old man shook it.

"Come on, no need to rush off. Finish your tea, and let's just chat."

* * *

Well, what can I say? They set us up comfortably in the guest barracks for Slayers. Unlike the regular barracks for new recruits, here there were individual rooms.

Our small two-room suite had just barely enough space for the both of us. But all that mattered was that we were inside the Center. Doubtful that King could reach us here. Imperial oversight, and all that. This place was unassailable and untouchable.

"Learned anything?" I asked Anna, who was going through some papers.

Yep. Shnoop didn't burn up absolutely everything. In one of the premises marked by Anna as an accountancy office, he was able to make off with a drawer of documents from the chief accountant. The department it was from was officially above-board. King's legal businesses went through it. And they were what Anna was studying now.

"I have two targets for you," the girl said. "Here and here."

She tossed two folders to me. I sat down and took a look.

"A pig farm and a slaughterhouse? Seriously, these are the best options?"

"Funnily enough, the slaughterhouse brings in thirty percent of his legal income, and the pig farm — twenty percent. And let me tell you, that means big numbers."

"Is meat that expensive nowadays?" I chuckled. "Maybe we're in the wrong business. Should I go learn to be a farmer?"

"Not a bad idea," Anna smiled. "But no. The numbers I saw can't possibly match what's really there. I have a rough knowledge of the meat market in the Empire. Basically, in order to provide that kind of income, that slaughterhouse would have to be four times larger, and working around the clock. And the pig farm would have to be at least ten times the current size. Something doesn't add up."

"Right," I nodded. "I'll take care of it."

I stared glumly at the last weapon I had left — the huge club, — and scratched my head. I didn't like the idea of lugging that big thing around. And buying more crap from Arkhip... Might as well throw my money away.

The firemen still hadn't called me. Probably still picking through the ruins. Maybe they'd find something there, but I couldn't be sure.

I sighed and hefted the huge club onto my shoulder, spending a little power to strengthen my body. I'd have to keep powering my body with energy while I carried it. But what can you do? A penny saved is a penny earned!

"Epic outfit," Anna said, grinning as she looked at me.

I looked at myself in the mirror.

Alright, so the tip of the club was bigger than my head. And with the spines sticking out, maybe

I did look a *little* comical.

"Don't hate the player!"

I waved the weapon a couple of times and accidentally knocked over the coat hanger by the door.

"Alright, I'm off. See you."

We were renting the property here, after all. It was all I needed to trash the place.

"Alright, good luck!" Anna said. "And be careful."

I left our room and headed down the corridor, then was met with a surprise at the porch — Helga, standing there with a thoughtful look on her face.

"Hey there, beautiful!" I chuckled, watching with pleasure as the girl blushed at the innocent compliment.

"Decided to move house, huh?" the girl asked.

"Where's the 'hello,' the hugs and kisses?"

Helga ignored my fooling around.

"I heard you didn't come here alone."

"Ooh, you have spies!" I grinned at her. "Yeah, that's my colleague."

"Colleague?" The girl raised an eyebrow in surprise.

"Well, yeah. Why, what did you think..?"

"I thought she was a pros..." Helga broke off. "Sorry, I'm rushed off my feet today."

"Oh, no need to apologize." I shrugged. "How've you been, anyway? I heard from Andrei that you're planning on leaving. I don't know what your mysterious task was here. Or what the hell you were doing here at all. But I get the picture your work is done. I'm surprised to see you still here, actually."

"I've extended my... business here," Helga said thoughtfully. "Are you staying with us for long?" she asked as if in passing.

"Depends how things go."

"And where's that monstrosity from?" She nodded towards the club. "Headed out to sell it?"

"Nah, decided to get a little exercise."

"A Rift?" Helga widened her eyes. "Like this?"

I looked down at myself. Alright, so my chainmail and armguard were gone, and I had no throwing knives left. So I was standing there all smart, in my civilian suit, with a huge club over my shoulder. So what?! Stylish, youthful, fashionable. Just right for raiding some Rifts.

"Want me to lend you some money?" Helga asked with a sympathetic frown.

"Whoa there, girlfriend!" I laughed. "Things aren't that bad yet. I'm not bankrupt. I have money. It's just that this," I swept a hand down my outfit, "is more than enough for me for now. After all, I have this beauty here on my team too."

I petted Caramel on the head. Helga's gaze softened at once.

"Hey, little friend." To my surprise, she came closer and stroked the panther's head before I had time to open my mouth.

Wow! And she didn't even bite her hand off. I could see Caramel accepted her as a friend. What had they got up to, for the panther to be so friendly with her?

"Want me to come along with you?" Helga asked, again as if as an afterthought.

"Thanks, but not today."

The girl's gaze darkened a little.

"Well, you know, your Grandpa made me agree to a few raids. So if you pull some strings, and something tells me you have them, then you can get yourself into my raid group. Looking forward to seeing you there," I said with complete sincerity, and realized that it was true.

The girl's eyes softened just a little.

"Well, alright. By the way, there's a surprisingly good bar here on grounds of the Center. If you suddenly feel like taking a night out..." Her eyes darted toward the window, where Anna was watching us.

"Are you asking me on a date?" I narrowed my eyes.

"Ugh, Galaxius, you're such a dumbass! You really know how to ruin everything!" Helga huffed angrily, then turned on her heel and walked away.

"Strange girl," I chuckled. "Come on, furball." I nodded to Caramel, who was growling at me unkindly.

You are a dumbass, I heard in my head.

"Oh, you're talking again, huh?" I said. "Whatever, let's go. Time to play some dirty tricks on some bad guys!"

The first target for one of those dirty tricks was the pig farm.

I couldn't see anything at all over its high

walls. The place was like a fortress. On the other hand, Shnoop could see inside them just fine. I sat off to the side and carefully looked at everything he showed me. Strange, but it really was a pig farm.

The more Shnoop crept around, the greater my surprise. Just an ordinary pig farm. Pigs grunting in their sties, sows feeding piglets. All clean, nothing amiss.

But when Shnoop got to the logistics center, matters took a turn. First of all, I saw that the logistics center was a kind of 'state within a state.' It had two vehicles for loading. Ordinary trucks at first glance. Judging by the thickness of the doors, they were armored at least as well as a Center APC. They were partly filled with oinking and screeching pigs, and just now they were in the process of loading. Shnoop crept further in.

Whoa! A stubborn pig was dragged into a cozy building, and the people sitting inside deftly packed up a jelly and stuffed it into the animal's mouth, forcing it to swallow. Then they put a small, barely noticeable stamp on its belly. After that, the pig was immediately sent out to be loaded up. Then another. And another.

"How much time do we have?" one of the packers asked, wiping his brow.

"We've only just started, plenty more to be done. Let's go for a smoke, then get back to it."

The men walked out, past the beefy guards.

And Shnoop immediately stuck his curious nose into the containers standing nearby. One was full of white jellies, another of red. Ton of jellies.

I chuckled.

"Bring those here, my friend!"

And bring them he did, though it took him several trips back and forth.

After counting, I realized that I was richer by two hundred and forty-three white and thirty-four red jellies, the total worth of which at today's prices was almost thirty thousand rubles!

As I counted the loot again with a grin, the screech of an alarm split the air. Shnoop was frolicking nearby, and I winked to him.

"That's all, no more need to go back there. We've done what we came to do. Now let's get out of here, fast!"

A question kept spinning in my head — why go to all that trouble to hide jellies?

And then I remembered the destination of the cargo — the Khanate of the Grand Steppe. Right! A permanent enemy of the Eastern Empire, they had a habit of attacking the Empire's borders whenever their warlike ruler got in a mood. From what I remembered, it was forbidden to sell weapons to them. And jellies were a kind of weapon too, definitely a dual-purpose item at best. They came under the ban, anyway. Whereas trading in foodstuffs was allowed. King had to be making a sizable profit on this contraband. Well, better leave the target in peace for now. Maybe I'd come back here again, and more than once or twice.

I didn't bother calling a taxi, just walked. Who

knows what connections King had, after all. And I knew I'd be suspect number one, considering the circumstances of the disappearing goods. No need to make his job any easier. I just hailed a passing truck and the trucker gladly gave 'Sir Slayer' and his fine 'kitty' a ride.

The slaughterhouse was on the other side of Irkutsk. I asked him to drop me off in the city center, which he did, and refused to even take any money for it. Then I looked thoughtfully at the sack of jellies. Couldn't cart them around with me, and it wasn't an option to give them to Arkhip either. I could hand them in at the Center. But maybe King had connections there too.

An idea came into my head that we'd pulled off recently in the park.

"Shnoop, go search!"

We were in an old part of the city, and Shnoop crept down to where there were numerous tunnels underground. Fifteen minutes, and he found a dry tunnel segment covered with a rusty grate and a just as rusty lock. Some service room for the local utilities. Didn't look like anyone had been down there in some time. After sending the sack of jellies there, I asked the little critter very politely to please, please remember where it was. I took a look around myself, taking note of the surroundings. I didn't want to end up like a dog who'd buried a bone and then forgotten where he put it. I'd have to start keeping bookmarks at this rate. Ha-ha!

Well, now for the slaughterhouse.

And again, our examination began with an

apparently real and straightforward business. A holding section into which the unfortunate cattle were driven to await the slaughter. Tiled sections partly splattered in blood, partly already washed.

Where was the catch here?

No sooner did I ask the question than Shnoop found himself on the carcass cutting floor. What a strange cow... I asked Shnoop to get closer to it. It was almost twice the size of an ordinary cow, and looked maybe three times as heavy. It also had six legs. And horns that a bison could envy.

As I watched, its skull was split open with a circular saw, and a white jelly was cut from the brain. That confirmed my suspicions. After that, they went on skillfully cutting up the carcass as if nothing was amiss.

Oh, now this was starting to get interesting!

Shnoop took our search further. And, of course, in a large secure hangar, he found a Rift.

You clever bastard, King!

Two men happened to be walking out of the Rift, and they looked nothing like Slayers. Judging by their transparent rings, they were simple workers. The rings were only there to let them into the Rift. They were bringing out the corpse of another cow on a cart.

"Rift farming, huh?" I chuckled.

Now that was something else!

It was getting dark. Large spotlights switched on around the perimeter. Electric current ran up through the wire fence. People moved on watch towers, aiming machine gun barrels in all directions.

Still, I needed to get inside. I sent Shnoop out scouting again with a specific goal. This time, my interest lay in the substation that powered this whole complex. I sent one Salamander that way, and a second to the fighters' barracks. And asked them to kill themselves.

A huge buzzing shock filled the air. And, unsurprisingly, all the lights shut off in the area. The only sources of light left were two merry blazes, one where the substation had stood and another at the barracks.

I ran up to the perimeter, filled my club with power and slammed it into the wall.

Shit! Overdid it a little — the whole section of wall fell in.

I chuckled. This club wasn't as bad as it looked.

Next, taking advantage of the panic, I just made a break for my target.

The guards were weakly Gifted, and I took them down without slowing. The idiots didn't even have infrared goggles in case they lost visibility. I didn't have any either, but I did have my infrared Shnoop instead, whose vision allowed me to see everywhere. We'd practiced it plenty in our past life. Yeah, it took extra energy. He sat on my shoulder and I just switched to looking through his eyes.

Ordinary workers were running all over the place. The Rift was open, and I ran into it. And headlong into some fully equipped fake Slayers, whose rings burned with a white light. Apparently they were strong enough to kill the local mutant cows. And one of them held a sword with a pleasant greenish tint. As my Shnoop would have said: "W-w-wwaaant!"

I smiled and slammed my club into the chest of the closest as I ran. Fair credit, he had experience, and had trained his Gift well. He managed to power up his armor in time, and instead of exploding in a shower of blood, he flew back and fell down unconscious.

The second one couldn't think of anything smarter to do than power up his body and attack me. A purple bolt flashed by my right side — Caramel flying into the unlucky gang member. They rolled away together. Before they stopped, the panther's claws were ripping through his armor. The first scream told me when his armor fell. A few seconds more, and the Slayer stopped twitching.

"You could work a little cleaner, you know," I said, frowning at Caramel, who walked off to one side and started licking her paws.

Really — the man was torn to shreds. I carefully took off his belt and scabbard and sheathed the sword that Caramel had knocked away from him with her first hit. I was right! Karsk steel! True, it was on the short side, but beggars can't be choosers.

Two white jellies. And that was all.

I walked up to the second man, still stunned. He was still breathing, albeit lying unconscious.

Looked like I'd broken the hell out of his ribs and they pierced his lungs, judging by the bloody foam at his lips. The man was done for. Well, unless he got a good healer right away. But he wasn't going to.

"Nothing personal, pal," I said with a chuckle, cutting his throat.

His cheap alloy sword went into my bag, and I pulled the ring from his finger, which turned transparent after the death of its owner. I turned it over in my hand. Like I thought — no identifying number at all. This person wasn't enrolled in the Center, and didn't train there. This was purely King's personal army.

I took two jellies from him too, and carefully examined his equipment. Ordinary riveted leather armor. Armor for our world, with no special bonuses at all apart from the special stink.

"Damn, boys, do you ever wash?" I grimaced, then climbed to my feet.

I saw cows grazing in the distance, and sighed heavily. I liked animals more than people, but I had no choice. Weighing both the swords in my hand, I smiled and just tied them to the back of my backpack, picking up my monstrous club again. Waving it a couple of times, I headed toward the herd. I wondered — would one hit be enough to take the head off one of those beasts? Better for them not to suffer, after all.

* * *

I emerged from the Rift as dirty as ever, bloodied, but entirely satisfied. I'd played my dirty trick on the bad guys, closed a Rift and even gotten some souls, even if I did have to slice up some animals in the process. The zone had been child's play. All I had to do was kill all the monsters, which I did.

Shnoop showed me that nobody was waiting for me outside. They must have been busy with the chaos in the slaughterhouse. I walked out and smiled. Then I took out a marker with my number on it, drew a happy smiley face on the label, and stuck it into the ground outside the Rift. Dusting off my hands, I quickly left the slaughterhouse, now far less financially viable than it was before.

Right, Anna was set up and under watch. And I'd kicked up the hornet's nest. Now I had to give things time to settle down. And in the meantime, hello, mysterious Empire of the Rising Sun!

* * *

King's bunker

King raged and stormed. He had nearly torn apart his observation room. Luckily, he stopped himself in time. That equipment was damn expensive. Instead, he tore apart the adjoining recreation room. Around him were the smashed remains of the billiard table and a multitude of bottles of expensive alcohol.

"Find him!" he shouted. "Find that son of a bitch and kill him!"

"But he's in the Monster Slayer Center, boss."

"I don't give a rat's ass! Storm the place! Blow it all to hell!"

"Ivan Ivanovich, do you really want to declare war on the Empire?"

Of course King didn't want that. He was just angry. That bastard had got him again.

"Place guards around the Center! Don't let a single one of those sons of bitches get by us. As soon as he shows up there, report to me at once. Send all our forces there!"

King's phone beeped. He glanced at it, and his face darkened.

"Dammit! Stand them down."

"Sorry, Ivan Ivanovich? Stand down... who?"

"All of them!"

King looked at the photo he'd been sent. In the background was a sandy beach, in the foreground a billboard: *Welcome to Odaiba Beach!* And, in the snow-white sand, a stick or finger had written:

2:1

CHAPTER 2

I HEARD ABOUT THE EMPIRE of the Rising Sun for the first time in my early childhood, when I watched anime-style cartoons on the TV. I remembered that the large-eyed girls and boys had made me laugh then. I asked my tutor — was this some special human race with the largest eyes in the world? As it turned out, it was the other way around. That was the first strangeness I discovered from the Empire of the Rising Sun.

Then, when I grew up and started training, I met a narrow-eyed Master from the Japanese empire, who easily took down three of our own Masters in an exhibition match. I also remembered that my father had been very disappointed. In the end, he paid some enormous sum of money for the Japanese visitor to train up his personal bodyguards.

I had always been interested in power since I was a young boy, as soon as I recognized myself in this body, and in my past life too. Human power first of all. Early on, I moved from kid's books to a focused study of the history of the Earth. That's when I learned about the Epicenters, and the fact that there were several of them on the planet. In Eurasia one was in the Eastern Empire, and the other just so happened to be in the Empire of the Rising Sun. And although the Imperials had full control over their own Epicenter, the Japanese had a real nightmare to deal with. After all, it's hard to control something several miles under the water. That's right — the 'Japanese' Epicenter, as it was called for simplicity, was over a hundred miles from the eastern shore of the Japanese archipelago.

And it was based on this very Epicenter that the scientists of the world learned just where the uncontrolled development of unclosed Rifts could lead. At first, from what I understand, there were ordinary Rifts there, and all the sweet little critters that emerged from them died instantly, crushed by the pressure of the profound depths. Some of them even floated up to the surface, when they didn't get eaten by the beasts of the deep first. For some time there were even fishermen toiling above the Japanese Epicenter, catching the lightly chewed corpses of Rift beasts.

From what I could tell, in some ways they really did have a tougher time of it than the EE. You have to reach a Rift somehow, but the waters were teeming with beasts. All they could do was guard the coastline.

And then, it seemed, the Rifts evolved, started to spew out beasts that could breathe and live under the water. Problems began with shipping. Monsters attacking civilian ships. Armed escorts had to be sent out.

But it didn't stop there. After some time, either the beasts started to mutate here or they changed in their source world of the Rifts. The scientists didn't have a clear answer either way. In any case, beasts began to appear who successfully left the Rifts and reached the shores of the Empire of the Rising Sun, since it was the closest land. They crawled out onto the shore and started making life interesting for the inhabitants.

On top of that, the bastards evolved to be even larger. Huge mountains of flesh started slithering onto the shore. The Japanese had to go to quite some effort to defeat them. I recalled that I even got hold of a comic about Godzilla in my childhood. That was what they called the first beast that suddenly appeared on the unprotected shores of Tokyo Bay. So many lives were lost then!

Currently, the entire east of the Empire was a multi-tiered defensive net complete with artillery and missile platforms, aircraft and endless garrisons.

Even the global community appreciated the usefulness of the Rising Sun. After all, if the monsters destroyed the Japanese islands, they would continue on to Korea, the Dragon Empire and the Eastern Empire. Accordingly, the strongest guarantor countries wrote a law on the neutrality of the Empire of the Rising Sun.

It particularly concerned their neighbors Koreans, who had constant squabbles with them. When the cunning Koreans once again took advantage of a mass attack by Rift monsters on the eastern shore to mobilize their own army and attack the Japanese in the flank, the Pacific Imperial Fleet made it abundantly clear that it would not stand for it. And the dragons took advantage of the commotion to nibble away at the northern borders of Korea. The Korean Empire had caused no more trouble since then. And the Empire of the Rising Sun had unwittingly become something of a permanent sword and shield of the eastern borders of Eurasia. It was no wonder that through all of this, the society's highest values were valor and bravery, and the education of children was aimed exclusively at the martial sciences.

As expected, Dolgorukova chose the most expensive hotel in Kyoto, Celestial City, and immediately rushed off to tend to her own affairs — reconnaissance work, as she put it.

I didn't stay in the room for long. Checking my smartphone and studying where I could go, I drew up a plan.

"Reception?" I asked, dialing a number on the room phone, which only had Japanese characters on it.

I spoke in English, and when I got a positive

answer on the third try, I celebrated.

"Send lunch for two up to my room, please. Meat and seafood." Praise be that they didn't ask me to be more specific.

Caramel was pleased with the delicious marbled steak they brought up for her.

After eating, I went to take a look at the capital of fierce narrow-eyed warriors. The coastline in Kyoto looked incredible. With my own eyes I could now see what I'd seen so much of online, read so much about. The sheer size of the coastal batteries was astounding. They were larger than any other naval cannons in existence, and made to order.

And not far away stood the Japanese fleet at anchor in the bay, mostly consisting of small destroyers bristling with depth charges. Patrol flotillas constantly kept watch between the islands and the Epicenter. In the case of an early detection of monsters, the entire standby fleet moved out to the signal and dropped mines down on the monsters' heads.

"What's up?" I looked at Caramel, who was pointing a paw at a ship.

She looked at me with her cunning eyes. "Meow?"

I sighed heavily. "No... They won't take us fishing with them."

There was a fish restaurant not far from us, and the whole pier smelled of fish. We were heading right towards it.

A little further out there were a few

battleships and cruisers sitting at anchor, but their task was to deal with monsters not far from the shoreline, in case any of them managed to reach the shallows, or, God forbid, the shore itself. The choice of smaller destroyers wasn't by chance. Sometimes it happened that a monster attacked ships, and then what mattered most was maneuverability. Or, if they were destroyed, then low cost. Losses are unavoidable in any war. If the general has a way of minimizing them, he uses it.

Most surprisingly of all, life in the city went on as normal behind all these fearsome fortified armaments. The small sandy beach was filled with people relaxing at their ease. The locals must have been used to the situation here, or maybe they'd just gotten tired of being afraid.

The panther sniffed the air a couple more times, then went nuts. What could I do? My pet was a greedy guts. No choice; we had to stop in at the restaurant.

After some fish and a seven-hundred-ruble bill, I went to the beach and sent a message to King. I paid by card, so I didn't have to carry the local currency.

And with the light sensation of a debt repaid, I decided to take a walk through the city, a little embarrassed by the constant bows I was getting from random passersby. At first I didn't understand what that was about, and then I realized that the ordinary nod of greeting from the people who for some reason didn't see my ring was very different from the waist-deep bow of those who did see it.

Seemed like they had more respect for Slayers here than back home. Makes sense; here in the Empire of the Rising Sun, the life of the common folk depended entirely on the mastery of the Monster Slayers. Despite the fact that the army and navy did most of the work, it was groups of Slayers who organized the defenses and the ultimate destruction of the monsters.

I didn't know what was going on with my cat today, but she got hungry again, and this time she was staring wide-eyed at some rolls that a young Japanese man with long thin whiskers was making right in a restaurant window.

"You'll get fat at this rate, and I'll never be able to find a boy cat for you," I said, shaking my head at her.

As I walked into the Japanese restaurant, I was surprised again. Firstly by the fact that the owner rushed up to greet me personally, bowing almost double. And secondly that he spoke in perfect Eastern Imperial and told me what an honor it was to welcome a Monster Slayer, and of course it would be his pleasure to treat me to his finest dishes for free. He really messed up there... Caramel purred in satisfaction. At the sight of her the owner began to stammer, and with eyes nearly bursting out of his sockets, informed me that his words extended to my pet also.

I didn't refuse, and after an hour of gorging ourselves on all-you-can-eat fresh fish, Caramel and I burst out of the restaurant like two stuffed geese. In the doorway stood the smiling owner with his two wives, waving us good-bye and nodding like bobbleheads as we went. Strange folks.

"Surprising culture, but I like it!" I said, waving a hand.

The hand with my ring on it. Three taxis nearly caused an accident, and their drivers almost came to blows over the right to take me where I wanted to go. And unlike the taxi drivers in Irkutsk, these ones didn't seem bothered at all by the presence of Caramel, just beckoned her into the broad back seat.

"Claws away," I muttered, earning myself a reproachful glance before the panther jumped softly in and sat down.

Caramel wore a fancy blue collar that Anna had found for her somewhere. And put it on her herself — I wouldn't have risked it. They really were becoming friends. Anna got the collar for one simple reason. Unlike me, she had studied the traditions and rules of my destination. In the Empire of the Rising Sun, people have a very negative perception of Rift beasts, which have taken the lives of many of their friends and family. That meant that someone might attack Caramel if she wasn't wearing a collar. Any attacker would be digging his own grave, of course, but I don't need that kind of trouble. Only the Gifted would realize that it was just an ordinary collar. But those same Gifted would also recognize that since it was ordinary, there must be a reason for it. As for normal people, the panther would look just as safe as if she were wearing a subjugation collar.

While we flew in on the plane — an army plane, actually, which the duchess somehow organized, since only the military risk flying close to the Epicenter, — Dolgorukova slept for most of the journey. She had been through a tough Rift the day before, the closing of which discharged her yearly duties. As for me, I spent the journey looking up places of interest to me. Including weapons stores.

The bladed weapons of the Empire of the Rising Sun were famous throughout the world. Europeans found them a little tough to use because of the unfamiliar balance. But for me, with all my past experience, it didn't make any difference what I waved around. So it was time to go see what the local craftsmen had to offer.

Judging by the information online, the first store the taxi driver took me to belonged to a noble family with an interesting Gift for working with metal. Their craftsmen had been making the best swords in the Empire for hundreds of years. I was let in by a guard who bowed deeply and emanated an easy aura of power of at least Veteran rank.

The guard's impassive face was smooth as stone. Actually, no — the edge of his trained eye twitched when it landed on the short sword I'd looted from that gangster. Apparently, that quick twitch of an eye was all the disdain the dispassionate guard was allowed to show. Sorry, buddy, I gotta make do!

I stepped inside. Hmm... Unexpected. A huge

hall, comfortable seats in a waiting area, multiple cute saleswomen who darted to me like moths to a flame. And in total, one, two, three... twelve different types of weapons were on display in the room, which had to be over two thousand square feet. Was this place really a store!? More like a museum!

The girls started twittering right away. I shot them a friendly smile and said clearly:

"East Imperial, English, German or Italian, please."

At that point one of them started to speak Imperial, the second German, the third Italian, and the fourth English.

"Wow, the full set!" I smiled.

Although I suspected that each of them knew all those languages. Just part of the job. On top of that... They looked fine as hell! Honestly, I tried not to think of how long it had been since my last sexual encounter. But soon, as fat Old Mac used to joke, it would start pouring out of my ears.

This place seemed like a top-class business. And the girls were top-class too. Short skirts, stockings, neat blouses. I frowned. What did they remind me of? Right — those dumb anime comics. The girls looked like this in those too. Only these ones had normal eyes, like Japanese girls should have.

"What would the gentleman like to see?"

"What would the gentleman like to buy?"

I interrupted them.

"Alright, you and you stay here! The rest of

you — thank you."

The other girls bowed obediently, and left us in peace. The other two seemed to be indescribably pleased at my choice. But I had made it quite simply. I just chose the ones with the biggest tits... I mean, breasts. Damn spermatoxicosis!

"The gentleman would like to take a look around first."

"What type of weapons is the gentleman interested in?"

"Let's start with the swords," I nodded.

"Please follow me, sir," one of the girls tittered.

And the second:

"Would you like some tea or coffee, sir? Perhaps champagne?"

"Sir will definitely take you up on your offer later," I chuckled. "But first, the weapons."

We walked up to the first pedestal.

"A stunning katana crafted by..." the girl said, launching into a long rehearsed speech, but I just stood frozen in astonishment.

The katana really was impressive. I could feel the aura of power it gave off. When an inanimate object can hold power on its own, that shows it to be the work of a master of the highest art.

I narrowed my eyes and looked closer at the weapon's aura. It burned particularly brightly in a few places around the pommel and blade. Right where there were runes of power inscribed, placed and powered by an unknown master. Even if I filled myself with jellies and poured all my energy into the thing, there was no way I'd damage it. Not unless I trained for years first. I scratched the back of my head, catching myself thinking of how to break the weapon.

I lowered my eyes to the price tag. There was a description written in all the languages I'd listed and more, and next to it was a price in the national currency. The sword was worth one and a half million imperial rubles. I wish I could say it was overpriced, but looking at the blade again, I decided the price was fair. I'd never seen a sword like it before. Even Arkhip's store with its exclusive items didn't approach these prices — to within even a million. Maybe there was a store like this one somewhere in St. Petersburg, but I doubted it.

"May I..?" I reached out a hand.

Obviously I wouldn't have enough money for it any time soon. But it looked so enticing.

"Of course, sir." The girl put on some delicate silk gloves, carefully took it off the pedestal and handed it to me.

Energy surged from the sword. I'd definitely never seen anything like it in this world, that was for sure! What did this mean? The sword itself was a kind of battery that could recharge its owner. Now that's what I call a blade!

"The gentleman may walk this way." The girl bowed again and pointed to a specially marked-off area with a little free space and no breakable objects at all.

Man's love for weaponry can never be understood. I couldn't deny myself the pleasure; I took a combat stance and performed a few moves. The sword sang in my hands. The thought suddenly occurred to me — could I just run out of here and take this amazing sword with me? I pushed down the urge in embarrassment.

Maybe I could send Shnoop in to steal it..? Hmm... No. The girl switched off some clearly complicated alarm system before she touched the blade. And secondly, that would be a little... Hell, it would be very, very wrong! You can't just steal a weapon like that. A weapon like that has to either be bought or won in battle. I liked the second option more. I needed to find some local Japanese guy and challenge him to a duel. Ha-ha! Go Galaxius!

I described some pirouettes thoughtfully, enjoying the whistle of the blade. As I reached the end of the combo, I froze, surprised to hear someone clapping. I turned and saw an old but still strong Japanese man walking toward me unhurriedly. All the girls bowed low at the sight of him.

I swore to myself, catching myself thinking that I'd just shown off everything I should be keeping hidden. Feeling such a fine weapon in my hands, I had let my power go to increase my speed. From the outside I must have looked like a blur in the air.

Goddamn it, Xander, keep a low profile!

"Yoshito Nakamuro." The man gave me a brief nod.

Upon his finger burned a family signet ring

with an unfamiliar symbol on it that said nothing to me. But the name said a lot. It was the name of the ancient family to whom this store belonged. He also wore a Slayer ring. It shimmered with a blinding blue light, showing his class — two. A powerful old man!

"Alexander Galaxius."

"Very pleased to meet you." The old Japanese man nodded again slowly. "And I am very surprised to see such perfect technique with a katana from such a young Slayer. Even Slayer Fifth Class, with all due respect for you, is a little fast for your age, young man."

"Well, I'm very talented, you know..." I said, coughing and not knowing what to do — offer to shake his hand, or..?

In the end, I just nodded briefly back at him. There was no way I could tell by the old man's face whether I'd broken the rules. I'd heard the Japanese were sticklers for decorum. But I just didn't know the details.

"Allow me to ask you a question, young man." The old man bowed his head slightly.

"Please do."

"Where did you learn those techniques? Clearly not here in our country. I would have heard of such a prodigy. And I also know that in the past ten years, there have been just three Great Magisters of such a level outside the bounds of our Empire. I wonder, which of them trained you, and doubtless spent several years of their life in so doing?"

"Who trained me? Well, I've had a few teachers," I said honestly. "Old Mac probably tried the hardest with me, and Grand Master Wulf taught me the basics."

The Japanese man frowned.

"I know neither of those names."

"It was all far away from here. And they weren't Japanese."

"Then that is even more surprising," the old man said. "You did not mention your title. Are you from the Eastern Empire? A count, a duke?"

"No, I'm just a baron."

At that, the wise old man twitched an eyelid.

"How very strange," he muttered.

I even started to feel a little bad for him.

"Like I said, Sir Nakamuro, I'm very talented. And I just don't have the money for this kind of weapon. Doubt I will have any time soon." I smiled. "Forgive me, I couldn't resist."

"The weapon is intended for human hands, skilled human hands. Whereas you have the hands of a virtuoso. You have done me honor by visiting my humble store." At this, the old man suddenly gave me a deep bow.

I handed the sword to the girl, who bowed also as she took it from me before walking away.

"With your permission, I'd like to look at more of your weapons," I said.

I hadn't had this much fun in a long time.

"I will gladly show you them all, personally." The old man smiled, sending the girls away with a motion of his brow. "After all, money can always be made, and far faster than mastery."

I chuckled. The old Slayer was right, no doubt about that.

CHAPTER 3

THE OLD MAN WAS RIGHT, and I liked his thinking. Money really can always be made. I've never chased it, I've always just known — money will come, and that's that. It's just a tool for achieving power and knowledge of the self, and it can help me feel better.

I had seen people in my past life who believed that the path to power lay in the exploration of asceticism Idiots... I came back from all manner of tough battles knowing that a tasty breakfast and warm women were waiting for me.

But them? They went back to their cave to eat porridge with no sugar, and sleep on a hard stone floor. And they really did like all that, but I never saw much power in them.

There were no ascetics among Hunters. We were taught maximalism, and, in some sense, arrogance. A Hunter has to show people their potential, and what their path can lead to. How could we attract new recruits otherwise? Ha-ha!

"What's that sword?" I asked, seeing an interesting bluish blade.

"That is the Eye of the Princess!" he answered, pride clear in his eyes as he beheld the blade. "My son created it in honor of a girl who got away from him. One of his first works of those that may be considered successful."

Hmm... With his permission, I took it in hand and appreciated it for myself. A good blade, no doubt about that.

And a hefty price too, at seven hundred and fifty thousand rubles.

I had a decent conversation with the Japanese man, and we discussed several subjects. I didn't even know what made him so interested in me. Maybe he was just bored, or my technique really did impress him. I don't think I showed him anything all that special. I couldn't have. If I started working miracles, then my body just wouldn't withstand it. Sure, if I had my seals, and a lot of them, then I really would show him... Ah, if only!

I could sense power from the old man too. If he wanted to kill me, it would be a fight to the death. I'd have to use everything I had, and even then there was no guarantee that I'd survive even if I won. Better odds running away.

"Take a look at this weapon," he said, leading me to a distant stand. "What do you think of it?"

It seemed he'd decided that some greatly respected master had taught me after all.

I picked up the weapon and tried to sense it. With my eyes closed, I ran my fingers along the blade and started to charge it with my energy, feeling out its properties.

"I think... that I shouldn't even touch such a weapon," I told him truthfully.

He laughed. "Why not?"

"Too tempting to sell everything I own just to buy it," I answered honestly. "True, it isn't perfect. I don't know what the flaw is exactly, but there is one. When you sell this blade, it'll let down its owner, and then he or his family will come to you and complain."

"Is that so..." He rubbed his chin thoughtfully.

This time I didn't answer with the truth. I knew just fine what the problem was, but I couldn't tell him. This blade was alive... The Hunters made blades like this, sealing the souls of very powerful monsters inside weapons and armor. It was considered the height of craftsmanship. But there was one nuance. We never bothered with weak beasts; they were unworthy of it, and there was no point in them.

Whereas the spirit in this weapon was of a weak beast, and I had seen it. It was an amorphous rat-like creature. Weaker than my Caramel, but that didn't even matter. Whoever made this blade was an idiot. You can't put creatures like that into weapons. A rat, even of godlike rank, is still forever a cowardly rat, and will always let you down just when you need it most.

Imagine my surprise when the old man took the sword in hand, and with a single chop of his fist, snapped the blade in two. The weapon was ruined.

"You feel bad to waste it?"

"In your money, its price was one million rubles, but I feel not an ounce of regret." Damn, his family sure must be wealthy... "Reputation is above all. I did not make it; I bought it. I could not put it up for sale, but was unsure what it was that I disliked about it."

"And you broke it based on the words of a random passerby?" I chuckled in amazement, looking him right in the eye.

"Correct!" he answered with a smile of his own. "A random young man with the eyes of an old wise man."

"Whoa!" I raised my eyebrows. "Haven't heard that before. Normally I just get told I'm a womanizer, or a dumbass, or sometimes a drunk."

"No shame in a love for old drinks and youthful bodies." He winked at me.

The old man and I spoke a little longer, and just as I was about to leave, something strange happened. He asked why I came to their country.

I answered that I wanted to visit their famous Rift, and that was why I was looking for a sword. But with these prices, I was better off challenging some nobleman to a duel and taking his toy off him.

He liked my joke. But I wasn't joking.

He already knew I was poor as a pauper. Good thing he wasn't the only one who could read people by their eyes; so could I. And his contained no judgment, disdain or pity, just interest.

He was bored, and I was someone who entertained him a little.

"Catch!" I heard just as I'd almost walked to the door.

I heard a whistle, and reacted like lightning. My hand shot over my shoulder and caught what was flying at my head, my fingers gripping the blade's edge.

"You can bring it back after the Rift. A good swordsman cannot use just any old sword," the old man said to me in parting.

Then the scabbard flew toward me too.

"Thanks..." I nodded to him, and left.

An intriguing old man, and so was his gesture.

He'd lent me a sword worth at least half a million.

If all the people here were so generous, then maybe I chose the wrong country.

No... Every land has its eccentrics. This guy just lived heart and soul in his profession as a weaponsmith.

I also detected two seeking spells. If anything happened, he could find his sword and get it back. I didn't think anyone else who picked it up would argue with the old man. Or maybe he wanted to know where I was going. There was also the chance that it would be used to track and kill me, but that just meant even more fun.

Ugh... Even in this country I had to call a taxi. Anna was right; when I got home, I'd have to figure out some transport. I tried to explain to the driver in three languages where I needed to go. He didn't understand a word, but I'd dealt with worse. I showed him my ring and pointed on the map to where I needed to go. When he saw the Rift, his eyes widened and he nodded his understanding.

There was a reason I went to the Empire of the Rising Sun as soon as I got an invite. I considered it a sign from above. And it was all because I was starting to slowly prepare for war, and for my doubtlessly great future, and for now I was studying and accumulating information. And so, what I needed was those slimes of mine who were so good at getting rid of evidence. Maybe it seems crazy to go all the way to another country for a little thing like that. But there was good reason for it.

I was an aristocrat, and a single unfortunate corpse could destroy my whole reputation and put me in prison for a long time. One day, I might come back to my manor and find the corpse of a duke's daughter there, for example. I'd have a minute, maybe less, to get rid of it.

Alas, Shnoop wasn't capable of carrying big things like that. And it didn't feel right to make Caramel eat a human body.

Getting into a Rift is no problem no matter where the hell it is in the world. The Slayers were a little more than a simple club. All I had to do was put my initials on a form and note my rank, where I was from... That was it. I had official leave to be there. Nothing but a formality.

As it happened, I could see a group of Slayers at the entrance to the Rift. There was a five minute queue, and that was only in one direction. But they were all civilized, no swearing or pushing. The Rift I chose was similar to the Anthill, only this one was two years old already. And nobody had been able to close it.

Seeing that I wasn't local, the soldiers at the entrance didn't ask me anything. All they needed was to see the signet ring on my finger.

When I entered the Rift, it was the same kind of show as in the Anthill. At the very start was a small base, and even a checkpoint for selling loot, that's how settled-in they were.

The place was interesting, of course, but I moved on. I wondered if you had to book your room on a forum here too. Whatever, I'd figure it out.

We didn't walk for long, maybe thirty minutes, around a place that looked like a canyon full of geysers. The place was damp, muggy, and in each cave I passed through there were several geysers that activated on a whim, spitting out mud and water in all directions.

The acid slimes didn't much like that, but ordinary ones were fine with it. The ones I needed were definitely here somewhere, only deeper in.

"Go on, find me a shortcut," I said to Shnoop.

"And try not to run into other human."

I followed after him, but we weren't allowed to go far. Guess that route wasn't popular, and people didn't go there much. That led to one of the caves being filled to the brim with slimes, sliding around and devouring all the vegetation they could find.

I could get through the last caverns on speed alone, but not this one. They'd grown like mushrooms in here, and they were already crawling toward me.

Now that sword really started to come in handy.

Caramel growled, and I counted at least thirty heads and then lost count. I hadn't fought against these in a long time.

I ran up to the closest one and stabbed it in the spot that should hold its core. They couldn't survive without the core, only collapse into a murky puddle. Then it was important not to step in the remaining ooze, which ate through everything it made contact with.

In fact, most slimes did that. It was how they fed, increasing their mass. But one of them did it faster than the others, and that was the one I needed — the green type, called the acid type.

The red types took a lot longer to devour their victims than the yellow or green.

There were also black ones, at least back in my world. Those were masters of absorption, but they had one drawback: they left a black trail of acrid slime behind them.

While I was thinking, the slimes sensed food and moved toward me more confidently, first creeping and then bouncing my way. They were of different sizes here. A small and weak squad might have ran away at first sight of the horde, but I didn't give a damn. My armor was charged, my sword was taking in my energy and seemed in no danger of breaking.

I ran toward them and started slashing in all directions. If you don't know how to use spirit sight, then these creatures are very dangerous. You have to cut at random until you hit the core. But I could see where it was...

I created a fireball and launched it at a small slime. It didn't even try to dodge, and an explosion followed. Jelly went flying through the air, and the creature's soul flew into me.

Damn, time to get back to a safe distance — that nearly hit me. My armor would withstand that kind of thing, sure, but the hell with the risk! I didn't like these enemies.

On my way here, I'd seen people going the other way with wounds like burns. One girl must have fallen into some slime, and her head looked terrible now. No hair left, all red and raw, and it hit her face too. She was lucky it was just a weak slime. The acid one wouldn't have left her any bones.

At first Caramel didn't hurry to attack, but then they started to surround her, and one got too lucky and almost reached her tail. Now that she couldn't forgive. She lit up red and started to draw energy from me at an accelerated rate. Covering her body with defensive field similar to my armor, she roared and rushed in to tear the slimes to pieces. The slimes felt no pain that I could see — they didn't seem to feel anything at all.

It took us ten minutes to kill them all, and we did it with our own hands and paws. No chance of any jellies here. From what I could tell, these things were completely financially useless. But from what I understood, there was a reward for killing them, to prevent this Rift from spewing out thousands of monsters into the city.

Just as I was about to leave, the geyser spat out more water and slimes. Oh, come on!

I cast an orb of ball lightning in my hand and threw it at the group of slimes that was just appearing. It didn't kill them, but gave them a good shock. Then a couple of sweeps of my sword and it was all over.

I'd wanted to summon my pets so that I didn't have to do all that dirty work myself, but Shnoop showed me that a squad was headed toward me that had gone deep inside and was now coming back. So I might have rumbled myself.

The squad of five wounded Slayers was trying to run from room to room, only killing when it had to, not staying in one place for long. But in one of them, they'd have to stay. One of the caves was huge, and the geysers within it were constantly erupting. One just continually spat out slimes, and from there they crawled around among all the other geysers and into other chambers.

I walked toward the group. Not that my heart yearned to help exactly, it was just that I was headed in that direction anyway. I'd just back them up if it came to that.

Before I got to the large chamber, they were already there. Standing at the very edge and looking gloomily at the monsters. What were they thinking? Why'd they go so deep in? Sure, they must have sacks full of loot, but was it worth it? Actually, I didn't even know what sort of loot could be gotten here. Maybe goo from rare slimes — it was sold by the jar here.

I started to feel curious, and sent Shnoop to check their backpacks.

I was right; they had vials made of special plastic in which they kept multicolored liquids. But not only that... Some of them had miniature slimes inside, like little slime babies. Looked like they'd get a good score for this raid, that is if they made it out alive, of course.

Fine, I'll help them.

Despite the fact that one girl was wounded worse than the others, they didn't abandon her, although she was currently acting as ballast on the shoulders of her colleagues. And that meant they had team spirit. Hunters, too, always came to the aid of their fellows, and never abandoned anyone in trouble.

After running to the right spot, I waved a hand at them. I happened to be standing on an outcropping, the cave below me. And to get down there, I had to slide down. They were standing at the edge of the room and could see just fine from there. All the walls were covered with green moss that gave off good light. I remembered that there was lots of that moss under the ground back in my world too, and we often used it instead of torches. You can just pick it up and wrap it around a stick.

Magic is all well and good, but there are creatures who sense it. And it's better not to give yourself away until you get where you need to be.

They'd started waving their hands at me and shouting. I couldn't hear what they were saying, but I knew a way I could.

"Get closer to them and show me," I said to Shnoop, and he slithered that way.

Shnoop didn't let me down. As for the language barrier... Yeah. They were shouting in Japanese, and I'm no pro...

They were pointing at the girl too, and waving at me. Asking me to save her? Or did they want to tell me that she was hurt? Maybe offering her as a gift?

I looked closer — she wasn't bad, pretty cute. But clearly not dressed for the weather, in torn armor and a leather skirt with a flared hem. Did anyone tell her where she was going? But that's girls for you — always looks over logic with them.

I slid down into the cavern, holding the sword ahead of me so it didn't get stuck, and realized that I'd have to buy myself some new clothes too. I'd been wanting to avoid that.

Damn, no choice now...

The slimes saw food and quickly started to

slither toward me. In the meantime, the Japanese put their heads in their hands and started to swear. If there was anything I did know in Japanese, it was the swear words. They thought I was going to get myself killed and leave them alone again.

The chamber was filled with enemies, and worst of all, none were the ones I needed. There were browns, reds, yellows, even a fire slime. The fire slime left a trail of soot behind it as it went, and exploded on death. An unpleasant enemy that I fired lightning at to blow up. As for the others, I figured I could deal with them later.

I charged my body with energy and started to dole out strikes. The sword flowed like an extension of my body. The very fancy toy sat in my hand as if molded to it. I knew it wouldn't let me down, and that meant I could work at full swing. Well, I say full swing... Really, I just worked at a normal pace — there were witnesses here, after all. Apart from fighting and putting down packs of slow slimes, I was also using Shnoop to keep an eye on the Japanese group, to make sure they didn't die or decide to cause me any trouble. For a while they looked at me with the kind of expression that said "Ugh, idiot!", but with each passing minute it changed more toward "WHO THE HELL IS THIS!?"

Oh, you bastard! Another fire slime spat flames at me and nearly hit; I had to bend back double to avoid it. Good thing I exercised all the time and kept myself supple, or else I'd have broken my back in half.

Caramel got revenge on the creature for me, firing blades of energy from her claws. She was clearly gaining in power, and had learned various spells. I just wished she'd use her own energy reserves for it instead of mine.

Yeah, she had her own energy, but she tended to think that hers belonged only to her and mine was communal. Girls tend to have special rules for themselves.

Nice to be winning, but my clothes took a beating from all the killing, splashes of acid landing on them and eating through them.

I wanted to summon a salamander and burn the whole place down, but it was a little too early for that. Once I got a little further in, I'd summon one then. Shnoop had already found where the green ones were. While the Anthill spread downwards, this Rift stretched off into the distance.

I couldn't even count how many I killed by the souls. Even weak as they were, I could feel the energy flowing from so many. Maybe there was some sense in staying a little longer in this country.

Incidentally, the people realized that I wasn't about to retreat, and now they joined the fight too. They happened to have an archer with them who was firing energy arrows, and every one of them killed a slime dead.

No idea how they could have had such a bad run with a guy like that on the team. Of course, I'd seen nine-foot-tall slimes in there too, but those I just avoided and that was that.

Actually, the raid had taken me a lot more time than I thought it would, and that grated on me. In the end I managed to help the Japanese, and even tried to talk to them. Only none of them understood a single word in any language I knew.

Shame... I had to lead them back, but they didn't trust me to help carry the girl. Naturally it all got a lot easier at the exit, where the healers ran up to us. An Imperial-speaking rep from the local Center came with them and asked me for my details, plus thanked me for the help. And promised that a letter of gratitude would be sent to my Center.

Only then was I able to go back to farming my acid slimes at an accelerated pace. To save time, I summoned two salamanders at once to burn through everything in my path.

A fun campaign... Two thousand, two hundred and thirteen souls of various slimes. Yep — an army like that could eat half a small barony.

My 'personal mission' was done, and now I could finally get on with Dolgorukova's job!

CHAPTER 4

Country Club 'Tranquility'
One day prior

ADMINISTRATOR AFANASY LUKYANENKO was very proud of his work. His ancestors, and he himself, had served their noble masters for a long time. As a boy, Afanasy had even been sent to an imperial institute to study economics and the hotel business. And now ten years had passed since he became the permanent director and administrator of the most elite club for aristocrats in Irkutsk. And through it all, he himself wasn't even an aristocrat. His was a position of high trust, and he lived up to it, enjoying the opportunity to mingle with the best people of Irkutsk.

Yesterday's incident with Galaxius had knocked him off balance a little. The arrogant little baron had dared to try throwing his weight around. Afanasy, although not an aristocrat himself, had seen plenty of counts, dukes and even princes in his club, and considered himself close to them. And though he himself could never attain even the title of baron in his life, he still considered the young man an upstart.

After a call from one of the beneficiaries, who didn't want to ruin relationships with the criminal underworld of Irkutsk over some unknown baron, Afanasy expelled the braggart from the grounds of their noble establishment. And — why hide it? — he had he enjoyed the sense of power that came with it. He walked through his domain squeezing the appetizing buttocks of the serving girls and taking the host's right to test out the dishes that were to be delivered to the aristocrats for breakfast that day.

Life was exquisite.

But then he heard a shriek, then another. The guards shifted. In the earpiece that he wore even as he slept, the guard captain's voice chirped.

"Afanasy Vasilyevich, we have a problem!"

"What sort of problem?"

"Huge rats have appeared out of nowhere. Rift beasts! They're chewing through the supplies, furniture, everything they can get."

"What about people?" To Afanasy's credit, he did care for his subordinates.

"It's strange — they aren't touching the people, they avoid contact, they're just destroying as much of our property as they can."

"Where did they come from? Did a Rift open?"

"I have no idea. There's a Slayer response team already on the way."

Afanasy, even with all his self-importance, was no coward. He picked up a double-barreled shotgun and powered up his armor. Yes, he was weakly Gifted, weak for fighting anyway. After all, all his potential was in his head. Without hesitation, he ran to the lower floors to help the guards.

The administrator fired twice at a screeching rat, one shot after another. The rat still didn't die, but didn't try to attack him, darting into another room instead. Afanasy swore and ran after it. The rat was dragging a paw, and he finally finished it off with two precise shots.

"Take that, bastard!" Afanasy smiled.

A guttural whine came from behind him. He turned around and saw another rat. It was bigger than the one he'd just killed. And, strangest of all, it wasn't running away from him. The rat stared straight at Afanasy. Stared most unkindly. And he could have sworn — if a brainless animal could smile, that rat would be grinning at him in that moment.

* * *

The Tokyo Imperial Academy was a truly impressive building, almost an enclave of its own. Its grounds spanned several hectares in the heart of the city. It used to be on the outskirts, but, for the past few hundred years, the city had grown around it. From what I understood from

Dolgorukova's explanation, it was hard enough just to get inside the place. You had to have a personal invite. Which explained the duchess's business here — she was trying to annoy and terrorize her rival, who didn't want to be exposed. I didn't know what Dolgorukova did, but we got a pass.

At the entrance, the guards asked our surnames and let us in. One of them stepped forward to escort us. From what I understood, the Academy combined both educational functions for aristocrats and an equivalent to the Irkutsk Slayer Center. Luckily, given the specifics of the Japanese empire, they were one and the same thing.

Aristocrats studied only the art of war. So the study halls and barracks were combined. People migrated back and forth depending on their course and task at hand. In my view, it was a great way to do things — everything in one place. Many young aristos all over the world dreamed of making it into the Imperial Academy. The Japanese were happy to welcome foreigners, although the conditions were atrocious. Considering the number of applicants, they had their pick. In addition to the difficulty of the entrance exams, the cost to study there was through the roof.

Depending on their potential, the locals could get scholarships. Given their constant losses in the war against the monsters, the state never had enough experienced fighters. So as to their own citizens, the lack of money didn't matter as long as their potential was good. Whereas they made foreigners pay through the nose. Good way to do it.

The duchess was excited, in a state of anticipation. Honestly, to earn my bread, I had spoken with her pretty seriously. We even set up a couple of exhibition sparring matches. Maria and her family's Gift was the Basilisk Stare. If the enemy can't resist it, he's completely paralyzed. If the enemy has a strong Gift, he's either stunned or slowed. A highly useful Gift, it seemed to me.

I 'held back' in our sparring session, playing the part of a rabbit in the headlights. The first time I didn't even defend myself, just turned to a statue. The second time I let myself slow down slightly. And actually, the duchess was at a good level. She had earned her class four. And her personal power was at Veteran rank, very close to Master.

I remembered again that most normal parents tried to train their kids from the cradle. Not so the Goddards, unfortunately. And Maria had three elder brothers too, who spurred her on hard. If it weren't for my past knowledge, if Alex Goddard's body had its ordinary consciousness in it, at sixteen he would have been an utterly useless creature, just like Goddard senior thought he was.

We walked along red carpets with perfect lawns, benches and places for meditation. Exotic old trees grew all around us, trimmed to perfection. A place of real beauty. But a little too perfect for me — I found myself missing a touch of chaos. But that's the eastern way.

Ahead we saw a crowd of people. At first I thought it was some kind of picnic, but it turned out they were all standing around a training ground scattered with sand. Teenagers are teenagers everywhere. A crowd of people had come to watch a duel. When they saw us they switched to a whisper, pointing and laughing quietly. I got the feeling that it was my pet Caramel causing most of the commotion. At least, the entire female half of the crowd pointed at her with looks of utter rapture.

Most of the audience was Japanese, with a few Europeans and even a couple of black people.

A short but solid-looking man stepped toward us with a low bow. The Slayer Third Class ring on his finger told us he was an experienced fighter.

"Allow me to introduce myself — I am Hakushaku Kuwabara Novojimo. I am a teacher of martial arts at the Academy. Today I will be acting as judge."

We greeted him respectfully and he led us to the arena proper. It was large enough. Roughly one-sixty by eighty feet. They probably practiced group battles here too. At the far end stood various mannequins and training tools. The closest section to us was a sparring area. Students were training there. When we appeared, they wrapped up their session and headed toward the viewers on the bleachers.

In the distance I saw Maria's sworn frenemy, who was ranting about something to a young man, unusually tall for a Japanese guy. The main gift of

Countess Anastasia Novodvorskaya was the ability to strengthen her body, and there was a reason she had been sent here. Apart from the fact that her parents were very rich, Anastasia was the only daughter in the family and had decided on her own to become a Monster Slayer.

When the pair saw us, they cut off their conversation and came closer. I compared the opponents. Maria was taller, but lighter. Her rival must have spent a lot of time on strength training. I couldn't see any excess weight on her, but her muscles were exaggerated and unfeminine.

"Seconds, present yourselves."

"Koshaku Hiroshi Minamoto," the young man nodded.

Minamoto... Minamoto... What a familiar name, I thought. *Where have I heard that before..?* And yes, the title of 'Koshaku' was similar to our 'Prince.'

The Japanese man looked confident, even arrogant, looking past me with disdain, but thoroughly examining Maria. I really didn't like the look in his eye. Unlike the other impassive Japanese, I could see him undressing the girl with his eyes, smiling a creepy smile.

"Baron Galaxius," I said.

At this, both our opponents and the judge himself stared at me in amazement. They were just short of dropping their jaws.

"Oh, come o-o-o-on..." the Japanese prince drawled. "Baron?!"

The judge said nothing, just nodded. But did

I see something flashing in his eyes... sympathy? He started declaring the rules.

The girls chose to fight to first blood. The lighter dueling option. Although Dolgorukova wanted to go 'until mercy,' I talked her right out of it, especially after I learned the reason for their conflict.

Novodvorskaya had only spread rumors that slightly embellished on information that Maria had told her in confidence. She didn't go into details, but the information was related to someone male. I didn't try to extract any more from her; all that aristocratic drama didn't interest me at all. No way would I have flown all the way across the world to demand satisfaction in her shoes. But I respected the duchess's pride.

Incidentally, duels to the death were strictly forbidden in the territory of the island Empire. Rising Sun citizens who violated the rules were severely punished. Foreigners were deported with a huge fine, or made to work off their crime. From what I understood, the Japanese placed a higher value on human life than any other culture, after being so long in permanent war with the beasts. After I learned that, I felt even more respect for them. I couldn't help but think back to our more 'relaxed' Europe, where noble aristos killed each other just for fun. Better to send them here, to the front lines. Or at least to the Perimeter near Irkutsk. One could dream...

The seconds, i.e. us, were asked to move to the side. Without a second thought I moved to stand next to Minamoto, who suddenly moved away from me with an expression of disgust on his face.

"Do not approach me, gaijin," he hissed.

I just chuckled and shrugged. The hell with him.

The girls were ready to fight, waiting for the judge to call the start. From behind, I heard:

"Hello, Baron."

I looked around. A short fat man walked up to me, a count's ring on his finger.

"Count Patrikeyev," he said. "Why travel halfway across the world only to disgrace yourself?" he asked me, smiling.

I frowned.

"What are you talking about?"

"Do you know who that is?" He nodded at the countess's second.

"No clue."

"He is the senior heir to the Minamoto clan — his family are close relatives of the Imperial Family. And right now, he's the official suitor of Countess Novodvorskaya. They have been training together for two years now. Your girlfriend has no chance."

"She's not my girlfriend," I said, feeling a vague need to correct him.

"Well, no, of course, not really. How could a duchess and a baron be together?!" The man beamed at me and chuckled. "I simply used the wrong term for your student."

"Well, we'll see," I said, smiling.

"Ha-ha!" The man clapped me on the shoulder. When he saw my grimace, he pulled his arm back at once. "Good luck!"

I nodded silently and looked at the arena, where the judge gave the signal.

The girls had known each other since childhood, and each knew perfectly well what the other was capable of. That said, they hadn't seen each other in over a year now, and in that time they'd had time to learn something to surprise the other.

The countess was using twin swords. In one hand she held an ordinary Roman sword, that very same family blade that Maria had come for, in the other — a wakizashi. And, by the way she held herself, she was plenty confident with the strange combo. Armor powered and energy driven into her weapon, she rushed to attack.

Maria had a European family sword and an elegant main-gauche in her other hand. And right now she was on the defensive. Thank God. It had taken quite some effort to convince her to do that. The girl was chomping at the bit, and wanted to finish this duel with a single blow.

On the face of it, with Maria at class four and the countess only at five, the former had the advantage. But in reality, it wasn't so. The countess's power was in her speed. With all due respect to the duchess, she just wasn't that fast. And so I developed a simple strategy for her — save your strength and just stay on the defense, all the while suppressing the opponent's will with your

Gift. It was a kind of fight to exhaustion. It was forbidden to use jellies during the battle, and only the most intelligent and enduring would win.

Both girls were strong. Both sides let some hits through. But their armor was holding up for now. At roughly minute five of the duel, I noticed that the countess was starting to get tired. She sensed it too, and started to press harder, rushing to finish off her foe. One, two, three blows passed through Maria's defenses, but her armor still held up. At minute twenty-two, I saw the first sign of near victory.

Novodvorskaya, after parrying Maria's sword with her shorter sword, made a rapid lunge, and in the middle of her action somehow faltered, freezing for a second and letting a blow through. She jumped two steps back, gaining distance. Anger and confusion flashed in her eyes. Maria's eyes, on the other hand, burned with fun and threat.

"Don't even think about it!" I shouted loud.

I read her thoughts and realized that she was about to launch a furious attack at her enemy. That wasn't the plan she and I had agreed.

Absolutely everybody turned to took at me, even the judge. I shrugged.

"What, am I not allowed?"

Advice from seconds was actually allowed, but considered poor form. On the other hand, what difference did it make? Winning was what mattered! I could survive the looks of contempt from the viewers somehow.

Fortunately, Maria heard me. Her legs, crouched and ready to leap, relaxed, and she took a step back, inviting the countess to attack. Beyond that it was just a matter of technique.

At the seven minute mark, the countess's armor fell. Maria drove her slender sword into the enemy's thigh with a tinge of sadistic pleasure, making the girl scream and fall to her knees.

The judge immediately appeared between them, and raised his hands to them without a hint of embarrassment. "The battle is over!"

I widened my eyes at his powered armor. The tutor didn't have to worry about a random blow landing on him. His armor would have withstood it easily.

"Duchess Dolgorukova is the winner!"

Maria smiled and leaned forward and said something to her former friend. The face of her opponent, contorted in agony, reddened with shame. All the same, she sheathed her sword without fuss and handed it over with a brief nod to Dolgorukova. Maria took it and raised it in triumph above her head. She couldn't help it. I clapped reservedly, noticing that most of the audience looked pissed. There were only a couple of shouts of approval.

Maria walked up to me. She was smiling, although she looked a little tired.

"Didn't I do well?" she asked me.

"You sure did," I answered. "Well, can we be dismissed now?"

"No, you cannot!" came a voice from the side.

I turned to look. Minamoto was staring at us, enraged.

"By the law of the Dueling Code of the Empire of the Rising Sun, I challenge you to a duel!"

And no, he wasn't talking to me. He was talking to Maria.

"What, that was an option?" I raised my eyebrows.

The girl looked a little upset too. The judge immediately appeared beside us.

"Do you need time to recover your strength, Duchess?" he asked as if nothing was amiss.

"Wait." I stepped forward. "You mean there's no option to refuse?"

The Japanese man smiled slightly.

"Of course not! By law of the Empire, the second has the right to take vengeance."

"Well, I'll be damned!" I said, looking appraisingly at the Japanese man.

Then I turned to the judge.

"Yes, we need to rest." I sat the girl down on a chair. "Relax. Take this!" I handed her a green jelly. "Will that be enough?"

Maria was in shock, but she'd already gotten a grip on herself. She squeezed the jelly in her hand, closing her eyes, then opened them again and nodded.

"Yeah, it's enough."

I walked up to the judge and asked him for an expanded comment on this unusual situation. As it turned out, there really was such a rule. Seconds had the right to take vengeance. If

Minamoto won, he would both reclaim his girlfriend's family weapon and take Maria's. If Dolgorukova won, she would take his family katana, which I was eying up with interest.

I crouched down next to her and tried to quickly discuss a new strategy. Naturally, I knew nothing about Minamoto, so the tactics stayed the same. The girl nodded and walked into the circle.

"Now you're really in over your head!" came the self-satisfied voice of the arrogant nobleman.

"Listen here, you!" I snapped, turning to him and fixing him with a hard stare. "Enough crowing! Or else it'll be you and me in the arena next." I kept on staring at him, and didn't give a damn that he was a count, his blood would still be red...

The lout chuckled with twisted lips, and seemed about to shoot back a witty remark, but something in my eyes gave him pause. He whispered to himself: "Madman..!" and walked back to his companions on the bleachers. Then I turned toward the fight.

It turned out to be a very quick one.

The Japanese man demanded a 'fight until mercy.' And, before I had time to say anything, Maria agreed to it. After four minutes she'd lost her dagger, and after another three a heavy blow knocked the sword out of her hand. Seemed like her Gift wasn't affecting her opponent, but she probably just couldn't concentrate properly. Or rather, her enemy wasn't letting her concentrate. Dolgorukova tried to switch to melee fighting.

The man, instantly plunging both swords into the sand of the arena, performed a takedown and then got her in a stranglehold. I saw him powering up his body and crushing Maria's armor, and I clenched my fists, powerless. The girl was fighting with all her strength, but even I could see she wasn't going to win.

"Give in!" I couldn't believe my own voice, but I said it.

Her armor was severely depleted. And considering how much power the Japanese man was pouring into the hold, he wouldn't even notice it when he broke her neck after her armor fell.

"Maria, surrender!" I shouted even louder.

But the girl, teeth clenched, just kept trying to get out of the hold.

"Judge! Stop the fight!" I turned to the judge, but the man raised his hands, showing that it wasn't allowed.

I surged forward, but someone grabbed me by the arm. I barely held back from giving him a slap. But it turned out to be another tutor, a kind of referee.

"You are violating the rules," he said to me strictly.

"He's going to kill her!"

That got me a derisive scoff.

"Don't worry, he won't. Minamoto the Younger is an experienced fighter."

I could literally hear the girl's armor cracking. And I didn't know how the man would manage to stop in time.

Crouching down on my heels, I summoned Shnoop. It didn't matter — all eyes were on the arena. It took only a fraction of a second to give the critter his task.

An instant later he appeared beneath the fighters lying in the sand, and without further ado sank his sharp teeth into the proud heir's backside. The man twitched reflexively, strengthening his grip. Fortunately, Maria's armor held up, but the stress made her lose consciousness.

"Stop the battle!" The attentive judge noticed the girl's eyes rolling back and instantly separated Japanese fighter's hands. "Victory goes to Koshaku Hiroshi Minamoto!"

The Japanese man looked at himself in confusion and felt his backside, trying to figure out what just happened. After the judge's words, however, he smiled in satisfaction, took the scabbard off the unconscious girl and took away the Dolgorukov family sword, lifting it high above his head. This time the bleachers weren't silent. Cries of joy resounded above the stadium. The man swaggered toward me and stretched out a hand.

I narrowed my eyes at him. "What do you want?"

"The countess's sword."

The sword lay beside me on the bench.

"Pick it up yourself."

The man hissed something in Japanese, but picked up the sword.

Just then, his comrades rushed in, clapping him on the shoulders in congratulations. He returned the sword to his girlfriend with a pompous bow.

I shot into the stadium and leaned down over Maria, forgotten by all. I carefully patted her cheeks. No break in her aura, no wounds either. Her circulation had just been cut off. The girl's skin was just starting to pink up, and then she came round.

"I lost, didn't I?" was the first thing she said.

"Not yet." I smiled.

Carefully, I helped her get up, then turned toward the judge, who had already decided that his work was done for today.

"Excuse me, sir, I have a question!"

He looked at me with narrowed eyes.

"By your rules, can I challenge that dumbass to a duel?"

The judge twitched an eyelid. Either at 'dumbass' or at the unparalleled arrogance I must have had to try to duel the heir to a princely house as a mere baron. He got a grip on himself and nodded.

"Yes, you may."

I quickly walked into the celebrating crowd, unceremoniously shouldering my way through.

"Hey, you, asshole!"

The Japanese man turned to me in confusion.

"Yeah, you... Time to pick on someone your own size. I challenge you to a duel! And, unlike Maria, you'll be asking me for mercy!"

CHAPTER 5

SILENCE FELL. They were all looking at me like I was an idiot.

Even Minamoto's eyes widened, either in anger or surprise.

"You!?" His noble face twisted in a sneer. "Seriously?!"

"Never been more serious. Come on, sad little samurai, let's get in the arena." I nodded towards it.

"I'd gladly teach you some manners, gaijin. But you have nothing to wager."

"What do you mean?" I stopped and turned back to him.

"What I said. You are a pauper!" The Japanese aristocrat laughed right at me. "Do you really think that piece of shit will be enough?" He nodded at the short sword that I'd taken from the gang member.

I had returned my wonderful borrowed katana to Nakamuro right after the Rift. He had taken the weapon from my hands with a slight smile on his lips, then thanked me for some reason.

"Where is your family weapon... aristocrat?" The last word was spoken with a mocking leer.

"I don't have one," I said, shrugging calmly.

Laughter rolled out through the crowd.

"Like I said — a pauper!" Minamoto grinned and crossed his arms, looking triumphantly across the sycophants around him.

"So you're a coward, then?" I asked calmly.

The Japanese man's face filled with red. He opened his mouth to say something, but then the tutor judge intervened.

"With all due respect, Baron Galaxius, Sir Minamoto simply cannot duel you. Tradition does not allow it."

"Sure," I chuckled. "Tradition. Where would we be without it?"

"I will gladly answer your challenge outside of the bounds of a duel for offending my honor," Minamoto said, flushed with rage.

Well, that option didn't suit me at all. I needed to get Maria's weapon back.

"Will my cat be sufficient as a wager for the duel?" I placed a hand on Caramel's huge head.

She glanced sidelong at me from beneath my fingers, and in my head I heard her voice:

Are you stupid?

"Just trust me," I whispered to her.

The cat snorted, and again asked me mentally:

If you lose, do you mind if I eat that cocky bastard?

"Go nuts," I answered just as quietly.

Silence reigned around us. The Japanese man was thinking.

At this point one of his comrades came up to him, then someone else, a girl, and they whispered something into his ear. Maybe they knew better than him about the going rate for a pet like mine.

"I agree," Minamoto nodded. "That is a acceptable wager. I will gladly take the only valuable thing you possess."

Thing!? Caramel hissed furiously in my head. *Can I eat him even if you win?*

I didn't answer, just stroked Caramel on the rising fur of her hackles, and silently walked toward the arena. On the way there, Maria grabbed me, alarmed:

"Alex, what are you playing at?"

"Relax, I know what I'm doing," I smiled.

"You shouldn't do this!"

Maria trembled with real terror.

"Calm down. Just enjoy the show." I smiled widely, and squeezed her shoulder. "Get used to trusting me, my dear."

Maria's cheeks reddened. She glanced at my hand. Her royal roots were showing, but she just smiled and mouthed to me silently:

"Good luck!"

"Luck has nothing to do with it," I said with a laugh, and then finally walked on. Her head was still in the clouds!

My foe and I moved to stand opposite each other.

Minamoto shifted into a combat stance, taking a two-handed grip on his sword and holding it a little off to the side. His pose looked relaxed. Guess he didn't understand who he was dealing with. Although his fight with Maria had been short, it was long enough for me to study his style. He was fast, very fast. And strong. Only I didn't sense that he'd used his Gift at all, except to strengthen his body. Whatever, let him try to surprise me with something new.

I took out my sword, which was vaguely reminiscent of an ancient Roman gladius. Mocking laughs and jokes drifted in from the crowd, but I couldn't blame them. My dull sword looked like a toothbrush against a dagger in comparison to the Japanese man's gleaming sword.

Sure, Minamoto's wasn't quite as nice as the one I had held in my hands recently. But that was understandable. Family swords, of which there were usually several in powerful families, were mostly made decades or even centuries ago, when technology wasn't as good. In principle, they were civilian and dueling weapons. A decent Gifted would take an entirely different weapon into a Rift. Like the type I saw in Nakamuro's store.

The judge gave the signal, and my opponent charged toward me. I stepped back and started to dodge furiously, sometimes carefully parrying a blow with my sword if I couldn't dodge it. For good reason I was worried that if I blocked too powerful a blow, I'd end up without a weapon. So I just danced around my enemy. Fatiguing and annoying him, judging by his eyes.

After fifteen minutes of dancing around, I saw that the man's face was covered in red spots. He was tiring, getting angry. Furious. He exploded with a series of rapid strikes in an attempt to reach me, but I dodged them all.

Booing and whistling came from the bleachers. Seemed the viewers didn't like what they were seeing. A couple of times I heard shouting:

"Fight, coward!" "Enough running!"

But that was the least of my concerns. The Japanese man had to have a Gift. I was waiting for him to use it. And finally, I got what I wanted!

Minamoto was breathing heavily when I suddenly sensed his aura exploding with power. He started moving in a blur even to my experienced eye, shooting at me and waving his sword with incredible speed.

I let through one blow, a second. My armor groaned, but held up. What a Gift. Plenty powerful.

I failed to block his next lunge, then darted off to the side and just ran toward the training dummies. The man started after me. I rolled away from him, then again, running away shamelessly.

The bleachers roared with fury, demanding that my cowardice be punished. I was just buying time. I'd seen a Gift like this one before. It had only one drawback — its short lifespan. And when the aura fell, it drained away significant strength from its owner. And that's just what happened.

I dodged Minamoto's next lightning-fast strike by almost bending back double into a bridge. And then it hit him. He slowed down dramatically, and his face suddenly turned worried.

I span around in a crouch and tried to kick his legs out from under him. He reacted just in time, jumping on the spot. But I had time to react too, and raised my kicking leg a little higher. I basically hit him in the air, sending him flying comically through the air and crashing to the ground. Then I jumped to my feet and brought all my weight crashing down on his sword arm. Two crunching sounds. First from the armor, then the arm.

To Minamoto's credit, he didn't scream in pain, just turned deathly pale, grabbing at me with his healthy arm. The rest was easy. I fell onto his chest, forcing my knee up beneath his throat and holding his good arm, then started steadily strangling him. His armor started to crack across all its seams, and the man struggled on in silence.

"Give in!" I hissed through my teeth.

The proud samurai's eyes showed only hatred. I pressed even harder.

"Give in, fool!" I said.

No use again. What, was he willing to die just to avoid accepting defeat? That didn't suit me.

With my free hand, I placed my 'pauper's' sword to his gut and pressed hard.

"You're the heir to a Great Family, right?" I chuckled. "Well, you don't have to surrender. But I'm afraid you're about to lose your honored title!"

I pressed harder. Even the audience could hear his armor cracking. In the last few moments, there was dead silence.

The Japanese man paled, his eyes darting around, looking ready to cry... Probably more from helplessness than fear. And I knew how he felt. Today clearly wasn't his day. Staring at me hatefully, he opened his mouth:

"Mercy!"

"The fight is ended!" the judge said, jumping in at once and unceremoniously pulling me away.

Which he easily did, since I eased off right away, standing up and smiling, watching as my noble foe stood up, cradling his broken arm.

"Do you mind?" I asked simply, pointing at Minamoto's weapon lying on the ground.

He turned purple. Pulling the scabbard from his belt, he tossed it to the ground. I shrugged, grinned at him.

"Well, I not above picking something up off the floor."

I picked up the katana, slid it into the scabbard and walked back to Maria, whistling happily.

As I approached her, I thought in passing that she could easily be a model, the kind of girls they draw with big eyes in the Japanese comics.

"How did you do that?" Maria asked in amazement.

I beamed at her.

"No hugs and kisses for me?"

The girl stammered and blushed. Well, at least I'd brought her old spirits back.

"Oh, I almost forgot."

I walked up to Countess Novodvorskaya, who was sitting with both swords pressed to her chest — hers and Maria's. She looked ready to burst into tears.

"May I?" I reached out a hand.

She automatically handed them to me. I took them and nodded briefly.

"Nothing personal, Countess. You fought well."

And I went back to Dolgorukova again.

Caramel's voice resounded in my head:

Well, can I eat that guy now?

"No, afraid not," I said, smiling. "Come on, let's buy you some fish instead. I think Duchess Dolgorukova is paying today."

That said, I wasn't allowed to leave yet. The tutor caught up to me, extending a hand.

"Someone wants to talk to you."

"Who?" I raised an eyebrow in surprise.

"A representative from the Minamoto clan."

I took the phone from him.

"Hey there."

"Baron Alexander Galaxius?" The man on the other end spoke in English.

"That's right," I said, switching to the same

language.

"My name is Haruki Minamoto. I am the Master at Arms of the Minamoto clan. And I am Hiroshi's uncle. Unfortunately, the clan leader is currently away in Kyoto. And I have the authority to negotiate with you for the return of the family weapon to the clan."

Chuckling, I automatically glanced down at the trophy sword I was still holding. That was all they were good for, really. Trophies that could be sold back for a good ransom. The rule had existed always and everywhere. Sure, the winner could refuse to sell it back, thereby causing further insult to the loser's reputation. Some did just that. I personally knew a couple of veteran duelers back in New Prussia who had whole collections of family blades from defeated foes. But I sure wasn't one of those guys.

"I'm ready to hear your offer," I answered.

"We are willing to offer you a blue jelly as ransom."

I stopped in my tracks. Holy shit! I quickly tried to recall how much they were worth. It might not be a rainbow jelly, which few had ever seen in the flesh. But even absolutely standard black and blue jellies were insanely rare trophies from very powerful monsters.

I covered the microphone with my hand and turned to Dolgorukova.

"How much is a blue jelly?"

"Whaaat?" Maria stared at me wide-eyed.

"How much does a blue jelly cost? Tell me,

quick!"

Maria knitted her brows together.

"I'm not sure exactly, but somewhere around a hundred thousand, give or take a couple."

Now it was my turn to go wide-eyed. This sword clearly wasn't worth that much. Although I figured that for the Japanese, a family weapon had far greater value than it did for Europeans. I silenced the greedy voice inside me that demanded that I keep haggling, and answered simply:

"I accept."

"Where can you be found?" came the answer.

I looked around.

"Well, we're just about to leave the Academy, and we're planning to get a bite to eat somewhere."

"If you don't mind, I'll send a car for you that will take you to the best restaurant in Kyoto. And the bill will be on me."

"I'm willing," I said. "We'll wait for the car by the exit."

"How can the driver recognize you?"

"We'll have an overgrown ginger cat with us," I chuckled, earning a derisive look from her.

"Understood. The car is on the way."

I hung up and turned to Maria.

"Looks like you're going to save some money today."

Seeing the girl's look of confusion, I added:

"Grub's covered."

"Grub..?" The well-bred aristocratic woman looked even more confused.

"I mean, we've been invited to a restaurant," I

corrected myself.

"By whom?" she asked in surprise.

"The Minamoto family."

"You mean, you humiliated their heir and took his sword away, and now they're inviting you to a restaurant?"

I laughed. "Yeah, I like this country too."

And then I realized I was still holding the phone. I turned to the tutor standing beside me as quiet as a mouse and offered it back to him with a small bow.

"Thanks."

The man took the phone and hesitated for a second.

"May I ask a question, Sir Galaxius?"

I nodded.

"Who taught you how to fight?"

I opened my mouth, at once remembering Old Mac, who was fast becoming a legend in this world, but then I just waved a hand.

"They're all long dead," I said simply, and thought for a second how nice it would be if they weren't.

I had no clue where my old world was. Had I just been moved through space, or through time too? When I died, Old Mac was still wasting his life away. I would have loved to find my past world. The old crew would be so shocked!

The Japanese man faltered again. Curiosity seemed to overwhelm his good manners.

"Would you like to join our Academy?" he suddenly asked.

Maria whistled next to me.

"Nah," I said with a smile. "I'm too old to be a student."

"I don't mean as a student," the man said, surprising me again. "I think the administration would gladly take you on as a teacher."

Someone snorted next to me. I thought it was Caramel at first, but no. The sound came from the stunned Maria.

"Thank you so much. I'm afraid I have to refuse," I said. "I have business back home. An awful lot of business."

The armored limousine that picked us up wove through the streets of Kyoto and dropped us off on a nearby hill. The best restaurant in Kyoto turned out to be an architectural ensemble on the slopes of the first line of the defensive perimeter, with a view out to sea.

A couple of tall men with powerful auras greeted us and led us inside.

The inside of the restaurant was split into separate rooms. We were led into the largest one, a corner room with open panoramic windows. At a table blanketed with enough food to serve at least a dozen people sat an old but solid Japanese man, gazing thoughtfully out the window. As we appeared, he stood up and nodded.

"Sir Galaxius, Lady Dolgorukova."

"Greetings, Sir Minamoto," I nodded. "Here we are."

Without further ado, I offered him the sword.

"This is yours."

The Japanese man hesitated a moment, looking at it, then took it and put it to the side, and turned a small box on the table before him toward me.

"And this is yours."

Of course, the thought that I was being scammed never entered my mind, but I had never seen a blue jelly in my life, so I opened the lid a little anyway. It was like a little blue sun was sitting on the velvet surface, so strong was the light emanating from it. It was larger than the white and red jellies, which were around as big as a large coin. This little blue sun was about the size of a tennis ball. And the energy it radiated was simply stunning.

I snapped the box closed. *Well, hello there, my future armor seal!*

"Eat, drink. All has been paid for." The old man gestured at the laden table.

"You won't be keeping us company?" I asked in surprise.

The Japanese man faltered for a moment.

"I must express my deepest apologies, Sir Galaxius, but I need time to overcome this shame. I did not have the honor to be personally present, but according to Master Novojimo, whose opinion I trust without question, you are an incredible warrior. The Minamoto clan has no quarrel with you. And we are grateful that you agreed to the exchange. And now, with your permission, I will take my leave."

I shrugged and nodded. The old man walked

out.

I scratched my head. "Such strange people."

A stomach rumbled beside me. I turned. Caramel was staring with starving eyes at a huge baked fish in the very center of the table.

"Do you ever get full, fatty?" I chuckled.

"Be nice to the kitty!" Dolgorukova said, jumping to her defense.

I stared at her in amazement and shook my head. I guess girls everywhere stick together.

* * *

Dolgorukov Family Manor
Somewhere in the Urals

Prince Ivan Dolgorukov gritted his teeth. His beloved daughter had embarked on some dubious adventure with that grubby Novodvorskaya girl without his say-so. And the little scamp had managed to trick him by saying she was going to Irkutsk to raid her yearly quota of Rifts. He had always had a rather skeptical view of that — after all, the role of a woman was to protect the family hearth. Men were the ones to do the fighting, which is just what his three elder sons did. But, on the other hand, people are mortal, and the ability to stand up for yourself has always been a valuable skill in the Dolgorukov clan.

Without the help of the family, Maria had been able to independently achieve Slayer Fourth Class. Among all their high-society friends and acquaintances, he didn't know a single other girl her age who had managed that. So he closed his eyes to it and just did all he could to keep her safe. But once he learned about the duel with Novodvorskaya, the senior Dolgorukov at first felt fury and a certain amount of fear, but then remembered the rules of the Japanese empire, where duels to the death were banned.

He relaxed slightly, but still felt ill at ease. He'd solve the matter of the ransom if she lost. But the hit to reputation... Damn it, she could seriously harm his reputation. And yes, he would most likely forgive her and smooth out whatever difficulties came up. But if there was anything Ivan Sergeyevich hated, it was things out of his control.

"Father," his middle son said, walking into his office.

In his thirty years, Sergei Dolgorukov had earned his command over both the family's security services and its inner guard. At the same time, his elder brother and first in line of succession was now protecting the honor of the Empire in the southern steppes as part of the Imperial Army.

"She lost, father."

The old prince's heart skipped a beat. He gulped spasmodically. Anything could have happened.

"Is she alright?"

"Yes, she's fine."

"Ahem. What a disappointment. I was certain she was stronger than Novodvorskaya."

"She is! Her she did defeat," Sergei said. "But the Countess's second stepped in. And the second was the eldest son of Minamoto."

"Dear God!" The Count's eyebrows, and thanked the heavens that word of the defeat came to him after the fact.

If he'd known that she was going into that fight, he would have used all his connections, even contacted the head of the Academy, to prevent the duel from going ahead. With all respect for his daughter, she had no chance against Minamoto. He raised his eyes to his medium son — a strong warrior. He, perhaps, would have a chance. The eldest, Vanya, certainly could have managed. But Maria...

Dolgorukov the elder sighed.

"Contact their family and negotiate the ransom."

"Understood." He nodded and started to walk out, and then his phone suddenly rang.

The young man picked it up and the expression on his face changed.

"Who?" he asked. "What surname? Got it, thanks. I owe you one." He turned back to his father.

He looked a little lost.

"Maria... The sword was returned to her."

Dolgorukov frowned. "That's bad," he said. "Far worse than I thought. Minamoto has decided to deliberately shame us, if he returned the weapon without a ransom."

"It wasn't Minamoto. Maria's second won

back her honor."

Now the old prince's eyes widened.

"And who was her second?"

"Baron Galaxius."

"Baron?" the prince asked.

"Yes."

"Galaxius?" the prince went on in disbelief.

"Exactly right," Sergei said, cocking his head at his father. "Is something wrong?"

"More like nothing's right. If it weren't for one 'but'. The Galaxiuses... Could one of them really have survived?"

Prince Dolgorukov sat at his table and drummed his fingers on it. That was some news... Where had she managed to find a Galaxius? That had to mean... One of them must have remained alive, and still with a claim to the family!

The implications swirled in his head, and he immediately realized that the boy was sure to have many problems. There was a reason that family was torn down by its enemies. Although he himself had nothing against them, he had kept an eye on their war in the news.

Then another obvious thought came to his mind. How strong was he, if he defeated Minamoto? And what linked the baron to his daughter?!

He pressed the button on the desk to call his assistants. "I want a full report on this baron on my table before the end of the day! Get to it!"

CHAPTER 6

I WON'T LIE, it was nice to beat that puffed-up samurai. All that bravado and such amateurish swordplay. The first dard-a-roon he met in my world would have eaten him up. They were six-armed creatures, and looked like anorexic humans. And they had a screw loose. When they found weapons, they never dropped them. For decades they honed their mastery, training and massacring the people of the hills and mountains.

Strange beings... Some people thought them the souls of warriors who never got to be reborn, instead sent back in this form. Insane and stupid, driven by only one purpose — eternal warfare.

"Are you sure you're okay?" I asked the girl again at the entrance to the hotel. "You got beat up pretty bad."

"Are you ever going to let me live it down?"

She wrinkled her nose. "So I underestimated the situation, it happens."

"Not to me," I said, laughing and opening the door to let her in.

"Sure," she said, rolling her eyes. I liked needling her. She'd been so sure of herself before, and now realized she'd gotten knocked down a peg or two. After a moment, she said: "I heard you ran into some trouble in the city yourself."

I wondered when she'd had time to hear that.

"Trouble?" I asked, almost skipping a step. "Why do you think that, Maria?" I shrugged with surprise. "I'm just relaxing here. All my troubles are just living life back in Irkutsk. Maybe they aren't so big and scary after all?"

The girl just sighed. She wasn't in the mood for fighting with words after that duel, and I could well imagine why.

She'd messed up, and that meant her father would surely learn of what happened, and she had a conversation waiting for her at home.

"Do you have more business here?" she asked me in the hall. "I think we'd better fly out tomorrow morning."

"I'll be ready in time," I said, smiling at her.

"Great," she said with a weak smile of her own. "But tomorrow we're going to the park, and I won't take no for an answer!" She realized that I wanted to object, and cut me off: "I had an awful day today, and as the one who saved my honor, you have to save my spirits too. And that means you have to feed me ice cream and take me on a ride."

"A ride, huh?" A smile spread across my face on its own.

"Uh-huh..."

I guess we had different kinds of rides in mind. But my thoughts weren't serious. Get intimate with a duchess? May the gods preserve me, and Shnoop steal me and toss me in the trash. I'm not crazy enough to give myself that kind of headache.

"I'll be all yours by the evening!" I said with a mocking gallant bow.

"Tell me, Galaxius, do many people want to kill you? Because I wouldn't be surprised."

"A few..."

I led Maria to her room and ordered Shnoop to keep an eye on her, to make sure nothing untoward happened.

Just in case, I asked her not to do anything stupid, to be a good girl and rest. The healers from the Academy had done a great job, and the Minamoto family offered its help too. All the same, she needed bed rest.

It was clear that this wasn't a physical problem, but more a psychological one. She was used to being strong, and now she'd been defeated, and so easily too.

If she'd been at full strength and energy, that wouldn't have happened. More experience wouldn't hurt either. But she'd gotten it wrong... As it happens, I didn't know about those traditions myself. I could be forgiven, but her... She definitely had some explaining to do at home.

As I went into my room, the first thing I did was order ice cream for Shnoop. I also ordered another portion of meat for Caramel; she never refused food. As for me, I didn't feel like eating.

In my pocket was a blue jelly, the sight of which made me want to laugh. There it was! My armor seal!

All I had to do now was cast the thing properly, and not break anything in the process and cripple myself for life.

I waited for them to bring everything to my room, then stepped out onto the balcony. There I sat down in lotus position and started to meditate, holding the blue jelly in my hand.

It gave off a pleasant heat, warming my hand, which inflamed my imagination even more, though it also made me stop and think.

Was I doing the right thing? There were ten other seals I could unlock. Shouldn't I think again?

No way!

That's how I work! Less thought, more action. He who doubts is first to die.

I entered into my fundamental self, and started to inspect my astral form.

My regeneration seal was working just fine, and had already proved itself well. I had poured plenty of energy into my body in the Rift with the slimes, and all the microtears healed over right away.

Alright, enough thinking, time to act!

After several hours of painstaking work, in which I had time to hate it all and even feel nostalgia for the old days, my first armor layer was ready.

I had chosen a very complex weave which consisted of ten words, and only when they all lined up the right way would the seal be fully-fledged. After that, I'd bet any money that I could surprise even a High Mage in a fight. Though not for long, of course.

Right now, the weave was around twice as strong as the armor I usually put on myself. And it ate energy at half the rate, and cast more quickly.

Now the most difficult part. Full concentration... And I clenched the blue jelly in my fist. An ocean of energy surged through my body! There was more than I could absorb, even more than I could use for any of my techniques, but I didn't need to use it. I was a wise Hunter who had already lived one life through.

I had created a channel in advance to convert the energy from unbridled ocean to obedient river, and direct it to where I needed, in particular into my seal.

It isn't enough to create a reliable channel; it also has to be controlled, so that it doesn't break and distributes energy evenly. There had seemed to be plenty of energy in the jelly, but I started to notice that it was running out after an hour of work, and I wouldn't have enough. Now that was bad!

I didn't expect that... Damn it, I shouldn't have made the armor so strong, then I would have had enough. Although, who am I trying to convince? I wouldn't have changed anything. The poor workman has to work twice. The armor that I had begun to cast was the same as what I had in my past life. I couldn't even count the times it had saved my ass. Only fifty percent of it was Order-standard, the rest I came up with myself, and had constantly refined over my long life.

I had to dive into my personal supplies and take the energy I needed from there. Shame, of course, but as long as there were Rifts, I could always find more.

So it was no problem; maybe I'd even manage a Rift in the morning, no point putting it off.

Glory o universe, I had enough energy, just barely. If it had taken a drop more, my Slayer ring would have fallen to a lower rank, and I didn't want that. Then I'd have had to spend all night in a Rift again and not come out again until I had my rank back.

Although the ring was clearly dimmer now anyway, so I'd have to think of something.

Whatever, all this was just details. The main thing was that now my armor seal was ready! On the other hand, I felt ready to collapse. Sweat flowed down me in a constant stream, and my body felt broken.

I poured more energy into the regeneration seal, and felt a little better. My energy channels had been overloaded.

I activated my armor through the seal, and admired a job well done. Now I could get some rest and relaxation, and better yet — eat, and eat as much as possible.

Just as I was about to call for room service, Shnoop appeared.

"Sssshhhhhh..." he began to hiss at me, straining.

"Being a snake? No? What game is this?" I said to him jokingly.

He didn't like the joke, and just started hissing harder.

"You constipated? I warned you! You can't just eat ice cream and nothing else!"

"Ssshhhstolen!!" he finally forced out, and furiously rolled his eyes in a fit of righteous anger. All four eyes at once.

No need to ask him what was shtolen. There weren't many options; I'd asked him to keep an eye on Dolgorukova, and now she must have been...

"Goddamn it... No rest for the wicked!" I sighed heavily. "Show me!"

And Shnoop showed me — at first the girl was sitting in her room and drinking wine in solitude, glancing sadly at her sword. When she went to the shower, I asked him not to show me any spoilers and instead to skip ahead.

Then she drank another bottle, and I could see it was going to her head, but that seemed to be what she wanted. In any case, she could have charged her body with a little energy to dissolve the alcohol.

Next he showed her deciding to go out and take a walk. Wow, what the... She didn't even take the sword with her. Hmm, she wasn't dumb. Maybe she'd had a lot of stress, and she was afraid to lose it again, but her brain should be working, right?

From here, the most interesting part began. She strolled around the city for two hours until she got lost. Then she decided to use her smartphone GPS to get home. But the damn thing had a fondness for shortcuts, and it led her into a less than prosperous part of town.

Skinhead men sitting on bikes, covered in tattoos. They looked like they were up to no good, and now a gorgeous woman from out of town was walking toward them.

They surrounded her, and without naming herself or saying where she came from, she immediately started fighting. Who knew that there were thirty men there, and among them some strongly Gifted?

The girl was knocked out. Now she was lying in some manor house on the floor of a locked room, and the men were deciding what to do with her.

While they decided, I watched through that clip of Shnoop's memory again on the way there.

Dumbass, Maria... If anything happens to you, they'll rip off my head before even asking whose fault it was.

I didn't know the address, and by the time I figured it out, I'd be too late. So I had to run there on my own two feet, powering them with energy. I nearly caused a couple of accidents when I darted across the road. There was no time.

Shnoop was already there, and watching it all! Caramel had also almost made it, and her job was simpler. If I didn't make it in time, she'd break in there and eat them all.

But it looked like I might make it! They were drinking still, and loudly discussing something. I didn't like the way some of them were motioning with their hands, indicating what they wanted to do with the girl.

Poor boys... Those ones would definitely be losing some appendages...

I could understand them all. They must have been celebrating, with such a hot girl falling into their lap like that. They had tied her up with a complex artifact chain. She was probably trying to suppress it with her energy. And in the room where she was held were four other girls, which meant this was nothing new for the kidnappers. Human trafficking was outlawed, but laws don't stop criminals.

As I ran to the right spot, I had to use my power twice on the way. Who just up and started waving knives at someone on the street who was clearly in a hurry with urgent business to attend to? And shouting in Japanese at him when he doesn't understand a word of it, too?

They were the fastest muggings in the world. They gabbled something at me, I kicked them in the gut, and they flew six feet through the air.

I took the knife off one of them, which I'd

definitely throw at something some time, but the second one had a butcher's cleaver. I didn't need it, but he shouldn't be walking around with it either; he might hurt someone. That was if he survived — I didn't pull my punches, after all.

I threw the cleaver into the river I was running by, and — oops, — I didn't watch where I was throwing it. It hit a fishing boat tied to the mooring. Now the boat was slowly sinking to the bottom. Oops. Well, what could I do? I'd wanted to throw it hard, and I knew there were no people there, but that boat... Oh, the hell with it!

By the building I could finally catch my breath, and asked Shnoop to show me what was going on inside. I hadn't seen the expensive car parked there before. And that meant some new characters had turned up.

So it was... A Japanese man in a white suit was shouting in rage at his subjects. Dolgorukova had woken up now, and been shown to the man. He knew right away that she was a noblewoman, that someone would come looking for her.

Now all they could do was kill her. I would have done the same thing in their shoes. Well... or kill her later. No way would I have done that!

But that thought seemed to have occurred to these guys. The oily man picked a sword up from the table, a katana that had its own name that I'd forgotten, and pushed it into the chief's hands. Since it was his mistake, he had to correct it.

I wondered, was this a very expensive car? Probably...

A fireball charged with my energy flew right into the windshield, smashing through it and filling the interior, then exploding. The driver was Gifted, but still died on impact. I didn't spare any power, and struck true.

The building was in the kind of place where there weren't likely to be any police or clan patrols. It was right next to the slums.

The explosion was noticed, and men came running out of the building. Armed men.

I stood behind the building in an alleyway and summoned an acid slime.

"Eat through the wall so I can get through and you're free!" I commanded it quickly.

When the job is eating, they're always up to it!

One didn't cut it; the building was well-built, with several layers of brick. But two worked out just fine! They quickly ate through and opened up a passageway for me.

And I stepped into the building mad as hell... The first person that crossed my path got sliced from his neck to his stomach. He was still holding his guts in his arms as I moved on.

By the table stood a man who was trying to count money amid all the commotion, probably for the boss. An old kitchen knife flew into his eye and killed him stone dead.

Many of them had ran out onto the street, and were now putting out the fire and looking for the arsonist.

Fifteen people were left in the building, and I

thought about how to proceed.

"Meow?" my cat piped up.

"Yeah, go kill whoever you like!" I said, waving her off. "Apart from the girls, of course."

Could never be too careful with Rift pets.

I walked up to the table and saw bags full of cash. It was yen, might as well be monopoly money to me, and I didn't think it was worth taking with me. It was bound to raise questions in the airport, and I knew well from my past life that the Mafia sometimes likes to keep track of their money. In my world they did it with a magic seal, but here — by the serial numbers on the bills. Then they waited for them to start showing up, even just a couple. On the other hand, what was I supposed to do with it? Destroy it? Big job... I didn't even know how much was here:

Two people burst into the room and ran straight for me. Now I'd have to not just kill, but defend myself. They had Gifts, and even I could tell they were strong Veterans — they sure waved their swords like they were, — and could cast medium armor too.

I deliberately took a hit from one of them on my own armor, my arms at my sides. His eyes widened, but he quickly pulled his blade away and jumped back. Damn, he ruined my experiment. He must have suspected some trap, but I'd just wanted to test my armor.

But his comrade with the dragon on the cheek wasn't so smart, and swung for my neck.

Incredible... I'd forgotten how strong it was,

how little energy it consumed. The attacker didn't even have time to see my finger flying into his eye and smashing through it.

A Hunter is a weapon himself, all his body a deadly weapon, he needs no lumps of iron. As I already said, we work hard on our bodies, and metal is just a bonus.

For some reason, the man's friend opened his mouth, then tried to run away, only ran into trouble instead. One paw-blow stopped him for good.

And suddenly I realized something. I was angry, and killing these idiots couldn't fix it, or even give me any adrenaline or excitement. Or even satisfaction.

So I decided to go crazy and started punching the walls to get some attention. I wanted a fight that would make my blood boil, make me want to laugh at nothing!

Alas, I didn't get any satisfaction then either, even when they all realized there was an outsider in the house and started to come back in. I cut them, hit them, sliced them, broke their bones... And they had no chance whatsoever. Ordinary trash who thought just for an instant that they were strong. It had been hard for them to knock out a girl who was already exhausted after two duels that day. Of course, she could recover with jellies, but that was dangerous to do too often. Better to restore energy the natural way.

Incidentally, she was now sitting on the second floor and listening to what was going on.

There were no tears on her face, but her red hair could have used a brush, judging by how tangled it looked.

The Japanese boss entered the battle too, and he was probably the most interesting opponent. But he wasn't even as good as Minamoto, though not far from it.

His head left his body after a few seconds. What was this foolishness? If you're an aristocrat, even low-ranking, then you have no business in the Yakuza.

When there were only corpses and girls left in the building, I summoned another slime to devour the dead. Then I went upstairs to find Maria.

As I went, I broke open doors and let the other girls out, who showered me with teary-eyed thanks in Japanese and ran out, scattering in all directions. I just shrugged — I hoped they'd be okay.

"What should I call you now, huh?" I asked her, stepping into the room whose door I'd just had to break down.

"Dumbass?" She smiled weakly, tried to laugh, but I saw a wave of relief in her eyes.

I stood there smiling silently.

"You going to help me? Or are we walking through the streets like this?" She reached out her arms, wrapped in chains.

"Hey, they suit you, you know..." She really did look cute.

"Father was probably right. It was a mistake to fly to this country for the sake of a duel. To get into all this trouble twice in one day."

She was pretty calm about it. Even if she'd wanted to get hysterical, she couldn't allow herself such weakness.

I walked up to the girl and tore off her chains, then picked her up.

She was too weak to walk down the stairs on her own.

"Thanks!" she said embarrassedly, holding tight to my shoulders.

"Close your eyes, we're going downstairs."

When has that ever worked? Not once as far as I remembered... She looked closely at all the corpses and bloodstains I'd left behind me. I ordered the slime to back off for a couple of minutes, not showing itself to her.

We walked along silently and emerged onto a lively street where I caught a taxi and we drove back to our rooms. The girl said nothing the whole way back.

"Thanks..." she said embarrassedly outside her room. "By the way, I wanted to ask — how did you find me?"

"The cat took you for a squirrel, and she has a crazy sense of smell!" I joked, but she didn't get it. "Pure luck!" I said after a moment, lying without a pang of conscience.

"Uh-huh..." she said, making like she believed me.

"Give it to me straight, do I have to stand guard outside your door? Or are you going to be a good girl and let me get a decent night's sleep without any misadventures?"

She laughed.

"I promise I'll have a shower as soon as I get in and then go straight to bed." Did I dream it, or was she looking to see how I'd react after she mentioned the shower?

"Great! Until tomorrow, then!" I waved at her, and then, just as I was about to leave, she rushed up to me from behind and carefully hugged me.

"Thank you again..."

"My pleasure, Duchess!" I said, reminding her of our status, and that there was no need to suffer from excessive gratitude. The difference between us was too great, and I was having a good enough time as a baron already.

In the morning I set off for the store with my swords and some packs of yen I had, and used them to buy a set of throwing kunai that could hold my energy, to replace the knives I lost in the explosion. And in the evening, as promised, I took Maria to the amusement park and fed her ice cream, to an envious hiss from Shnoop. In that moment, I think he regretted helping to save her.

* * *

From the secret life of the Hunter

An unwritten rule of the Hunters was: "eye for an eye, tooth for a tooth." Xander was always known for his ability to fu... to break or lose his weapons. Jokes were often made about it at his expense.

But there were all kinds of situations, and usually, Xander wasn't at fault for what happened.

His jokester friends liked to recall one incident in particular. In a forest lake, there had settled a huge water monster, which had begun to drag in any cattle that came down to the water to drink. The locals put up with it for a long time, but when the monster carried off a couple of young women who were scrubbing laundry in a nearby brook, they hired a Hunter.

History is silent on where Xander's sword disappeared to, but at some point he ended up going hand-to-pincer with the Lake Crawler. The river monster twisted around and bit the Hunter on the ass. At which the enraged Xander did exactly the same. It wasn't just the strength of his arm and armor that made this Hunter famous — his teeth were a fearsome weapon too! In the end, the monster was defeated, and the Hunter's grinning friends, to whom the locals described the whole battle in detail, decided to give their fierce companion a rude nickname for a while — Assbiter.

CHAPTER 7

THE MILITARY AIRPLANE soared into the skies above Tokyo. I clung to the window to get another look at the interesting city and country below. The country really had been fun. A lot of fun. And I'd be sure to go back there as soon as I built up the power to stand up against those giant monsters.

My Hunter thinking kicked in, putting up a clear division in my mind between humanity and everything that threatened it. A laudable position. Only, when I got back to Irkutsk, I'd have to alter it a little. After all, when you're fighting on one side, you don't usually have to worry about being stabbed in the back. And the 'humanity' in Irkutsk, or at least a part of it, happened to be out for my blood. Oh, well — that was for later.

Maria was being unusually quiet. After the duel and the time we'd spent together, she was starting to see me through different eyes. After the restaurant, she even innocently asked where I was headed next.

"Where am I headed? To a house of ill repute!"

Sure, that sounded pretty shameful for a noble aristocrat. But Xander wasn't above that type of thing at all in his day. When you're surrounded by monstrous beasts for a week straight, or even a whole month, and the tension in your body grows and your head feels ready to explode, then when you finally make it back to civilization, any woman is like a queen. And in the Empire of the Rising Sun, it just had to be done.

When I returned that sword to Nakamuro, I asked about the subject without a hint of shame, and the old samurai, with complete understanding and without so much as a smile, gave me some recommendations for where to go.

Long story short, after a quick trip there, I was now feeling relieved. In all senses of the word. Maria's reaction, on the other hand, was like... Ha, it's funny... She reacted like Helga, who was always accusing me of sleeping around and having low standards. What the hell did it matter to them?

Anyway, Dolgorukova suggested that I not return to Irkutsk, but instead fly over to her home. She passed on a personal invitation from her father, who wanted to express his gratitude to me. But I refused. I tried to be as gentle as I could, telling her that I'd go visit as soon as I got the chance. Because I had my final hearing on the fate of my manor in three days, and I needed to be in

Irkutsk. Maria agreed outwardly, but I could tell she was upset.

In the end, we exchanged warm good-byes and I flopped down into the taxi, unpleasantly surprised at the sidelong glance the driver shot at Caramel.

Right — no more friendly Japanese taximen. Better get used to it, Xander...

We moved toward my new temporary home.

As always, I sent Shnoop ahead to tell me what was waiting for me — which was at least two cars, parked outside the Center. Judging by the fact that each of them contained only two weak Gifted, I doubted it was a capture group. More likely just recon.

When my taxi appeared in their field of view, the watchers picked up their phones and started furiously making calls. There, now King knew I was back in town.

The guards greeted me at the entrance, and the watch officer told me that the boss of the Center had asked him to tell me to go see him at my earliest convenience. I nodded and headed for 'home.'

Imagine my surprise when, as I approached the barracks, I saw Anna sitting on a bench and chattering away peaceably to Helga. I'll never understand women. Back when I was leaving, Helga had been looking daggers at her. Now they looked like best pals.

"Hey there, girls!" I smiled widely as I walked up to them. They shut up the moment they saw me.

Anna smiled widely and fairly sincerely, waving at me.

Helga's smile was darker, with a hint of some sadness to it. All the same, she gave me a slight nod too.

"I brought some gifts for you both," I said, eliciting a cry of excitement from Anna and a look of confusion from Helga.

I took out two silk kimonos that the geisha at the house of ill repute had convinced me to buy.

Honestly, my jaw had nearly dropped when, after the main purpose of my visit was done, the geishas had begun nattering away at me happily, asking me about my life. I was relaxed and satisfied, so I let slip that I knew a couple of girls back in Irkutsk. To which they said that I just had to bring back some gifts for them. And as a gift, they immediately suggested some kimonos, modeling them for me on their own perfect bodies, and offering to help pick out the best sizes and designs. I ended up agreeing, although the weightless silk cloths cost me two thousand rubles each. Yeah, that's right. Obviously I picked one up for Anna. But as for why I bought one for Helga too — I had no idea.

I didn't want to risk buying one for Maria. Our relationship wasn't close enough, although I liked her, of course. Both as a warrior and a woman.

And again, the reactions were like night and day. Anna twirled with glee, clutching the kimono. She even let me give her a kiss. On the cheek, of course. Helga, on the other hand, looked at it like a boy might look at a doll — with confusion. At least, that's the analogy that occurred to me. Maybe she had something else in her mind. But in the end, she suddenly gave me a faltering smile and said:

"Thank you, Alexander."

Alexander. She was so... proper.

I needed to take a shower. I left the gleaming Caramel with the girls.

Why gleaming? Because that whorehouse I visited was deluxe-class, and attended by some of the highest-ranking members of the Empire. The place had everything for their convenience, including a grooming salon for their pets. Caramel seemed to have had a massage, her fur brushed and her nails done. The fierce cat was a little shy about it, but I could tell shes loved it.

And yes, the traitor easily decided to stay with the girls, muttering to me mentally:

Go, run your errands.

I washed, then saw with surprise a Slayer uniform hanging nearby. It had no distinguishing marks on it and seemed to be my size. Given that I had no clothes left again, I chuckled and pulled it on. It fit perfectly. Anna's handiwork, no doubt.

Next I went to see Khrulyov. Very polite of him, to invite me 'at my earliest convenience.' But why upset one of the most powerful people in the Eastern Empire? Not in terms of his strength — although he was at Master level, — but of his position.

"May I come in, Sir?"

"Ah, Alex! Of course, come in!"

Look at that. Alex now, not Galaxius. I took a seat.

"I won't ask, I'll just pour you some tea right away," the old man said. "With honey, of course."

I just smiled and said:

"Thanks a lot! Gladly!"

I'd already found out that the old man kept his own apiary here. The honey was his own. He was insanely proud of it. Although he didn't tell anybody he was a beekeeper in his spare time. It was a kind of open secret. Everyone knew it, but they all played dumb. They just gratefully accepted the treat. As it happens, far from all his guests were treated to the honey. It was an honor for a rare few. As it happens, it really was good honey.

"I've heard about your... adventures on the islands."

I smiled.

"Somehow I knew you would have."

"Well, naturally. All the Slayers of the world keep in contact with each other. As you know, the threat we face is shared by all humanity. So we always share information between ourselves. Particularly as the Slayers are an organization above governments. Whatever wars might take place between humans, the threat of the beasts comes first. Take a look." He turned his monitor to me. "Your reputation is eighty-seven! You can now take up to fifty people into a raid. Incredible for one so young. A little more and you might reach the maximum raid leader rank."

I smiled skeptically. The old man caught my expression and suddenly laughed.

"Right, right. Who am I talking to? A man who does everything solo."

He sat down and looked at me.

"That uniform suits you, you know. All you need is some decent badges."

"Please don't start, Sir," I said, smiling.

"I had to try," the old man said with a smile of his own. "You'd be a difficult subject. The boys wouldn't have time to pin enough badges on you, with all the Rifts you close. What is it, every day one more, two more?"

"Don't exaggerate, Sir," I chuckled. "Even I have limits."

The old man laughed again.

"Even I have limits..." he echoed. "Now that's what I call a sense of your own greatness. No limit to perfection!"

I shrugged.

"I don't think I'm great. I'm just stating a fact."

"Exactly my point," the old man said, nodding. "Many make like they're hot stuff. But Galaxius just does his job. Could do with more like that."

He was silent a moment.

"I imagine you know why I invited you here."

"Yeah, to tell me how I have to slave away to work off my stay." I smiled.

"You put it harshly. But you have the idea,

yes. I've picked out a Rift for you. Look."

My tablet squawked. I took it out of my bag.

"You have all the information you need, and I've sent you my preferences regarding the group as well. In principle, the final selection of the group is at the discretion of the raid leader. But there is one person there that you cannot remove."

"Let me guess... Helga?" I smiled.

For some reason, the old man's smile slipped. I leaned toward him and whispered conspiratorially:

"Maybe you could enlighten me, Sir. Just who is she exactly?"

The slight smile returned to the old man's face again.

"Those who need to know do know. Those who don't, they have no need to."

"Heh, you're a real philosopher!" I chuckled. "Fine, all the same to me."

"So, when will you take care of the Rifts?" the old man asked, his tone businesslike now.

Now it was my turn to laugh.

"You really don't mess around! I haven't even looked at them yet. Give me two or three days, unless it's super urgent."

"No, it's not urgent." The old man shook his head. "What I'm giving to you 'burnt out' half a year ago already, maybe more. That's why I picked it for you."

Suddenly, he clapped his hands.

"Alright, Galaxius, dismissed!"

"Yes, sir!" I said with only a slightly mocking

salute.

The old man laughed at the sight of me.

"You'd make a great regular Slayer, Galaxius."

I silently turned on my heel and marched out of the office.

Behind me I heard the old man's quiet, but satisfied laughter.

* * *

At the exit from the Center's office building, Androsov was waiting for me. He looked less than pleased.

"Well, where have you been?" he asked, his face set in a grimace.

"Glad to see you too," I said, offering him a hand, but for some reason he didn't take it, just kept looking pissed off. "Come on, Andy, that's enough!" I smiled. "Firstly, I'm sure you know where I was. And secondly, the monsters in the Empire of the Rising Sun are too big for your soft princely ass."

Androsov tried to look offended, but didn't do a great job of it.

"Well, want to get a drink somewhere today?" I asked. I'll tell you what it's like there, in the land of the Rising Sun. And you can tell me your good news from here."

Androsov frowned at that, but then suddenly smiled for the first time.

"Actually, I came to give you the same

invitation. And not just for drinking. We have an occasion."

"No way!" My eyebrows went up. "What occasion?"

Androsov took his right hand out of his pocket and showed me his signet ring, which shone with a milk-white glow.

"Whoa! Slayer Class Six Count Andrei Androsov! Congratulations, buddy!"

I hugged him. When I pulled back, Androsov was already grinning with all thirty-two of his teeth. It was against his nature to stay angry for too long. He couldn't stay angry at all, really. His whole display was all show. "Actually, it's Duke now..." he said with a hint of embarrassment. "With my Slayer rank came an increase in my noble standing."

I laughed. "Don't let it go to your head. Alright then, Duke, the Center bar..?"

"Forget that!" Androsov's face turned serious again. "I can afford somewhere better!"

"No doubt..." I said. "And where might that be?"

"Well, we have a slight hitch there. I wanted to go to Tranquility, but it sounds like something happened there. They promised to sort it out by the evening, but they didn't sound too sure. So a little later tonight, I'll get in touch and let you know."

"Hope you won't ask me to wear a tux this time." I grimaced.

"Still don't have enough money for one?"

Androsov chuckled.

"Got the money. Just can't bring myself to spend it."

"Alex, Alex," my friend said, shaking his head. "Sooner or later you're going to have to get one made. Nobles won't let you through the door in the Capital without one."

"Well, when we get to the Capital, we'll talk," I said. "By the way, you don't mind me bringing two ladies, do you?"

Androsov frowned suspiciously.

"Well, Anna I know. Who's the other one?"

"Oh, just... An old acquaintance."

"What are you up to this time, Galaxius?"

"What do you mean? Maybe I'm just bringing one for you?"

"I have a fiancée! How many times do I have to tell you?"

"Well, a bride's a bride, but you'll like this one."

"If you've decided to bring me a whor... a chick... ugh, you're a bad influence, you know! A girl! If she's for my sake, then tell her not to come."

"No, no, Andrei. This girl will be invited just for my sake." I smiled widely.

"Fine, then," Androsov nodded. "In light of your recent events, I guess you need a lift there?"

"No, I'll figure something out."

"You sure?" My comrade frowned. "I'd rather my only friend not get shot by the mob."

"Your only friend?" I needled him, but with a warm heart. If I had anyone in this world who suited the moniker 'friend,' then it was Andrei. "Like one old alcoholic I knew used to say — dream on."

"Strange acquaintances you have," Androsov said with a sidelong glance.

"Some of the best, Andy," I said, remembering Old Mac, who, even with all his passion for the demon drink, could still stand up against the Emperor himself in a contest of power.

I clapped him on the shoulder, then headed for my barracks.

* * *

Anna and I waited for the car at the Center checkpoint.

Shnoop had reported that King's watchers shifted into action when they saw me. But no, boys, not today.

An armored limousine bearing the Morozov crest rolled up to the entrance. Two large armored cars accompanied it, front and back. While the limo stopped, guards armed to the teeth jumped out of the other cars. Shnoop reported that King's fighters were a little taken aback. The chauffeur opened the door and we climbed in.

Duchess Morozova was beautiful.

"I told you you didn't need to wear a ball gown," I said with a smile, taking in the stunning girl with her perfect haircut.

"What do you mean, ball gown?" She looked down at the waves of white silk. "This is just semiformal wear."

I chuckled. Anna looked like a servant next to her, in a red dress. A very attractive and alluring servant, but still.

Myself, I wore a suit. A nice suit. Another surprise from Anna. While I was gone, she'd found time to get it made to order. And, even more surprisingly, it fit me perfectly. Two and a half thousand rubles was all the pleasure cost me. But I looked like... Well, either like a second-rate aristocrat or a successful businessman. Whatever, anything was better than a tracksuit.

"Oh, Alex, I'm so excited, just so excited!" Svetlana clapped her hands. I felt my breath taken away again as I looked at the delicate, carefree girl, knowing how much power lay within her.

"If only you knew how excited I am." I smiled, catching a look of confusion from both women.

Don't look at me like that. A friend is a friend. I love giving my friends surprises.

The party did, in the end, take place at Tranquility.

The cars of the princely family were allowed into the grounds without question, unlike taxis. The outer perimeter and the inner grounds looked the same as ever.

At the entrance, the well-dressed doorman let us in. The manager walked over to greet us. He looked a little rough. I could tell that healers had worked hard on him, but his arm was in a sling, and the right side of his face sported a fading yellowish-blue bruise.

"Duchess Morozova, so nice to see you! Countess Goldsmith, my regards! Baron Galaxius? Ahem, greetings..." The manager's face changed instantly.

"And good health to you," I smiled. "What happened here?" I nodded at his beat-up appearance.

"Some minor difficulties. But we smoothed them out." The man smiled thinly.

"I hope nobody suffered." I grinned at him. "Except you, I mean."

The manager pursed his lips, but still answered.

"There were no other injuries."

"Well, that's just great!" I said with mock relief. "How strange... What mysterious trouble managed to sneak its way into the best defended club in Irkutsk?"

The manager's face twisted again like he'd eaten a lemon. He let that go without comment and just beckoned us in.

Today, Androsov had rented the whole place. That Slayer ring seemed to given him a little more confidence too. I doubted he'd earned the money for this fete in a Rift. Considering he now had a family guard following him around, I figured he'd condescended to allow his daddy to pay for this banquet.

Honestly, I didn't get why he didn't reconcile sooner. Family is there to help, after all. Why refuse in the first place?

I'd voiced the suggestion to him a couple of

times, but he always just waved a hand at me with a smile. I wouldn't do things that way myself. If I had a family in this world... rather, when I had one — I would fully trust it and provide all kinds of support. Family is family!

People were standing around in small groups. But when they saw us, a hush descended. We looked great, of course, no sense in being humble. I looked at myself in the big mirror in the foyer. The girls held onto my arms daintily. And as for me... Whoa! I saw various feelings in the eyes of the onlookers. A baron with a countess and duchess might have looked funny, if only that baron's surname wasn't Galaxius. The only people in the high society of Irkutsk who didn't know about me by now had to be living under a rock. And they wouldn't have gotten an invitation here anyway, so screw 'em.

Androsov stood with his back to us. Next to him I saw my old acquaintances — Helga, young Smolin, Sinelnikova, Viscount Schrader and a couple of other familiar faces.

Helga was the first to see me, and she narrowed her eyes at me. Pavel stood facing me too. I put a finger to my lips, telling them to stay quiet. They frowned in confusion, but did as I asked.

Once I'd walked right up to them, I grabbed a glass of whiskey from a passing waiter, then shouted loudly:

"To the new Monster Slayer — Duke Andrei Androsov! HURRAH!"

Andrei turned to me to accept my congratulations, smiling, and then his eyes fell on Morozova. His smile wilted, a glazed look of shocked horror spreading across his face.

"Surprise!" the petite girl said, clapping her hands.

Androsov didn't know what to do. He was holding a glass of champagne in his hand. He looked around until his eyes stopped on me with that same horrified look.

I deftly took the glass off him and chuckled.

"Go on! Go kiss your bride."

"Right, right." Androsov walked up to her and carefully embraced her.

"Hello, my dear!"

"Hello, darling! Isn't it wonderful that I'm here?"

Another sidelong glance at me.

"Yes, my beloved. Wonderful, without a doubt. But why didn't you warn me you were coming? I would have met you." Androsov's voice was shaking. He was nervous as a court servant seeing the Emperor for the first time.

"Your friend Alex met me off the plane."

Another sullen glance back at me.

If he kept on like that, he'd hurt his neck.

"We decided to make it a surprise for you."

"Well, it worked," Androsov said through his teeth.

"I see no joy on your face," I said, grinning at him, and gave his glass back. "Hey, you there!" I called out to a waiter. "Champagne for everyone!

And for the new Slayer — a glass of vodka! This is a great moment in the life of every person, and Andrei is of course happy to share it with you. He has told me many times that there's nobody closer to him than you. He just didn't know when he'd get to class six. Otherwise he would have invited you himself. But my intuition happened to kick in at just the right moment."

Champagne was brought to everybody. I raised a hand and shouted again.

"Who has some spurs?" I turned to the others.

Unsurprisingly, Helga had some. Two silver spurs clattered into the glass, and I offered it to my friend.

"Well, then — to our new Slayer! Hip hip, hurrah!"

The hall erupted with shouting, and Andrei drank down the vodka with a grimace, catching the spurs in his teeth.

The time for my vengeance had come. I looked at Androsov's reddened face. He seemed to have relaxed a little, and was now looking lovingly at his fiancée. He hadn't lied to me — it was obvious he was crazy about her. And so was she about him.

"You know what I've found out, guys?" I said to him conspiratorially. "It turns out that if Svetlana becomes a Slayer, then you can actually register your marriage at the Center itself. It only takes two hours. I have a good rapport with the head of the Center — Gramps, we call him, — so I think we could get it all arranged quickly."

I winked at both the young woman and the

stunned man. A whole ocean of happiness and hope splashed in Maria's eyes, and she clutched her betrothed tightly. Androsov's lips, on the other hand, whispered silently at me:

"You're f...ed!"

Ugh, how uncultured. And he an aristocrat, no less!

I smiled broadly, shrugging at him.

"Well, I guess you two have plenty to talk about. Guess I'll go enjoy the party. Waiter! Stop! Give me vodka! And one of those black caviar rolls! Actually, make it two!"

* * *

Dolgorukov Family Manor
Somewhere in the Urals

Ivan Sergeyevich couldn't stay angry at his daughter for long. Actually, he couldn't be angry at his only daughter at all! Their long-awaited and unexpected daughter had been born when Dolgorukov was already at a ripe age. His three elder sons were in the family business, but Maria was just daddy's girl.

And now his daughter was drilling her father in an attempt to get out of him everything he knew about the Galaxius family. You see, Ivan Sergeyevich had a hobby — he liked to dig through the genealogical tables of Imperial aristocrats. The Emperor himself sometimes consulted his advice on debated issues of inheritance.

"It is a *very* strange family, Maria. Very ancient, and very strange. You see, the Galaxiuses were close to the first Emperor, and helped him attain the throne when the Empire... Well, you know the history yourself."

Maria nodded silently and went on listening, not interrupting.

"Right, so... They had a very unusual Gift — a unique one, you might say. The Summoner's Gift. They could tame Rift beasts, and at one time they had a whole army of the godforsaken creatures. Incidentally, our army was once defeated by a raid of the steppe peoples. And only the Galaxius manor stood between them and Irkutsk. So the family released their... Ahem... pets. The proud steppe warriors galloped their way out of here in double time, heh-heh..."

The prince took a sip of the reinforced wine he liked so much from his silver goblet. Then he cleared his throat and continued.

"The trouble was that these Galaxiuses were, how can I put it... unhinged, to say it plainly. Entirely unhinged. They had their own Code of Honor, and they followed it come hell or high water. Regardless of their connections or their profits. Some couple of hundred years ago, the senior Galaxius challenged the Emperor himself to a duel over some trifling matter that was, in the opinion of the head of the family, unbefitting of our ruler. They barely managed to hush it all up..."

Ivan Sergeyevich stood up and started pacing back and forth across his office, his hands behind his back.

"They gained many enemies, a great many! External enemies, not internal. And, like little children, they harrowed the southern borders of the Empire and failed to see the threat growing behind them. Seven Families gathered all their strength and treacherously attacked their mansion. A terrible slaughter followed, although the victory was hollow... The seven Families lost half their heirs and best fighters in the battle, but the Galaxiuses were almost entirely eradicated. Only the women and children remained. The women were taken either by force or argument in the hope that they would bear children with that unusual Galaxius Gift. As far as I know, they didn't. And so that great family died out... At least, so everybody thought, until now..."

"Da-a-ad..?" Maria asked.

"Yes, yes, I'll help him, I said so already!" The old prince smiled into his gray mustache. "Even a little more than you think. I have a certain item in my collection..."

He pressed a button on his intercom.

"Kseniya, my dear, call Sergei up here! Tell him I have some urgent business for him to attend to!"

CHAPTER 8

THE PARTY WAS A LOT OF FUN, not counting the angry looks I kept getting from Androsov.

After I got a little tipsy, I dragged him off to a corner and asked him what his deal was.

Andrei, also a little drunk, admitted helplessly that ever since his childhood, when their parents had agreed on their 'strategic marriage,' he had felt ill at ease about it. It wasn't that he didn't like Svetlana — he really loved her, he just felt 'unworthy' himself.

Because of the girl's powerful Gift, and because of his own non-combative one. That was one of the reasons he ran off to Irkutsk. Now that he had some experience, he'd realized that his Gift was actually IMBA as hell. First of all, the whole raid felt much more confident in the knowledge that a powerful Healer was there to get them out of scrapes. And second, it turned out he could not only ease pain, but also cause a great deal of it to his enemies. That made him feel a little better about the situation. All in all, Andy was growing up right before my eyes.

A call from Rafael caught me by surprise.

"Alexander, your court hearing takes place tomorrow, at eight in the morning."

"Tomorrow?" Damn, that meant I'd lied to Maria when I told her I couldn't visit their family manor yet. "There was supposed to be a lot more time left!"

"Yes, there was supposed to be more than two months left," Rafael said, his voice irritated. "Something is happening, Alexander... The judge has been changed and the times moved up."

"Is that good for us, or bad?" I asked the professional.

"No idea yet. I'm trying to figure that out."

"Well, are we ready for the hearing?" I asked.

To that, the old Jew gave a quiet laugh.

"What a question, Alex! You could wake me up in the middle of the night and I'd be ready for any of the cases I'm working on. You don't have to worry about that."

"Glad to hear it!" I said with a sigh of relief. "Until tomorrow, then."

"Until tomorrow," Rafael said. "And you... That is..." He hesitated a moment. "Be careful as you move through the city."

That old fox! I didn't bother playing dumb, just answered simply:

"I'll try."

* * *

So as not to invite an assassination attempt from King's suicide attackers, I rented an armored car from the Center, which took me right to the city court building. It was amusing to watch the cavalcade of cars and the confused faces of their brutish drivers, trying to figure out over the phone what they should do. Just as I expected, King didn't risk giving the order to attack an armored car from the Center, so I got to the court building without adventure. There was also the possibility that the idiots would come in and arrange a slaughter on the inside, but by the time we drove up to the court, I felt calmer about that.

Once more, Rafael Goldsmith lived up to his reputation as a smart man. He knew where he was going and who he was meeting with. The court was already surrounded by serious-looking men with the Goldsmith crest on their breastplates. The local guards cast slightly fearful glances at them. They had practically encircled the building.

Knowing Rafael, I figured he probably had one or two snipers stationed near the building too. And yes, Rafael definitely knew who was who in Irkutsk. Because, after one of his fighters let through our armored car, holding his assault rifle barrel to the floor, he moved to block the road and raised his hand palm-forward to stop the goons driving after us. The mobsters didn't even get out of their cars, just turned around and parked up nearby. Nice. At least here my flank was well guarded.

I met Rafael right at the entrance. We greeted each other, and I thanked him for the extra guards, which got a jolly laugh out of him.

"What do ya think you're thanking me for, Alexander?" Rafael asked with a grin. "You think I'm covering your ass here? All due respect, but your ass is worth nothing to me. All these measures are for protecting my own priceless backside. After all, if there was a fight, I'd be the first to go down. So I'll answer you with a clean conscience — no problem."

He smiled, and we walked toward the courtroom. Two guards walked ahead of us, and two more followed behind. Judging by their auras, they were plenty powerful.

"Here's the plan, Alexander — you sit there and say nothing. When I talk, you nod." He smiled again. "That clear?"

"Crystal. Did you manage to find out anything about the sudden changes and what they mean for us?"

Rafael darkened. I could tell he was used to having everything under control, and he didn't like this situation one bit.

"I never did figure out where the wind is blowing from, and who really ordered the case against us. A little birdie whispered to me that the Dolgorukov family is involved in today's situation. It's possible, of course, that they ordered it. But their reputation is perfectly clean. Would you happen to know anything about it?"

I smiled, and breathed out somewhere inside. Maria, that little rogue! She must have decided to repay me after all. Well, at least it looked that way to me. We'd have to see how it all went.

And it went just great. Rafael had prepared for the proceedings. The judge had exhaustive information: the profile of Slayer Fifth Class Alexander Galaxius, with a particular focus on his incredible reputation for his short time in the Empire, his letter of recommendation from Center commander Duke Khrulyov, and the fulfillment of the greater part of his Rift debts in an unbelievably short period.

At that point I smiled. That old partisan. He hadn't so much as winked to tell me that Goldsmith had contacted him.

Next came the payment to cover my tax bill, of thirty thousand rubles, which I transferred while still in Japan as soon as I got the request, leaving me almost broke. Again. And finally came some documents that I didn't see personally, but which confirmed my right to own the asset.

I was clean all over. The state prosecutor and the tax inspector who were supposed to be my opponents didn't even open their mouths for the whole hearing. To the judge's questions, they only answered that they had no more questions of their own. Which was strange, of course, given how hard a time the state usually has letting things go. As expected, the judge took my side.

After the gavel fell, the Galaxius manor on the shore of Lake Baikal was officially returned to my possession. And I was declared the new head of the Family, with all accompanying authority and right to wear the family signet ring.

Goldsmith looked mystified, but very pleased all the same.

"A wonderful outcome, Alexander. Well done!"

I shrugged. "I had nothing to do with it."

"Sure, sure, you keep saying that!" Goldsmith laughed, his profession rendering him unable to believe such tales. "So, our contract is now ended." He offered me his hand. "My secretary will send you the remainder of the bill. Be so kind as to not leave the payment too long."

I smiled.

"Sure thing," I said, shaking his hand.

The short and skinny Rafael suddenly hugged me surprisingly tightly.

"One other thing, Alexander." His expression suddenly turned harsh. "I know that you have drawn Anna close to you. She and I..." He hesitated. "...have a complex relationship right now. But that doesn't change the fact that she is my daughter. For various reasons, I will not help you two. But if something happens to her, then be ready to see me in court."

"In court?" I smiled. Damn this old lawyer. Everything was so inhuman with him. "Firstly, I'll take care of her. And secondly, I'm not afraid of seeing anyone in or out of court."

At that, Rafael allowed himself a smile.

"Somehow that sounds like the truth. Good luck to you, Alexander. You know where to find me."

"Thank you, Mr. Goldsmith."

"Oh yeah, one last gift, Alexander. You need to pick up the judge's decision. It'll take around half an hour. Some of my guys will wait here until you're ready to go. A little bonus for you, as an honored customer."

"Thanks."

I walked to a cafe and ordered coffee and eclairs. Then I took a seat in the corner and started thinking about my situation.

Out of the corner of my eye, I saw a man heading toward me. Power poured off him. He looked older than me, around thirty. Tall, thin, green eyes, shock of bright red hair. But the face and crest definitely reminded me of someone.

With no clue at all, I stretched my lips into a smile before the man introduced himself.

"Allow me to introduce myself, Sir Galaxius. Duke Sergei Dolgorukov."

I gave Maria's brother a firm handshake.

"May I sit down?"

"Of course, Duke, of course." I nodded. "What fate brings you here? And thank you for the help, by the way, although I didn't ask for it."

Sergei allowed himself a smile.

"Right, Maria told me as much. That you'd be sure to say something like that."

I shrugged.

"Well, it's true. I could have handled it

myself."

Sergei shook his head.

"You look like an aristocrat, yet you have no understanding of the simplest things. It is not money that solves things in this world, but connections. If you have the good luck, or in this case the personal success, to enter new circles, then it is a sin not to take advantage."

"With all due respect, Duke, I have a different policy. It's always simpler to go it alone. That way you only have to answer for yourself, and don't have to worry about anyone close to you dying."

"Maria said that about you too."

"She seems to have said a lot about me." I frowned. "But I don't know anything about you."

"In brief, I am head of the security services and commander of the guard of the Dolgorukov family. If you take advantage of my father's kind offer and come to visit us at our manor, you will be able to get to know us more closely."

"You flew all the way here to personally convey the invitation that Maria already extended to me?" I smiled.

"Among other things. Actually, the main reason for my visit is this..."

He took a small and simple wooden box out of his jacket pocket. I opened the lid. On a burgundy base sat a dull signet ring of blackened gold. And on it was a crest, which... Holy shit! No, no way! HOLY... SHIT!

The elegantly crafted grinning face of a small, but *very* nasty critter stared up at me from the box. A honey badger. The most stone-cold bastard in the whole Universe. The secret mascot of the Hunters. From *that* world... A coincidence?

As I looked inside, I saw the family motto: *Honor Above Life!* I chuckled involuntarily and relaxed a little. What a dumb slogan. A little different from the position of the Hunters, but! There were some Hunters like that too!

I pushed away those strange thoughts. What mattered was that I had the family ring of Galaxius in my hand, and I put it on right away.

Sergei moved back, watching me with a smile, but his face tensed when I put the ring on, and then he froze.

A light aura of power encircled the ring and the gold began to glow, transforming to look freshly polished. And I sensed my inner energy supply expanding.

The ring had found Galaxius blood, and accepted its new master.

* * *

Arkhip had asked me very insistently for me to stop by his store. So I said good-bye to Sergei after thanking him sincerely, got back in my swanky armored car from the Center and directed the driver to *Arkhip's Legendary Armory.*

Honestly, between the court and other recent events, I was a little short on cash. Wouldn't hurt to get my stashes of weapons, gear and jellies. But I really didn't like traveling through the whole city with a tail of King's people following me. I had to do something about that. The situation was starting to tick me off.

"Greetings, Alexander!" The big storekeep offered me a ham hand. "I've heard nothing except tales of your travels on the Japanese isles."

I shook his hand and smiled.

"Has anyone not heard of them yet?"

"I suspect not," he said with a deep laugh. "You know that our Empire and theirs have a love-hate relationship. The Japanese envy our wealth. And our Empire envies their warriors, and constantly uses its riches to lure their best fighters over here. If it weren't for the Japanese mentality and unprecedented loyalty to their work and country, we would probably have stolen all of them. And then the Empire of the Rising Sun would be devoured by monsters, and the eastern border would move to the shore of Korea and the Empire. Of course, the Minamoto family would have preferred to keep what happened secret, but there were too many eyes. By the way, what did you get for his sword?" Professional interest flashed in the old man's eyes.

There was no point in hiding it, since Maria and the Minamotos knew already.

"A blue jelly."

Arkhip's eyes narrowed in confusion.

"I don't get it. You let 'em off easy. I'm sure the senior heir had the best sword in the Minamoto clan, worth at least half a million. Whereas a blue jelly is worth around a hundred and fifty thousand right now."

I smiled.

"And I guess you have one for sale, huh?"

"How could I?" Arkhip raised an eyebrow. "It's a very rare item." Then he narrowed his eyes at me. "Is yours for sale? I'll give you a hundred and sixty-five, above market average!"

I laughed.

"See. That's exactly why. A thing can exist and have a price. And yet not be for sale anywhere. And that raises its value quite a lot."

"So what are you going to do with it? With all respect to you, you definitely don't have a high enough max energy for it. It'd be like filling a car up with a whole fuel tanker — ninety-nine percent of it would spill out of the car's tank. But I can find a buyer for you. For maybe even more than a hundred and seventy thousand. There are powerful aristocrats in the Empire with a permanent demand for high-grade jellies."

"Thanks, friend. But I'm afraid it's gone already."

"You sold it? For how much?" The storekeep sighed. "I bet you got taken for a ride."

"Simmer down, I didn't sell it."

"So where is it?"

I wiped the smile off my face.

"Enough questions, Arkhip."

The storekeep cut off.

"Ahem... Sorry... I didn't mean anything by it."

"And a good thing, too," I said, smiling again.

"Anyway, what did you want?"

Arkhip pursed his lips a moment. "An order came in. But it's clearly a set-up."

"What makes you think that?" I asked.

"The rights to raid a Rift have been purchased. An official ad placed. A reward declared. Only they seem to be refusing everybody who applies. Even official Center fighters."

"What, you can do that?" I asked.

"Sure, Free Slayers can buy exclusive rights for a short time. If they don't handle the job, then it makes no difference to the Center, they just send their own Slayers out a little later. But in the meantime, the Rift is 'on order.'"

"And what kind of Rift is it?"

"Level five. Nothing special officially. Apart from the price. And that's another oddity. Usually, Rifts like these are rented out for high-demand monsters or Rift ingredients. Here, there's nothing really but the rep reward for closing the Rift. So not much."

"Where is it?"

"Look." Arkhip pressed a button and brought it up on his monitor, turning it to me.

Unsurprisingly, it was outside the perimeter, in a relatively safe zone not far from the army posts, on an abandoned farm. And the payment for closing it was fifteen thousand rubles — more than five times higher than the next highest reward at the Center.

I scratched the back of my head. If something looks like a duck, walks like a duck and quacks like a duck, then surely it's a duck. But the thing was, by putting such a high price on a cheap Rift, King — or whoever it was — was making far too obvious a bet on my greed. They must know I'd notice that, and be ready for it. And for some reason, that fact didn't bother them. And that bothered me. I'd have to prepare very carefully.

"I'll take it!" I said.

"Well, then let's try," Arkhip said. "Sign up."

I submitted the application, and a few seconds later the message came up: "Application accepted!" and the countdown began. The minimum deadline — one day, as standard.

I smiled.

"Well, thanks!"

"No problem," Arkhip said, giving me a strange look.

"What?" I asked in surprise.

"You're playing a dangerous game, Alexander."

"But a fun one."

I smiled. The storekeep didn't smile back.

"I don't see anything funny about this. Or fun either. Your life is at stake here, you know. You have some big players working against you, and too many of them. One day they'll just mob you."

I smiled to myself, remembering the mass of souls I had saved up within me. An azure dragon, for example, would barely notice a crowd of ordinary humans and their firearms. And I had plenty others to go at, too. Although, unfortunately, the supply was finite. In order to catch monsters of the same quality in this world, I *really* needed to level up.

"Thanks, Arkhip, once again," I said, offering him a hand.

"Are you sure you don't need anything?" He looked me up and down, taking in my unarmed appearance. "I heard your apartment got blown up, along with your personal armory."

"You seem to have heard everything," I said. "No, I don't need anything for this Rift. I'll stop by after."

"Oh, by the way..." Arkhip smiled. "About that miner's kama sutra of yours!"

I laughed. "Oh yeah. How much did you get for it?"

"It hasn't sold yet," he said with an embarrassed grimace. "The expert, the French marquis, was found dead in his room after certain... ahem... experiments. Seems like he was trying to repeat something from the tablet, but it went wrong."

"Goddamn!" My eyebrows shot up. "What now, then?"

"The stone has gone on to England," the big man said with a shrug. "There are, ahem, certain interested experts there as well!"

*   *   *

Tokyo Port District
Warehouses of the Blue Cherry Company

The medics kept pulling out more and more corpses, and it seemed like there was no end of them.

The victims bore cuts and gunshot wounds, and many had traces of strikes from Gifts. All the bodies and their parts were thickly covered in tattoos, as was so popular in the local mob.

Two policeman watched the medics tiredly as they loaded the remains into the corpse trucks, which set off one after another toward the city morgue.

"Someone decided to do our job for us, Lieutenant, sir?" asked the younger cop, a sergeant's stripes on his shoulder.

"Looks that way," his senior partner answered. "Two Yakuza clans lost their bosses today."

"What were they doing here together?"

"You know what. Slicing up their territory." The lieutenant chuckled. "But instead, they were sliced up... into little pieces."

"So what now? The slaughter starts? The clans won't just let this go — it's a matter of honor."

"I doubt it," the older man said, still smiling. "Did you see the blood on the walls? The notes in blood, I mean."

The young man nodded. "Sure did. But looks like East Imperial, and I don't know it."

"Well, I do. They say where the other side can go to get their revenge."

"So where is it?" the younger one asked.

"Some address in some imperial city. But that's not the most interesting part. The seconds are being promised by the Long Arm clan... 'Dolgorukov,' in East Imperial.

CHAPTER 9

I FELT LIKE A GODDAMN HOSTAGE! I could move around inside the Center as much as I wanted, but all the exits were watched, and you can't just go out to take a ride around in a Center APC.

First of all it's expensive, and I had less than ten thousand rubles left after paying my taxes and everything else.

And secondly, no matter how well disposed to me Khrulyov was, using an armored car as a taxi would be a bridge too far.

But I was seriously concerned by one of the groups that lay in wait for me at one of the exits. A huge armored jeep with St. Petersburg number plates and three big thugs inside.

They kept apart from King's people, and the latter kept their distance too. Shnoop had once managed to listen in on a conversation between these and two other incomers, but it was always the same ones on watch. And their trunk was packed full of powerful weaponry.

I sighed and went to pay tribute to Uncle Simon — the head of the Center's car fleet.

Uncle Simon, an old class-four Slayer, was a crystal clean individual. He was utterly impossible to bribe, so I had to go to him cap in hand and beg. Officially, through the website, I wasn't allowed to rent an armored car to go for a ride round the city — I had to try to solve it on the ground.

"You again, Galaxius?" the old man muttered, wearing his signature worn overalls splattered with machine oil.

"Hey, Uncle Simon!" I said, plastering a smile across my face, as friendly as I could make it.

"Need another APC for a joyride, huh?" The old fleet chief frowned and crossed his arms.

"Well, you know my situation. If I take a taxi, I'll get shot. And bystanders might get hurt too. I just need a one-way trip."

"What do you mean, one-way?" The old Slayer narrowed his eyes. "Decided to commit suicide, have you?"

"No, I have a plan. This is the last time I'll ask. I promise!"

The old man grumbled in annoyance.

"What does Petrovich see in you? Fine, one last time!"

"Thanks!"

After half an hour, the APC dropped me off by the Rhapsody restaurant at the edge of a large city park, with a winter terrace garden with an exit into that park. A wide open space.

"Are you sure you're coming back on your own?" asked the corporal, who I already knew.

"Yeah, Vasya, don't worry about it! Dismissed!" I handed him two ten-ruble notes. "Some beer money, as always."

"There's no need, Your Lordship," the corporal said, like he always did.

I smiled.

"What did I tell you?"

"That when people offer you money, you should take it. And say thanks." The soldier smiled. And took the notes. "Thanks!"

"Enjoy. You understand what to do, right?"

"Yes, sir!"

The armored car drove off, and I chose a table by the window and near the exit to the park, which right now was closed due to the poor weather. There were no customers nearby, I made sure of that.

I ordered a coffee and started to wait, examining the surroundings through Shnoop.

The 'Kingsmen' stood in the distance and spoke to their superiors, but took no measures. Their weapons included shotguns and assault rifles, but since this was almost in the city center, they surely didn't want to cause any bloodbaths.

The ones from Petersburg, on the other hand, went to some considerable effort. They worked smoothly. The duo went to the kids' amusement park, empty in the autumn time, and climbed up onto the roof of the House of Horrors.

A cold autumn rain drizzled down. There was almost nobody walking in the park, and without particularly hiding what they were doing, the duo took out and set up a sniper rifle on their vantage point. The gunner took out a magazine, the rounds gleaming with reddish light. Very expensive rounds, those, specially made for hunting Gifted. These were no mere thugs, and their gun was the professional deal too.

The third driver stayed in the car and kept the engine on, waiting for his companions.

"Mind if I smoke?" I asked the waiter, nodding toward the closed doors.

"Of course! Would you like an ashtray?" The waiter unlocked and opened the doors.

"No!" I smiled.

"Why not?" He looked surprised.

"I don't smoke," I said with a chuckle and stepped outside, raising my head to the sky. Cold droplets started to land on my face, and I smiled. Sighing deeply, and at first walking, then breaking into a run, I headed straight toward the would-be assassins.

The gunner's spotter got nervous. "Fire!"

And then a dead squirrel dropped out of thin air onto the damp hat atop the sniper's head.

"What the hell?!" The sniper's eyes widened as he threw the critter corpse from his head, then turned back to the rifle and felt... air in his hands.

But their confusion lasted only a fraction of a second. They were both pros, and they immediately grabbed their pistols and opened fire on me. I ran on, weaving like a hare, charging my armor to the max, and for good reason. A couple of shots made it through to me. The bullets were also 'anti-magic' — I could only imagine what it'd be like to get a hit from the elephant gun that Shnoop stol... appropriated.

My first kunai found its target, not breaking through the armor, but knocking its owner off the roof and right into a bush.

The gunner dodged the second knife, but I jumped onto a carved wooden horse, and from there leaped up onto the roof of the House of Horrors and slashed with my powered sword up from below. Armor cracked. Sword cracked. Good-bye, shitty weapon! Good-bye, strong opponent!

Grabbing the gun from the already dead hand of the falling man, I opened fire on the second assassin, who was just crawling out of the bushes. Yeah, I could shoot straight too! Unlike mine, his armor didn't withstand the special bullet. The fireball he wanted to throw at me fell into the damp grass, hissed and left a burnt spot where it fell.

I turned toward the waiting jeep. The driver had seen enough, and his hand reached for the shifter just as a strange furry creature with burning blue eyes appeared in front of him.

"You liiee! Wwwooon't leeaave!" Shnoop hissed, pressing the button to unlock the doors and pulling at the lever to open the door itself.

The huge ginger paw of Caramel, who the corporal had dropped off not far away while all these goons were 'lying in wait' for me, opened the door as if she owned the car, and the second paw pulled the unlucky driver right out of the driver's seat. Long white teeth joined in the man's throat.

I smiled... Look at that, now I had a ride. All I needed now was a driver.

* * *

I was sick to the back teeth of all these transportation issues. Especially the Irkutsk taxi drivers, who loved their cars so much that they refused to take Caramel, so unlike the polite Japanese drivers. The idea of getting my own means of transport with a personal driver had taken final shape in my head. And it would be far easier to move around the city in an armored car than in an ordinary civilian vehicle. Considering what King did to my apartment, he was more than dumb enough to blow me up along with a taxi driver.

Anna couldn't stay under my watchful eye for all time either, she needed to move around the city as well. And although I might be able to stand up for myself, the girl might have trouble. Her Gift, just like the rest of the Goldsmith family, was incredibly useful for civilian life, but absolutely useless for combat.

Some joker had called it the Gift of Genius, and that wasn't far from the truth. The brains of people with that Gift worked faster, more powerfully, had a better memory and unrivaled analytical abilities. But in battle, it was worth squat. Sure, she could cast some weak armor, but so could any other Gifted with even the slightest training. On the other hand, with so much money, the Goldsmiths just hired themselves a small army and seemed to get by just fine. But I didn't have an army, and someone had to keep Anna safe.

As I shoveled through everything she'd found in my absence, I looked over the list several times, and kept coming back to the case of the Magister hopelessly sentenced to death. And it wasn't that there were no better candidates. I mean, of course he looked great compared with all the others, but the others could be hired without issue. This one we had to save first. Pain in the ass.

I took another look at his case file. A young man looked up at me from the photograph, completely bald, with a strong square jaw. An old scar crossed his right eye. His gaze emanated pure calm. Andrei Potapov. Commoner. Captain of the Imperial Army. Next came some vague description of his service, deployments and military biography, publicly available stuff. But attached to it was a file that Anna extracted from her own sources.

As young as twenty-five, Andrei had risen to the lofty height of commander of an elite unit, Imperial Special Operations Force *Wolfpack*. And his code name was, unsurprisingly, Wolf. The list of his awards and achievements was truly impressive. And that was only the small few of them that Anna could find out, which was normal considering the delicate nature of the Imperial elite forces' missions. The short profile included a warning in red: *Inclined to argue with superiors, always has own opinion. Impatient with incompetent commanders. Tendency to debate orders.*

I smiled. No wonder a fighter that good had hit the ceiling of junior officer ranks and was still working in the field. Although, as I looked at young Wolf's face, my intuition told me that the last thing he wanted was to push a pen at HQ. And yes, his personal power was around Magister, with the potential of rising to Great Magister, almost unheard of for someone without noble blood.

At that moment he was housed in solitary confinement in a special-grade cell at the jail at the Irkutsk Military Garrison. I frowned as I looked at the length of his stay. He had been there for over half a year already. I knew it myself, but there was a note from Anna to say it too — the special-grade cells weren't just secure units. The prisoners within them were under the influence of a suppressing field that prevented them from using their Gift. The shittiest part was that it sucked the energy out of you, destroying your Gift. In principle, if a Gifted is held there too long, he rots away.

I wondered, had his mastery suffered much in half a year? I figured that right now, he was probably at the level of a Veteran. Just so long as he didn't drop all the way down to Apprentice... These were strict laws, made for real criminals.

And something told me that Potapov wasn't one of those.

The official indictment said the following:

Disobedience of orders. Armed rebellion leading to the death of a higher-ranking officer of the Empire.

After that just came notes from Anna that she'd gotten from her own sources again. The picture wasn't complete, but what seemed to have happened was that Potapov's group had been injected deep into the territory of a neighboring enemy state with a combat mission. Considering that he was in Irkutsk now, his mission was either in the eternal enemy state of the Khanate of the Grand Steppe, or in the Dragon Empire, which raided the southern borders of the Eastern Empire with enviable regularity.

But only two out of twelve of his combat group returned alive — him and one other, gravely wounded. And it seemed he had some questions for the administration that organized the fateful raid. His group had completed its mission all the same. There was a note about that. But as soon as he got back, Andrei fell out with the commander of Eastern Group Imperial Special Forces, Major General Duke Tarkov, and this falling out resulted in the sudden and apparently tortuous death of the Duke.

And then there was a surprise. His court hearing was due to take place soon, and there was a ninety-nine percent chance that the judge would sentence the honored soldier of the Empire to death. Anna somehow managed to get her hands on the case file, of which the main and most interesting piece of evidence was a video from a CCTV camera, showing Captain Potapov breaking the Duke's neck with his bare hands.

As a piece of evidence, only one copy of the recording existed, and it was stored in the military prosecutor's office.

I had nothing better to do after all. My kidnapped jeep, along with the small armory I found inside it, was under the tender care of Uncle Simon, who clicked a tongue in approval when he saw my new acquisition. He gravely promised to find any listening devices inside and to officially change the car's registration to my name. There had to be some punishment for attacking a Slayer!

I waited until nightfall, then walked out through the rear gates of the Center. Shnoop told me that King had sent more fighters, sitting four or five to a car, already armed and equipped. The hunt continued. But I had no desire to play their games just then.

When I reached the fenced-off imperial garrison, I sent Shnoop out scouting. He found the cell I needed. However, getting him inside cost us a great deal of energy. The magical suppression field worked both ways, after all.

All the same, through Shnoop's eyes I could now see the fighter lying with his eyes closed on a simple wooden cot. He was emaciated. And it probably wasn't down to being underfed, although I was sure they had no delicacies on the menu. It was all down to the power drain from that hellish device.

His cheeks were sunken, his eyes glistening. All the same, he was clean-shaved and absolutely calm, which I liked right away. Shnoop popped up next to him for a second, then disappeared again, emitting a sound like: *Pshhht!* And yes, the fighter still had his reflexes, because he instantly rolled off the bed toward the unusual sound, jumping to his feet and taking a combat stance. He looked around in confusion, then picked up the sheet of paper that Shnoop had dropped.

The gist of my message was simple. I offered to free him from prison in exchange for a five-year working contract, paid, of course. I included a rough outline of his rights and responsibilities. I figured a guy like this might find it important not to partake in anything criminal, so I gave it to him straight. He was going to be a driver and bodyguard in the service of a small, but very proud noble family. His main job would be to ensure the safety of those in his care. At the end I wrote that if he agreed, all he had to do was say 'yes,' otherwise shake his head.

The bald man stood up, then for some reason walked to the narrow barred window and looked out, up at the starry sky above Irkutsk. He sighed heavily, turned around and said to the air:

"Yes! I agree."

I chuckled, then handed a package to Shnoop

when he reappeared, asking him to visit the inmate again. The little son of a bitch was on form today.

"Sshhhhurrrprise!" he shouted loudly, appearing above the prisoner's head, and dropped the bag of food that had been lovingly prepared by Anna. Tasty food, but not much to sate the hunger of a man tortured by long starvation.

Again, Potapov didn't miss a beat, just caught the bag out of the air before it landed on his bald head.

Shnoop didn't leave just yet, but watched him from a nearby corner instead. No doubt he was giggling to himself, convinced his little prank was the cutting edge of humor.

The bald man looked into the package and then back at the air again. And suddenly, the happy smile of an adult child split his face, contrasting strangely with his fearsome appearance. And hope now flashed in his eyes.

Looked like we'd be working together!

* * *

King's Hideout
Irkutsk

"What?! They said what?! Give back their money?! The hell with them!"

King raged and stormed. Again. His comfortable life had gone down the crapper since that boy turned up. Such a tempting and seemingly simple contract had turned into insane losses. Both in human and financial capital.

And although the former wasn't a big deal — there were plenty of people looking for employment, after all, — the latter was simply a disaster.

In less than a month, Galaxius had killed off half his legal business, driven a wedge between him and the steppe peoples, and ruined his relationship with his aristo backers.

The latter had canceled with a note — 'we are disappointed,' and they wanted him to give their money back. His reputation! It was already stained as it was, now it was blackened. The young up-and-comers weren't sleeping, they were just waiting for him to make a mistake.

"This is personal! No way in hell!"

"But the money..." his assistant began hesitatingly. "Maybe we should return it?"

King thought for a second.

"They can go hang! Return it! This is my war now." He laughed sadly. "A war against a single boy!"

"If it makes you feel any better, the Petersburg bunch messed up today too," his second assistant said, wringing his hands.

"Yes? How?" The chief mob boss of Irkutsk raised his head in interest.

"Three assassins, all Gifted. Died during an attempt on Galaxius's life."

King's face broke out in a wicked grin.

"That's good. How many of them came here in

total?"

"Eight men, five of them Free Slayers."

"So they're going to catch him in a Rift, then?"

"Most likely." The assistant shrugged.

"We need to get to him first!" King snapped, slamming a fist down on the table. "Stop at nothing! He's just a boy!"

"There's a snag there too." The accountant, also his expert in public relations, coughed embarrassedly.

"What snag?" the boss asked, irritated.

"The investor called... He demanded... Sorry... Asked... That there be no more mass casualty incidents. Otherwise they'll take measures."

"Take measures?!" King exploded. "Pathetic dogs! Have they forgotten who feeds them?!"

"With all due respect, Ivan Ivanovich, they haven't forgotten!" the clerk said, raising his hands in a calming gesture. "They're trying to smooth over the incident, but they're under pressure!"

"From who?!"

"The Dolgorukovs and Androsovs!"

"Oh, come on!" King threw up his hands. Those surnames were famous all across the Empire. "What do they have to do with it?"

"Androsov the younger is currently at the Monster Slayer Center, and Dolgorukov's daughter was recently in Irkutsk too. Not to mention her brother — the head of the family's security services and commander of the guard. He left a strange message that he asked the investor to pass to you."

"What is it?" the mob boss roared.

"Forgive me," the clerk said, tensing, "but you'd better read it yourself."

King outright tore the sheet of paper from his assistant's hands and unfolded it. On it was written:

The Yakuza thought they were the biggest dogs in town too. Now there are two fewer clans in the Empire of the Rising Sun. Perhaps it's time to bring some order to Irkutsk, in the name of the Empire and Emperor.

With no respect, Duke Sergei Dolgorukov.

CHAPTER 10

"NICE CAR." Uncle Simon nodded to me as I came to pick up my new ride in the morning. "Not like our Tiger, of course, but the Japanese have always been well known for reliability."

"I did offer to buy a Tiger from you," I said with a smile, throwing out more bait. "But you just wouldn't sell."

"You're a smooth bastard, Sir Slayer Fifth Class," the old mechanic said with a chuckle. "A Tiger is a fighting vehicle. And they're made to order specially for the Center, you know."

"Never mind, I'll get one one day," I said, looking wistfully at the Center's armored cars.

Uncle Simon chuckled.

"Well, good luck with that! Now, to business!" He clapped his hands. "You're in luck. This is a police-issue Doyoda. And as you know, the Japs have a lot to deal with sometimes. So their government doesn't skimp on equipment. This is basically a semi-military vehicle, so you picked well out of what was on the market. As it happens, you probably won't find anything like this up for general sale, actually."

I smiled at 'picked out.' As if I'd been scouring websites. Just the ordinary civilian version of that car cost around thirty thousand rubles. As for this special model — I had no idea. So yeah, fair to say I was 'in luck.'

"Point is, I'm familiar with the model," Uncle Simon continued. "I know all its weaknesses. I've reinforced the suspension — there were a couple of weak spots. We pulled out the bugs too — there were a whole three of them! And removed the air bags."

"Why'd you remove the air bags?" I asked in surprise.

"Oh, you young'uns," the old Slayer said, laughing. "Picture it: Your car is armored and reinforced with a magfield. Someone fires an RPG at your engine. Your car survives the explosion, but the air bag smacks you in the forehead. What good is it?"

I scratched the back of my head and answered uncertainly:

"Well, yeah, not much, I guess."

"That's what I'm saying. Anyway, you owe us four thousand five hundred and forty-three rubles. Send it to the Center account."

"Hot damn!" I chuckled and shook my head.

That was almost half the money I had left. But it was my own fault. I'd told Uncle Simon to pull out the stops, and pull them out he had.

"You know much about combat vehicles?" Uncle Simon frowned, watching for my reaction.

"Not particularly," I said with a shrug.

There had been no such technology in my last world, and here I'd always just taken taxis or, back in Prussia, a car belonging to the family.

"Ugh, the youth of today!" The Center's chief mechanic rolled his eyes. "Look here." He pulled open the hood. "This receptacle is for white jellies. They give a boost to the engine by transferring energy to the fuel. And this one here is for red jellies. They maintain the shield, adding power to the armor and overall defenses. This car ain't easy at all to break through. Just make sure you don't get them mixed up! If you put a red jelly in the fuel system, the whole engine will burn out! And if you put a white jelly into the shield system, anything will be able to break through it."

"Um, alright, got it..." I said uncertainly.

I was embarrassed to admit it, but I really wasn't much good with the technology of this world. But I did know that jellies had more uses than just restoring energy. They could be used to upgrade weapons and armor, to create artifacts. The white ones were the most basic, and were often used in transportation. The red ones made sense for defense. I also remembered that orange ones were used in military turrets. A charge from one of them could cause a real Sodom and

Gomorrah. I couldn't even imagine what higher-class jellies might be used for.

"Got it. How do I know when it needs more jellies?"

The old man briefly put his head in his hand, then grabbed me unceremoniously by the sleeve and pulled me into the car. He pressed the engine start button. The engine roared, the car started, the instruments came alive.

"Here, for dummies! The white meter shows the white jellies, the red meter — the red ones. When it drops low, it's time to add more. Got it now?"

"Yes, sir," I chuckled, feeling a little awkward. "I definitely get it now."

The white meter was almost at the top, but the red one had only a third remaining. Either they were saving some money or they'd gotten into a fight somewhere. I just happened to be carrying five red jellies with me. I took one out, placed it in the container and closed the hood. For a quick second the engine revved into overdrive, then went back to idle again. I took the time to go look at the indicator — over half full now. *Damn, magical cars are expensive toys,* I thought, scratching my head again.

"Thanks for the help, Uncle Simon. Drinks are on me!"

"Heh, you're all talk..." the Slayer grumbled.

"But seriously, I know you won't take money off me. So let's go get a drink tonight, on me. If all goes well, I can introduce you to my new driver and bodyguard."

Uncle Simon grimaced.

"Hope you've found someone good. Any suit could manage this ride, but still, you want someone with skill."

"Somehow I think you'll approve of this one," I said with a chuckle, then clapped the old Slayer on the shoulder and climbed into the driver's seat.

After driving hard up to my barracks, I honked a couple of times like I was picking up a girl. Curious faces appeared in the windows, one of which was Anna's. I waved at her, and a couple of seconds later she came out, along with Caramel.

"Hey, furball, you stay home!"

The panther shot me a reproachful look.

"We're going to a polite establishment. You won't be needed there. Take a walk for now."

There are no squirrels here, her voice said in my head.

"I know! Thank god. Otherwise you'd get us kicked the hell out of this place." I laughed. Alright, go get some sleep. Or whatever it is you do."

The panther snorted, turned around proudly and walked back inside.

Anna climbed into the front seat.

"No no, girlfriend. Sit in the back," I said, remembering that there were no air bags in this car anymore.

"Huh, why?" She raised an eyebrow at me.

"Never mind... Get in the back."

The girl grumbled something under her

breath, but obeyed and switched to the back.

The Kingsmen had had the misfortune of witnessing me taking care of the Petersburg boys yesterday, and it seemed to have dampened their enthusiasm somewhat. At least, their combat units had disappeared. There were only three surveillance cars left, parked at all the exits from the Center. It seemed like the order of 'eliminate Galaxius at any cost' had been changed to 'keep an eye on him and wait for the right moment.' Well, good luck to them!

The GPS navigation was working fine, and plotted us a route. After five minutes, we were standing outside the building of the military prosecutor's office. Shnoop quickly looked around and noticed no danger. Anna and I stepped out and walked to the entrance.

"Good health, your lordship," the guard said. "Forgive me, but who are you and what is your business here?"

"This is Countess Goldsmith," I said, nodding to Anna. "She is the lawyer in today's hearing on the Potapov case. It's registered, you can check."

The guard checked his tablet, then nodded.

"And who are you?"

"I'm..." I smiled. "Just her driver and escort."

"Go on through."

Anna had laid some great groundwork on this one. In a military court, the presence of any lawyer at all, let alone a civilian one, was ridiculous. Usually there was just the accused and the state prosecutor, who also acted as military judge. That was it. But there was no direct edict against lawyers. Anna had somehow gotten the garrison's approval. So we were led into the courtroom. Well, I say courtroom. It wasn't like a civilian court with a viewers' gallery with a bunch of chairs for an audience. Just an ordinary conference room with a table, three members of the military court sitting at it. There was a chair for the accuser and a cage for the accused, which he entered through another door.

"Who are you?" the judge asked, raising his head.

"I am Potapov's lawyer," Anna said, stepping forward without hesitation.

The man, with a colonel's stripes on his shoulder, grimaced like he had toothache.

"I see. But it isn't his turn for a while yet."

"We'll wait... with your permission," I said, taking the initiative, grabbing Anna by the arm and sitting her down on the only free chair. I stood next to her, leaning against the wall with crossed arms.

Four withering gazes from different ranks of military men stared at me.

"You aren't even military!"

"Correct," I said, demonstrating my signet ring. "But we are nobles. And I am a Slayer, too. Any objections?"

"A noble lawyer for a military criminal." The prosecutor, a major, chuckled. "Now I've seen it all."

"You may remain," the committee chair

rumbled.

Next came a parade of defendants, one by one.

The committee was nothing if not efficient. A short speech by the accuser, a sentence pronounced, and the defendant was led out. Each one took no more than five minutes.

My mind was just starting to wander when a familiar name brought me back to reality.

"Former Captain Potapov."

I raised my eyes. Andrei was brought out. He wore cuffs and manacles which looked solid enough to hold a bull. What were measures like that for?

Wolf was still emaciated, and barely moving. He reeled as he climbed the step to sit down in the cage. The guard tried to hold him up, but that just got him a snarl. A snarl nasty enough to make the guard jump back and put a hand on his holster.

I smiled. He lived up to his nickname. Even a wounded wolf puts the fear into the sheep.

A loud screech echoed through the small room, making everyone grit their teeth in irritation. It was Anna, without a hint of embarrassment, dragging her hefty chair across the floor to take a closer seat. She sat down in it, carefully spreading her skirt on her knees, took her folder in hand and smiled sweetly.

"You don't mind, do you?"

I think every single one of them absolutely did mind. But firstly she was a woman, and secondly a countess. So they just nodded silently.

The accuser read out the sentence. And then Anna stepped into the case. It was sheer pleasure to watch her work. She tore them up like a wolf herself. The only evidence was the video recording that Shnoop had stolen the day before. And without that, all they had was the fact that the Duke had died at a moment when, as Anna put it, 'by absolute coincidence, her client was standing nearby.'

The prosecutor reddened and swore. The judges frowned. But in the end, Potapov was declared a free man, stripped of his rank and barred from service in the Imperial Army in the future. Apart from that, for some reason they gave him a fine of five thousand rubles, with the following explanation: *Unintended act or inaction leading to the death of a superior officer.*

Anna smiled and nodded, agreeing. I had six hundred left in my account, and I was starting to panic a little. But Anna took out her personal card with a smile, and the secretary charged the fine to it then and there. The committee spoke amongst themselves for a minute, then nodded — he was free.

The guards released Wolf from his manacles and cuffs, and he stepped out of the cage. Skinny, exhausted, a little confused. But all the same, he looked happy.

"Get him out of here before we change our minds," the colonel murmured.

"Hah, as if!" I laughed and walked up to Wolf, offering him a hand.

"Hey there, Andrei!"

His handshake was strangely firm for his withered condition.

He opened his mouth to say something, but I interrupted him.

"Questions later."

He nodded his understanding and followed us to the exit.

"Good day to you all," Anna said with a smile and followed after us.

After stepping out onto the street, we walked up to the car and Wolf silently reached out a hand, palm up.

"Keys."

"What?" I looked at him in surprise.

"The car keys, if you'd be so kind."

"Why?"

"You hired me as driver and bodyguard. It's my responsibility to drive the car."

I looked him up and down.

"Don't you think you should rest a little first?"

"I'll rest in my grave." He waved his open palm insistently.

I chuckled and dropped the keys into his hand.

Potapov opened the back door and gestured us in theatrically.

"Please!"

"Hah, full service!" I smiled.

"Merci!" Anna nodded, and slipped inside.

I shut the door after her and sat in the front, next to the driver. That got me a look of judgment.

"It's safer in the back."

"Thanks, I know." I smiled back at him. "Haven't forgotten how to drive, I hope?"

"I really hope not." Wolf laughed grimly, then pressed the start engine button.

His experienced eye scanned the dashboard. The air bag error didn't escape his notice.

"Air bags removed, good," he said.

I faltered again a little. Looked like everyone except me in this world knew how armored cars worked.

"Where are we headed?"

"The Monster Slayer Center. You know the way?"

"Naturally." He chuckled. "Strap in..." He hesitated a moment, but in the end added: "Commander!"

I didn't bother arguing, and fastened my seatbelt. He did the same.

Its wheels skidding, the car slid forwards and elegantly veered out onto the road, merging into the traffic. The armored jeep surged ahead, gaining speed. I reached up and grabbed the handrail.

"Whoa, whoa! We're in no rush!"

"Well, I'm not rushing." The fighter laughed.

I chuckled. Seemed I'd made a good staff choice.

Seven minutes and twenty seconds later, we stopped outside the Center guard post. And Half a minute later by the barracks. A glowering Androsov met us there, who I'd practically begged to come.

"Hey, Andy!" I smiled.

"Hey to you too," Andrei nodded.

"I see you have some new wrinkles. That's what happens when the wife comes to visit!"

"Enough jokes, Galaxius," Androsov muttered.

For the life of me, I just couldn't understand his bashfulness over his fiancée. He was Slayer Sixth Class now, and potentially one of the most powerful Healers in the Empire. If he was so madly in love with his bride, then what was the problem? We hadn't had a chance to get a decent drink and have a chat about it. But I figured I'd have to get around to that soon.

"What did you want? Why the urgency, the secrecy?"

"Allow me to introduce," I said, nodding at Potapov, who stepped out and leaned against the hood as if by chance. It was obvious he didn't have much strength left. "The driver and bodyguard of the Galaxius family, Andrei Potapov."

"Is that so?" Andrei smiled. "About time you hired somebody. You don't look so good, pal." Androsov shook his head.

"Your Highness," the bald man said with a bow, seeing Androsov's signet ring, showing him to be son of a prince.

"Yes, that's exactly why I called you here. I need you to get him back in form."

There was a strange sound next to us. It was Wolf. I looked at his round eyes. Sure, the special forces had their own healers, but they were weak Gifted who healed battle wounds in a mostly conservative manner. The greatest healing family of the Empire was available exclusively to the high aristocracy.

"I don't know much," I went on. "But I've heard there are methods."

"There are methods." Andrei nodded thoughtfully, walked up to Potapov and started to feel the man's body.

Even in the sunlight I could see a yellow light suffusing Androsov's palm.

"Hmm," he murmured. "A Master?" And then he straightened. "Rather, a former Master. Right now he's Veteran, and barely above Warrior at that. Who did this to you, Andy?"

"The special cells, Your Highness," Wolf answered.

"Rough," Androsov said, scratching the back of his head. "This'll take more than one session. Actually, he should really be in the hospital."

"No way," Wolf murmured.

"Why not?" Androsov asked in surprise.

"I can work just fine in this condition. I wasn't pulled out of jail to sit around on my ass."

Androsov looked at me in amazement and shook his head, but said nothing. I just shrugged and smiled.

"Fine. Well, then I'll perform the initial session with you right now. I'll clear your energy channels and kickstart your regeneration. Later, I'll slowly guide your recovery. Maybe we'll manage it a little quicker, we'll see." He patted himself on the chest in annoyance. "Why didn't you tell me why you called me here? I would have brought jellies."

"I have some. This enough?" I pulled a little bag out of my chest pocket which had four red jellies inside.

Androsov used them all.

"Enough for now."

"What else do you need from me?" I asked.

"From you? Just let me work in peace," Androsov answered. "Go take a walk. Half an hour should be enough. And give me the key to your room."

"It's not locked," I smiled, whistling.

Caramel stepped out onto the street lazily. She didn't like being locked up. And why lock her up anyway? In case of thieves? Ha-ha...

Anna and I took the panther and went toward the stadium and shooting range, around which there was a small park in which, to Caramel's great displeasure, there lived no squirrels.

I took out my phone and pressed a couple of buttons. Anna's phone pinged with a notification. She glanced at it and raised her eyes to me in surprise.

"I still owe you around three hundred rubles, I'll get that to you later. Thanks!"

"You're welcome," she said with a smile.

"I wanted to ask you something," I began.

"I'm staying with you," Anna said with a simple nod.

I nodded back at her. I had no more questions. We just walked on, enjoying the unusually warm autumn day.

Androsov called.

"Come back. I'm done."

We walked back. Wolf was sitting on my bed, staring at his hands in amazement, clenching and unclenching his fingers. He glowed all over with some strange aura, and somehow even looked bigger, more solid. Probably just a visual effect. Energy can't turn into flesh. At least, not as fast as that. I knew that for sure. Androsov, on the other hand, looked pale.

"How'd it go?"

"Fine." Andrei nodded, rubbed his sweating brow and looked at me strangely. "I was wrong. He was a Magister. A damn Magister! And not even a nobleman! Where did you find him?!"

"Gotta know where to look." I chuckled, remembering the man's case file. And decided not to mention that Wolf had a potential of up to Great Magister. Androsov would fall faint, or try to steal the unique man away from me.

Andrei shook his head.

"Well, he's a solid Veteran now, with no ifs or buts. And yeah, now I'm sure that I can get him back to Magister. Did you know his potential?"

"I did." I smiled.

Androsov smiled back.

"Well, of course you did. You always know it all."

"Need walking to your room?"

"Get lost." Andrei rolled his eyes. "I'll make it on my own."

"Got any plans for the night?" I asked, immediately earning a suspicious look.

"Why do you ask?"

"Well, if His Highness would condescend to it, we'd like to take him to the local bar tonight."

Androsov smiled.

"He would condescend. Svetlana just happens to have gone back to her manor for some business."

"So a bachelor party is in order, then?" I laughed.

Anna sniffed with distaste behind me.

"Something like that." Androsov rapped me on the chest. "Alright, I'm off. I'm going to go take a lie-down.

"Wait. Doesn't Wolf need to rest?" I asked.

Androsov laughed.

"Rest? Right now, he's better off running! He has surplus energy that he doesn't know what to do with."

"Alright, see you later!"

Androsov walked out of our room, and I turned to the others.

"Alright, girls and boys!" I clapped my hands. "I need to take a trip out. I'll be back tonight."

"Where are you going?" Anna asked at the same time as Potapov, jumping to his feet.

Guess I had two nannies now.

"I just have to go close a Rift quick and I'll be back."

"I'm coming with you!" Wolf looked in embarrassment at his prisoner's orange jumpsuit. "Only, maybe I should get changed first."

I guessed his measurements. In his heyday he must have been bigger than me, but now he was a lot thinner.

I took out a clean Slayer jumpsuit.

"Come on, try this on."

"I could use a shower first," the bald man said again.

"Alright, I'll wait."

"Don't even think about leaving without me, Commander!" The man said, suddenly frowning.

I had to admit, the thought had crossed my mind, but I felt bad about it. I clapped the man on the shoulder.

"Don't get your panties in a twist, I'll wait."

Thanks to Anna, I had some new socks and underwear. So after five minutes, Wolf stood washed and clean in a Slayer jumpsuit and a pair of solid boots.

"Right," I said, a thought coming to me. "Let's go for a little shopping trip first. Then straight to the Rift."

"Alex," Anna spoke up.

"Yeah, yeah, I know — be careful. Come on, Mel." I waved to the panther.

She slid outside.

"Hey, wait!" I said, suddenly remembering. "Come here."

I sat down on my haunches and waved to Wolf to do the same.

"Mel, this is Wolf. Wolf, this is Caramel. He's on our side, Mel. Got that?"

I got it already, came my pet's annoyed voice in my head. *Let's go.*

I laughed. "Move out."

We headed to the car and I opened the trunk, where the entire arsenal of the would-be assassins had been left behind.

"Familiar with these?" I asked.

Wolf gave me a wry look.

"I'm familiar with absolutely every firearm on the planet, no exceptions. So yeah, don't worry."

He took out a huge sniper rifle, pulled the slide open, looked into it and grimaced.

"Former owner should have his hands cut off. Didn't look after this thing at all."

He picked up a magazine full of rounds and whistled.

"These don't come cheap!"

"Yeah, I know."

I had pulled off the assassins' belts along with their holsters and weapons. Without a second thought, I'd completely cleaned out their pockets of money and spare magazines. Aside from that, they didn't have anything valuable on them.

"Sidearms," I said, nodding to them.

Wolf chuckled and examined the three pistols one after another.

"Their owners might have been chumps, but these pieces are top-notch," he said, pulling out a magazine again. He glanced in and chuckled again, seeing the red glow. "Got any normal rounds? Or are we fighting the Gifted?"

"We might be," I said. "But there are normal ones in that bag there."

Wolf thought for a moment, then kept the antimagic rounds in one and loaded another with ordinary rounds. He fastened both holsters on the broad belt at his waist. Then holstered the guns and smiled.

"Now I'm starting to feel a little more like my old self again."

"You're going to feel even better in a minute," I said. "Get in."

I jabbed at the GPS screen and set a route.

"This is where we're headed."

We drove to the site of the recent bloodbath, where Shnoop was carrying off the equipment of the unsuccessful killers into his caves.

"Wait here," I said.

"But..."

"It's safe here right now, believe me," I interrupted him, and climbed out.

Sending Shnoop into his cache, I got him to pull out something that I'd like.

"Now come here, Wolf."

He walked over. I opened the trunk again.

The bald man's eyebrows shot up. "How did this get here!? When?!"

"Forget it." I smiled. "I'll explain that later. Anything you like?"

Shnoop had pulled out a case of grenades, two assault rifles, one carbine, two bulletproof vests and some of the helmets that weren't too...

blood-splattered.

Another expert selection process. In the end, before me stood a warrior in a bulletproof vest, bristling with spare magazines and grenades. His hands had a firm grip on a carbine rifle.

I was surprised, and glanced at the two assault rifles, which looked far more imposing.

"Why not one of those?"

Another broad smile from the commando.

"Hard to explain. But in short, that one's a hunting rifle," he said, nodding at one of the assault rifles, "although an expensive one. The second one's German, solid, but a little outdated. This, on the other hand — this is a Whirlwind." He gestured with the short-barreled rifle, with an unusually high caliber and large magazine for its size. "This is our toy. Honestly, I'm pretty surprised to see you with one of these. They don't usually see action outside the special forces. Believe me, this is a damn good gun."

"I believe you," I said, nodding. "What about a helmet?"

The bald man grimaced. "I don't wear helmets."

"How come?"

"Just superstition, I guess. It ain't my head that's going to get it."

"Right," I said, laughing and nodding at the scar crossing his eye. "They already tried that!"

The bald man shrugged and answered without a smile:

"Yeah, that's what happened last time I put a

helmet on."

"Can't argue with that. I hope you know what you're doing."

"Oh, believe me, I do." Potapov smiled. "Well, where to next, boss?"

"Next we're headed to close a Rift, which you'll get a nice little bonus for. And there'll be a few less bad people in the world."

"Bad people?" Andrei frowned.

"Well, they think they're luring me into a trap, and they want to kill me there. What do you think — are they bad people?"

"No other name for 'em," Wolf said with a wicked grin, pulling back the slide of his Whirlwind.

CHAPTER 11

IN THE BEGINNING, I hadn't planned on taking Wolf with me at all. Why risk a man, let alone such an important one? And yes, actually, I did consider him highly important.

Not everyone can understand this, but I was sick of living without my own transport, always relying on taxi drivers. They could be pretty unreliable. So what if there are some monsters running around in the woods? How is that an excuse to just tear out of there and leave your customer in the lurch?

Ugh... I was starting to get angry. Enough of that.

"Do you have any intel on the ambush?" Potapov asked, interrupting my thoughts. "Or am I going in first and you following behind?" He wore a borrowed transparent Slayer ring on his finger with no number on it, just in case. At first I'd try him out in action, and maybe later I'd ask Khrulyov to register him officially.

"Wolf, I know you were a hotshot commander and all that. But I'm in charge now. You'll need to learn to trust me. You'll see, your life will get complicated, but very fun." I chuckled, clapping him on the shoulder.

"Got it... I'll wait!" He kept on standing beside me, peering into the space around us.

I hoped he did get it.

But before two minutes had gone by, he piped up again.

"There's a chopper flying a few hundred yards out. It sees us," he said to me impassively. "There's no signal in a Rift, and if we go in right now, they won't be able to tell the ones inside about us. But then they could block our retreat.

Ugh... Rough..."

I couldn't get used to the fact that right then I looked like a kid with almost no experience. Wolf was doing the right thing, trying to keep me safe, but where was the trust?

"We wait," I said, reassuring him. "Unless you have something against getting some fresh air in the woods?"

"Better than a cell," he said with a shrug.

I didn't want to hurry. Why? I already knew what I needed, and now I was thinking up my next plan.

Inside, the Petersburg lot awaited me, and King's people were lying in wait in the woods. That or somebody else had decided to get involved.

Any fool could see that they'd decided to press me on two sides. If the Petersburg lot put me down, the others could swoop in and finish off their weakened competitors and say they died in the crossfire. And if not they failed, the others could try to finish me off instead.

I just needed to think about what to do...

Hmm. There were plenty of options, but not only did I want to act as effectively as possible, I also wanted to give everybody a chance to have some fun, not just myself.

It was considered poor form among Hunters to take all the game for yourself, even when you can easily handle it and your comrades are weaker than you, and need to level up.

Have respect for your allies — that's what we used to say, and every Hunter followed the rule without exception. After all, one day, an ally you reinforced will cover your ass in another brawl.

Alright... After standing another couple of minutes, I'd figured out how best to proceed. There were twenty of King's people in all, but by all appearances they were weaklings whose plan was just to shoot at me, chase me into the Rift and hold me there until reinforcements arrived. Or maybe they were even a recon division.

"Here are your orders," I said, finally turning to my allies. "Wolf and Caramel, you're going that way. Around five hundred yards that way, those idiots have set up something like a camp, where there are cars and a group of people who really want to kill me. I suggest we kill them first. Any objections?"

Caramel sat there and watched me closely. Wolf also just stood there and asked no pointless questions.

"Oh yeah! I forgot to say. Caramel is senior!" Now I'd given them all my orders.

"Got it!" Wolf said with a nod, and moved out in the right direction.

Is he an idiot? I heard Caramel ask in my head.

Even Caramel was surprised that he didn't bother arguing about who was boss, and about the fact that I was sending them who knows where.

No, he just knows what the chain of command is, what orders are! You could learn a thing or two from him. The panther snorted derisively, and I leaned down and stroked her head. *Keep an eye on him and help him if necessary, just don't get up to any mischief.*

She accepted my petting begrudgingly, then snorted again and trailed after Potapov.

A cat watching over a wolf. I wondered who I'd get in my team next — a beaver, maybe, or a raccoon? Just so long as it wasn't a squirrel, ha-ha...

I waited for them to disappear into the sparse undergrowth, but didn't enter the Rift myself. I could already see through Shnoop's where our enemies were lying in wait, and what they were planning to do.

True, right now they were just sitting around

bored, but one was standing lookout. They didn't know exactly when I'd turn up, after all.

Caramel kicked off the action. One of the Kingsmen walked off to the side to talk on the phone, and death jumped out at him from the bushes. Then the second one died when he went to see what all the noise was about.

And the cat deliberately scratched the bark of a tree not far from him. When he saw the scratches and raised his rifle, it was already too late. The panther jumped onto his head from the tree and the man died before he could even cast his armor.

All well and good, but she was draining a hell of a lot of energy from me throughout all of this. She didn't want to take any risks, and decided to boost her defenses.

Shnoop missed the first shots, but as soon as he heard them, he darted toward them to show me what was going on. It was Wolf, who had already shot four men with the sniper rifle.

Hmm... He was skilled! Almost no delay between the shots. When did he have time to aim? Four shots — four bodies.

He'd chosen the strongest enemies, reading their auras in advance, and, as they talked, he struck. He planned it all out perfectly, and chose himself a position in a tree top. I'd like to see how he climbed up there. Wolves don't climb trees! Especially not with weapons like that on their shoulders! Now I could hear the gunfire.

No need to watch further, I guess. Otherwise I might start wanting to help. The last thing I saw was Potapov leaping down from the tree, carefully putting away his sniper rifle and taking out his Whirlwind.

I'm a nice guy and all that, sure, but there are some times when niceness just gets in the way. This was his exam — he had to pass it himself. I think he knew that just fine, even if he didn't ask any questions.

He was a total show-off, a hundred percent sure of himself, and even seemed to consider himself stronger than me. True, he accepted my authority, not to mention my extraordinary Gift, which he still didn't quite understand. But I noticed him looking at me, analyzing me.

If he could handle it, then he'd definitely be useful. He was a good man, with his own ideas of honor and morality. I doubted a man like that would shirk his duties or do anything that would taint his honor.

Alright, that was that dealt with. I hoped they didn't steal the car while we were all busy, or else I'd send them a worm that climbs into the body through the mouth and lays hundreds of eggs inside. And the human or animal becomes a trypophobe's nightmare.

Or I'd just feed their bodies to the slimes, that's a classic.

When I entered the Rift, nobody attacked me right away, and I felt sand beneath my feet and a scorching sun above my head trying to burn me to a crisp.

I was in the ruins of an ancient temple,

nothing of which was left but a few walls and massive columns.

I had roughly two minutes. When I took two steps forward, I hit a barely visible tripwire that was there to tell someone that a guest had arrived. I could have stepped over it, but why bother? More fun this way.

I ran off to the side and created an illusion by the columns, made it look like it was just studying the hieroglyphics. After all, they probably thought I was stupid and careless.

Incidentally, I had no weapons. My last sword had broken, and I didn't want to shell out for a new one. I hadn't bothered bringing that club with me either, the one I beat those mutant cows into a pulp with. I figured that if it was too dangerous here, I'd be better off retreating, and if it was easy, then I'd find myself a sword right here. And I was right... The people who were waiting for me had swords, not very good ones, maybe worth around ten to fifteen thousand each at the most. They'd do for a while, anyway.

These bastards had closed the Rift themselves.

I walked off to a small dune and created another illusion, hiding me from them.

When the 'guard' brought the others, I hurriedly charged my illusions to make them last longer.

After checking their photo to make sure it was me, the enemies moved to act.

I watched as one of them rolled down off a

dune and called out to me for help, making like he was wounded. His friends hid behind the temple ruins, which were elevated.

Damn it... Come on, Shnoop, let me listen! I sent him a mental command; I couldn't hear what this guy was saying to my illusion.

A second later, and I could hear it all.

"Help me, kid! We were hired to mine some ore, but there was a cave-in," he said, wheezing. "A damn column crushed my fellow workers. Help us, please! I'm just not strong enough to move the damn thing off 'em!"

Oh, great performance! He even made begging eyes, and bit his lip until it bled in anticipation of my answer.

My illusion nodded its agreement and the man started up the dune, reeling. My illusion followed.

He fell down three times, and kept asking me to hurry.

Most importantly, he'd taken the risk of coming down without a weapon, to gain my trust.

Alright, fine, say I believed him — but what did they plan to do when I got up there? My armor hadn't gone anywhere...

Either they were retards or they had only one guy with any acting talent. When he'd almost reached the top, he waved to his comrades.

"Come on!" he shouted at the top of his lungs.

At his command, his friends climbed out from behind their cover and threw some very interesting spears at my illusion.

Ugh, now that was a hiccup... Shnoop hadn't shown me those. They must have been stuck in the sand in this place. The spears were artifacts, with a weak energy charge of their own.

They flew straight into my illusion and right through it, and when they touched a hard surface, they suddenly detonated in three mighty explosions.

The booms sent fountains of sand into the sky and in all directions, some of it even reaching me.

A perfect moment, I realized, and ran toward them, banking slightly to avoid the spot where they were throwing spears.

I climbed up and saw that two had already jumped down, probably hoping to finish me off. But the 'actor' and another were stood looking for me. And so carefully that I managed to get behind them.

"So you like throwing things, huh?" I said, loudly enough for them to hear as I stood behind them and smiled.

They span on their heels instantly, just in time for a fist-sized slime to hit one and a kunai to land in the other's head.

Alas, the kunai broke. I'd charged it with enough energy to break through the armor and kill the guy, but... My toy was gone, and it was a long way to get another.

The slime, at least, didn't break. Like the kunai, it was charged with enough of my energy to break through the defenses and stick to the actor's face.

He tried to pull it off, but his fingers sank into the jelly-like mass and started to dissolve, and the little pancake stayed just where it was, spread across his face. An unpleasant death, to say the least.

I threw a kunai at the face of the first one that climbed up here too, but didn't kill him. I wanted to save my energy, but did decide to finish off the second one.

Weak, pathetic armor on these. They all had the same cookie-cutter weave. Probably a local invention from some genius of the criminal underworld, who took big money to train gangs and street thugs, convincing them that it was just as good as aristo armor.

In reality, it sucked... It was such a confused weave that its main weak point ended up in the head. Sure, the back of the head would be one thing. Don't show your back to the enemy and you'll be more likely to survive. Here it was almost like it was deliberately made to let any killer take them down with a single shot.

The last one seemed to have figured out his chances. He ran for the portal. Where did he think he was going? No cars nearby. Was he counting on the woods, on slipping away and reporting the failure? Or maybe they had some reinforcements?

Fine, run away... In the meantime, I stepped out of the Rift.

Shnoop darted over to Wolf and showed me that he was handling it just fine. Not a scratch on him.

"Find Wolf and take him on the trail of that runaway. There's some ice cream in it for you. Got that?" The little guy sat on my shoulder and rubbed himself against my cheek.

"Yessshhh shhir!" he said with a mocking salute, then disappeared.

"Wait!" I barked before he was fully gone.

"Whaaat... Shomeshing elshe?" His disgruntled little face reappeared on my shoulder.

Sorry, little guy! I forgot to tell you your whole task.

"Before doing what I said, first take the guy's phone away!"

"Yeshhh!" he hissed, and disappeared.

Now I was satisfied.

I took a comfy seat and just watched the hunt.

Wolf knew what he was doing, and Shnoop didn't show himself to him, although sometimes he did hiss a warning in his ear like "Behhhiiind youu!" and then disappeared again.

I wasn't sure that the guardian even realized what that was, but that was another test. Would he lose focus, try to figure out what it was, or take it in stride? He knew basically nothing, and all he did know could be written off as assumptions. That's how trusting a man I am.

Trust, but verify. If he'd had a tattoo of the Order of Hunters, it would all be different.

The funniest part was when he drove one of the enemies like a wounded beast, chasing him around the woods for twenty minutes. And when

Wolf put a gun to his head and told him to surrender, the man grabbed him by the hand and made him pull the trigger himself. Or at least help it along.

Very interesting... That meant he didn't want to be taken prisoner. What a surprising coincidence! A satisfied smile spread across my face.

I had no plans of taking him prisoner and torturing him. I'd just forgotten to tell Shnoop to whisper into Wolf's ear that it was fine to take no prisoners.

Guess he thought I wanted some alive. But Wolf didn't seem bothered. He looked at the dead body, shrugged, then hefted it onto his shoulder and walked toward the Rift.

Without knowing it, he had gained another point in my estimation. Not leaving evidence is an admirable trait. It meant I wouldn't have to send a slime there.

With a clean conscience, I returned to the Rift and gathered up everything I liked, then piled it up by the entrance. There were two swords, two axes, two of the remaining explosive spears, a couple of knives and ten white jellies apparently looted from the local monsters.

"How was your hunt?" I asked my bald bodyguard, sitting outside the Rift.

He realized I was looking in the direction he came from, and laughed.

"Longer than I'd like, but got something, at least." He shrugged and threw the corpse at my feet.

"Do I look like a necromancer to you?" I raised an eyebrow. "What do I need with this guy?"

"Clues," he said as impassively as ever.

I kept my eyes on him.

"Good work. Throw him into the Rift," I said to him, and he did it.

Next I was in no particular hurry, because this time I sent Shnoop to check the Rift for any interesting artifacts and such.

I knew there must be some, in an ancient place like a temple.

"Bring the car closer and gather up all the loot," I said to Wolf, and then headed into the Rift myself to pick up my spoils.

He got the picture without explanation. This fighter knew what he was doing. He had already gathered everything he considered valuable of the weapons from those of King's people who he'd killed, and brought it all here. It was obvious he was a military man. He took the weapons, but no personal effects. Although he did hint to me of clues.

I walked into the Rift and carried all the items out, stacking them up by the car. I threw them from that side onto the ground, pulling my hand out, and he was already packing them away.

Then I sent Shnoop to gather everything useful and valuable in the woods on the dead Kingsmen.

Now that'd be fun, to watch Wolf's face when he turned back to the pile of weapons and found it had gotten bigger.

Then Shnoop brought me a bag. Really... A shopping bag, thrust right into my hand. He must have stolen it some time before. And he'd put various little trinkets he'd found in the Rift inside. I knew right away why he'd done that.

What was it they used to say? If the people are poor, then the temple is rich? There were a hundred and three different coins inside. Gold and silver. No copper, but there were metals that I couldn't immediately identify.

There were also all kinds of charms, almost all broken, amulets with no magic left, simple trinkets which I hoped were still valuable.

There were also all kinds of figurines of divinities or just important people — who knew with these otherworldly religions?

I thought that was all, but the little one brought me two more bags like the first. Now I really whistled! They were filled with all manner of loot too. By my humble estimation, there were many thousands of rubles in my hands. And since I was temporarily broke again, I was really counting on that income.

I'd have to buy Arkhip a good bottle of cognac for this juicy tip. There was a tradition among Hunters of giving gifts to those who bring good fortune.

"Tired?" I asked my bodyguard, and laughed. He was clearly sick of loading all the loot into the trunk.

"No," he answered, and went on working.

"By the way, do you happen to know some place where I could sell all this?" I clearly didn't need so many weapons.

"I do, but I wouldn't recommend it," he said, suddenly looking concerned, even. "You can never have too many weapons, and different ones are useful for different missions. I wouldn't call this too big an assortment. They could all come in handy in time."

I hadn't thought of that. Looked like Potapov had a hard time saying good-bye to guns. We'd need to urgently find a warehouse, or more underground caches. But how could I explain that to him?

After looting everything worth taking and sending Shnoop out scouting, after which he just spread his paws in a shrug, we climbed into the car and headed back to base. I had a drinking session booked with Androsov and Uncle Simon, but there'd no doubt be other people there too.

On the way there, I checked the Slayer site and read up on who had registered that Rift, and whether I should close it officially. To avoid problems down the line if someone decided to accuse me of storming in and killing everybody.

"Stop!" I shouted at my driver, who stepped on the brakes and brought us screeching to a halt.

"An attack? Where?" He immediately took out his gun.

He seemed to be getting used to the fact that I tended to see more than most.

"No," I said with a shake of my head, then

smiled. "Not an attack... Something better! Head toward the Anthill Rift, and step on it!"

"Got it," he said, relaxing and shifting into gear. My comrade in arms even seemed a little disappointed as he turned the wheel to drive out.

Good thing the car had a navigation system that knew all the routes. And it wasn't a civilian version, but the Slayer edition, where all the Rifts were marked with special markers and routes with posts.

"Speed up! There are no beasts around," I said, dismissing any need for care.

"Got it," he answered, and put his foot down.

The speed pressed me back into my seat, but that was just what we needed!

I had just read on the forum that something unbelievable had happened, something that we just couldn't ignore. Another Rift had opened up within the Anthill Rift, and now all hell had broken loose!

And wherever hell breaks loose, there's opportunity for a Hunter to get stronger and richer.

Oh, how I love this world! It's every bit as good as my own! Two Rifts for the price of one! Just perfect!

* * *

Monster Slayer Center
Irkutsk
Slayer R&R Station, or in simple terms: The Boozer

Now-Duke Androsov sat with Viscount Schrader at large a table, sipping dejectedly at his beer. Hans was retelling some old tale from his homeland, but Andrei was only half listening.

He had strained himself earlier today, even if he hadn't shown it to Alexander. What he did for Wolf today was something that only two or three dozen people in the whole Empire could do. And that should be something to be proud of, but he had no energy to celebrate.

He thought that Galaxius would tell him something interesting today. The strange baron had suddenly become his best friend. But Alex was late, which wasn't like him at all.

"Hey! Heard the news?" He raised his head and saw a smiling Helga as she walked in, who had first picked up Anna with the aim of, as she put it, "crashing their bachelor party."

"What news?" Androsov asked tiredly, dispassionately.

"Disaster at the Anthill!" the girl said excitedly, sitting down on a bench and gesturing to the waitress. "Another Rift opened up inside it, and the beasts broke out and had themselves a slaughter. And some of them made it all the way outside. The army isn't enough anymore, and additional units are being recalled from the Perimeter. They're bringing the Air Force back from the front line. All our response groups are already headed there. Looks like there's a localized Armageddon going on over there right now!"

"Ugh, damn it..!" Andrei paled, grabbed his tablet and phone. He tapped something on his tablet, and with shaking hands began to jab at numbers on his phone.

"What's up?" Helga asked in surprise.

"Galaxius! He's late! And I bet my family signet ring that he's somehow mixed up in this!" Andrei brought his phone to his ear.

Anna gasped beside him, and Helga looked at him strangely.

"Hello! Anthill checkpoint? Hello? This is Duke Androsov! I need information on Slayer Galaxius! Has he entered the Anthill..? What?! How many..!? Yes, goddamn it!"

The usually calm Andrei threw his phone at the wall. It was a decent phone, combat-ready, so it wasn't harmed, and Hans managed to dodge just in time.

"What did they say?!" Anna and Helga asked in the same breath.

"He went in," Androsov said in a tired voice. "Almost four hours ago. They said that for the past two hours, only monsters have been coming out of the Rift. Not a single Slayer has come out in that time..."

CHAPTER 12

"NO FURTHER, YOUR LORDSHIP!" The ragged-looking army man held up his hands to stop me. His helmet sat askew on his head, which was wrapped in bandages here and there, blood already seeping through them.

"What's the situation, soldier?"

"A Rift opened up inside..." the private began. But I interrupted him.

"I know about that. What kind of beasts?"

"Gigantic beetles. Just take a look over there. Hard to kill as roaches!"

I looked behind him and saw a destroyed machine gun turret. The corpses of soldiers lay around it. And in the middle lay a huge bug a little larger than Caramel.

Off to one side, the small village of mobile homes that had grown around the Anthill was in flames. Screams were coming from that direction, along with swearing and shrieks of pain. I couldn't hear any explosions or shooting.

"We already fought off a few waves," the soldier said.

"Where are the Slayers?"

"Some of them went in. Some," he looked at me strangely, "came right back out again."

"No need to judge them," I said with a frown. "Everyone has to admit to their limits sooner or later."

"Forgive me, Your Lordship!" The soldier quickly stood to attention. "I did not mean to…"

"Forget it. I'm off…"

"May I have your last name for the register?"

"Slayer Class Five Galaxius," I muttered.

Wolf trailed after me.

"Do you really think that the Slayers running away are in the right?" Potapov asked me grimly.

"Well, how can I put it, Wolf..? Honestly, I think they're the worst kind of cowards. But a part of me, somewhere deep down inside, says that they were just acting rationally. By leaving when they did, they still have a chance of leveling up and coming back. But a dead Slayer can't level up anymore."

"But they abandoned people!" Wolf said, still frowning.

"Exactly," I nodded, putting an end to the unpleasant subject.

I crouched down next to the bug corpse.

It's good to be a Hunter. There are very few

unique creatures in the world. Feels like all the universes create by the same pattern and model. If you've seen ten different types of bugs, you've seen them all. I knew just where to find its tiny brain, which was its nerve center.

"Look!" I motioned Wolf over. "This is where you need to shoot. Ideally with something high-caliber."

"Got it," Potapov said with a nod.

I stood up and walked further past the ruins. Looked like part of the village had taken artillery fire from the guns stationed outside the Perimeter. I was starting to get the impression that the local defenders had called for fire on themselves. If so, that was worthy of respect. Everywhere were corpses, blood, metal mixed with earth. The entire area around the Rift looked like the barren dead surface of the Moon, covered in craters.

"Commander?"

"Yes, Wolf?"

"Will you let me come with you?"

I turned to him and chuckled.

"The fact that I gave you a ring doesn't mean I'm ready to lose you."

"I can handle it, Commander!" Wolf frowned.

"Tell me, buddy, how well do you handle swords, axes, maybe a spear?"

Wolf seemed at a loss for the first time.

"Not really my skillset. I'm an expert in firearms, actually. But I'm good with knives too. And I can throw them." He thought a little, then added: "And real well, too!"

I chuckled.

"Knives, you say?" I clapped him on the shoulder. "Maybe we'll make an assassin out of you yet. But not today. You stay here and wait for me. If it all goes to hell, head back to the Center. Find Anna, she has all the papers. Our contract will be considered complete. She'll send you your money too."

Wolf literally growled.

"I don't like that plan!"

Now I burst out laughing.

"Believe me, I don't like it either. But remember what I said about trust? Then listen — I know I'm going to come out of there. And not empty-handed, either. You cover my flank, soldier!"

"Understood."

I moved my eyes to Caramel. She opened her mouth and growled. A furious cry resounded in my head.

Don't you think about it! Don't even dare!

I chuckled.

"Where I go, you go too, huh?" I patted her gently on her big head. "Fine, let's go. High time."

We walked into the Rift. The internal staging area had also been destroyed. The very first wave must have overwhelmed the internal defenders.

I had two trophy swords hanging at my side, a dozen kunai in the band at my chest, which I'd get more than one use out of if I was lucky. And my own power hadn't gone anywhere either.

I sent Shnoop ahead, and Caramel and I

carefully followed behind him.

This place was already a kingdom of death — ant death in particular. The broken corpses of ants lay all over. Several of the stunned beasts ran toward us, but were quickly eliminated.

I hoped that the inner Rift wasn't too deep down. Judging by the fact that its beasts were making it outside, it probably wasn't.

Actually, this was an extremely unlikely event. I had heard about this kind of thing in a rare moment when I wasn't sleeping at the lectures. Usually, the beasts dealt with each other on the inside, and usually didn't make it to threaten humanity on the outside. After some time, one side got the upper hand. Then the Slayers went in there and cleared the whole place.

But this time something went wrong. And, remembering the almost crushed bug on the surface and the small bodies of the ants, I realized that the front-line units of the ants just couldn't compare. Maybe the soldier ants could show better resistance, but they were lower down.

The waves of crazed fleeing ants grew more frequent as I went deeper into the Rift, and their size increased too. Caramel really let loose. I even got involved myself a couple of times. The spirits raged in my inner vault. Shnoop picked up the few jellies that dropped. All going to plan. Only I couldn't seem to figure out where the damn Rift was.

We started finding Slayer corpses, torn to pieces and partly eaten by the beasts. However, judging by the fact that the corpses of broken bugs lay next to them, I could tell that the young men and women hadn't given their lives easily.

I looked thoughtfully at an axe lying next to a broken sword and realized it was time to gather some loot. Summoning Pinky, I handed him all the light bags I'd gotten from Arkhip. They were made from a really thin material. I think he said something about otherworldly spider's silk. They folded up into a little pouch, taking up barely any space in my backpack. But in their unfolded state, they were highly durable.

"You're our mule now, Pinky," I chuckled, patting his little pink head.

He nodded in apparent agreement.

An axe and two daggers went straight into a bag. I also threw my own backpack in there, which was hindering my movements. I picked up all the Slayer tokens and rings that I could find. And we moved on.

I saw an injured soldier ant in an adjoining tunnel branch. Smaller ants flocked around it, paying us no attention at all. I got the feeling they were trying to give it first aid.

Pinky moved forward for some reason too, but the big ant snapped its pincers, nearly biting the pink parlayer in two. The little thing whined and ran to hide behind me.

"You're from our anthill now! Better get used to it, poor little guy! These ones are strangers to you now!" I chuckled.

The ant looked in confusion toward his

former brethren, then shivered behind me like a beaten dog. I even started to feel a little sorry for him.

"Come on, settle down! We're not so bad! Fun, that's the main thing!"

The first beetle soon arose before us. It was missing two of its six legs. Someone had cut them off, but the beast was still crawling straight at us.

Caramel darted before it, distracting its attention. Meanwhile, I approached from the side. I tried to judge where the creature's tiny brain was located. Then, charging my sword with power, I stabbed it right there. Chitin cracked, the sword cracked, the bug died.

"Goddamn it!" I swore.

My first serious opponent, and I was a weapon down already. Looked like I'd have to be more careful. I realized why there were so many broken swords lying near the Slayer corpses. Few weapons could withstand collision with the hard shells of these beasts.

On the other hand, there were a whole two red jellies in the bug's head, which made me feel a little better about the situation.

We went further in. A wounded bug crossed our path. Its entire right-hand row of legs was broken off, and it couldn't move properly anymore. This time I was more careful, and put the creature down without breaking my weapon.

"Keep a look-out for where these critters are coming from, Shnoop. We need to figure it out."

Seeing the image that Shnoop showed me, I

swore furiously. Four Slayers were fighting in a small cave. Three more bodies lay behind them, either injured or killed. And five more bugs were bearing down on them.

A girl fell with a scream right before my eyes. A big man standing next to her, splattered from head to toe with green blood, deftly pulled the wounded girl onto his back and dropped his huge axe down into the shell of a beast. But the next beast knocked the big man off his feet. They didn't seem to have long left.

"Run!" I shouted; thankfully, the battle wasn't very far away.

We made it just in time. Caramel leaped onto a beast and started shredding it with her claws. I could feel the energy flooding out of me and into her. But I couldn't blame her. It took a lot to break through those carapaces.

I took down the second bug. Caramel and I pulverized the third together. Another one hesitated, caught between us on two sides. And then Pinky surprised me — with a high-pitched shriek, he cast himself at the beast's feet, sweeping them out from under it. I planted my sword in the bug's brain. And wouldn't you know it? That sword broke too. Of course.

I turned to the stunned Slayers, who held themselves up on willpower alone. The big man limped forward, blood seeping down one of his legs, then offered me a hand.

"Thanks, buddy! You showed up in the nick of time."

His ring burned with the yellow light of a class-three. A strong Slayer! I looked him up and down. He didn't look like much of a fighter.

"Viscount Smorodin, Commander of the Second Slayer Response Team," he said by way of introduction.

"Baron Galaxius." I shook his hand and smiled. "Slayer Fifth Class."

"Galaxius?" The big man narrowed his eyes. "*The* Galaxius?"

I shrugged. "Probably."

I looked at what was left of the group. Only three of them could move unaided. They could more or less stand on their feet. The others were lying on the ground and groaning in pain. Two had stopped moving, either dead or unconscious.

"The way out is clear... for now," I said. "If you hurry, you might get them out."

"We're a Response Team, Baron!" the man snapped from his vantage point almost a head higher than me. "We have a mission from the Center!"

"Look at yourself, fighter!" I said, snapping back at him. "Your mission from the Center is to shut this Rift, not throw your lives away! You were brave folks to come here. But that's enough for today. Anyway, who'll pull out your injured comrades?"

That last seemed to have an effect. The big man frowned, then nodded.

"Sergei, Sanya, gather up the wounded." He turned back to me. "We're coming back here,

Galaxius... As soon as we get the wounded out."

I chuckled.

"If you ask me, you're better off staying out. But decide for yourselves. Just be careful, Viscount. Oh, and..." Here I hesitated a little. "Could I ask you for a sword? As you can see, my last one broke. I'll give it back if it survives, and if it breaks then I'll pay you back what it's worth."

The big man offered me his two-handed pole-axe, but I shook my head no. It was good steel, and it would have taken a beating, but just wasn't my style. Not the best weapon in close quarters.

"Thanks, but I'd rather take a sword."

"Sergei, take Fyodorov's off him. He won't be needing it anymore." One of the still-standing Slayers took the dead man's sword and handed it to me.

I pulled the blade half out of the scabbard. The metal shimmered with a bluish light. Good ore! The best green Karsk steel, supposedly among the most durable alloys. It might stand up for quite a while.

"Thanks. Like I said, I'll give it back later."

"No need, Baron. No need. We'll compensate his family for its cost ourselves. Consider it thanks for saving us."

"Whatever you say. Alright, guys. Get out of here, hurry."

Loot doesn't gather itself. And I very carefully and justifiably broke open the brain-cases of the bugs that my team had put down. At the same time, I tested out the sword. It held a charge pretty well.

Something poked me in the side of the leg. It was Pinky; he'd brought me the leg of a bug, placed it on the ground beside me and was gesturing at it.

"What, is that for me?" I laughed. "You want to feed me up? Thanks, little guy, but I'm not hungry."

I petted my new pet's chitinous little head. The Slayers cast strange looks at me as they carried out their comrades. Right, a dude talking to a pink ant — did he have a screw loose?

We moved on. Shnoop couldn't seem to find that damn Rift. But the number of bugs greatly increased. The sword held up. I held up. Mel held up. Even my armor held up, although it was a close thing.

A couple of times I summoned some of their dead fellows against them, but my inner vault of energy wasn't endless. Here I had to choose between summoning beasts or fighting by hand. I quickly judged the situation and chose the second.

As I stabbed through yet another skull, I saw that my ring flashed with an orange light. There it was, Class Four again! No point trying to hide it anymore, I guess — I was already getting enough confused looks as it was.

We went further. Shnoop showed me an interesting room again, with a multitude of ants being torn to pieces by several bugs. It was like they were trying to protect something important.

I squeezed a red jelly in my hand, my third for

the day, renewing my supplies of energy. I sighed, then sped off into the tunnel branch. By the time we made it there, all the ants had died. And, with great pleasure, the three remaining beetles were chowing down on a clutch of ant eggs.

A high shriek burst out nearby. Pinky, quickly working his little legs, darted forward and tried to grab the beetles by the legs, clearly trying to destroy them. Only his strength wasn't really up to it.

The first blow from one of the beetles sent him flying. The only thing that stopped the giant pincers from cutting him in two was, surprisingly, Caramel, who knocked the arrogant beetle down with her body and slashed a clawed paw at its head. To my amazement, Pinky learned exactly nothing from the experience. He rolled back onto his legs and rushed back into the action.

"Are you trying to get yourself killed?" I shouted, throwing an ice spear at another beetle that wanted to attack Pinky again.

I didn't kill it, but clearly slowed it down. And that was enough for me to run up and break it open with my sword. Caramel dealt with the first one. We took down the third together.

I heard some strange sounds, turned around and couldn't hold back a smile. Have you ever seen a little puppy furiously ragging around a big slipper or a soft toy, making like his big papa guard dog? Well, Pinky was at that moment tugging with all his might and ferocity at the leg of an already dead beetle.

"Alright, alright, that's enough!" I said, walking up to the ferocious pink thing and carefully pulling him off the corpse. "You have a warrior's heart, little guy!"

Pinky walked up to the desecrated clutch of eggs and gave a piteous whine.

"Sorry, buddy," I said, feeling awkward for some reason, although I myself had stolen several thousand of these eggs in the past.

I walked up and picked one of them up, a green one — the cheapest type.

Pinky twitched, but then froze in place.

I was surprised once again.

"You mean, if I take these eggs, that's fine? But these ones you try to peck to death?"

The ant walked up to me and just silently prodded me in the waist with its head.

"Damn, now that's what I call loyalty!" I petted him once more on his hard head.

Caramel snorted nearby.

"What, old girl, getting jealous?" I smiled.

At that she snorted again even more derisively. Her thought resounded in my head:

When hell freezes over!

"Alright, let's move on. And you, little pink warrior, stay close by."

Shnoop finally found the entrance to the inner Rift. Trouble was, bugs were pouring from that direction. There was no other way there. We'd have to fight our way through.

I swore and squeezed yet another jelly. My head was starting to spin a little, and I reeled —

all the signs of energetic overload. But I knew my body well — it would hold up a little longer. And if I threw up — well, to hell with it. At the end of the day, I had one of the best healers in the Empire as a friend.

We ran straight back into battle. First I threw all the kunai throwing knives I had, putting them in 'explosive' mode. An expensive decision, and the Empire of the Rising Sun was far away, but it had to be done. Twelve throws — twelve corpses. I even started to feel a little pride.

Then the second wave came at us, across the bodies of the first. I span as fast as I could, showing true feats of agility. The panther darted to and fro beside me. My armor creaked. Caramel took some hits too, which caused another surge of energy from me to her defenses.

They were starting to overwhelm us. Pinky ran up beside us with a shriek, seeing that we were in trouble. And then I got a wild idea. I connected the little critter to my energy channel and started to feed him with energy, and stuffed two more red jellies into my mouth, swallowing them straight down. There was no time to squeeze them in a hand. I was bound to get stomach ulcers. Yeah, that's right, a whole two of them, one after another.

The ant was began to glow with an aura of power, and right before my eyes he ripped a beetle's leg straight off with the cartilage. But then two more threw themselves on him. Now it was my turn to get crazy, afraid for my pet, and I threw all the energy I had into his body. There was a crack, a bright flash of light flooding the area for a moment and blinding us all.

And before my eyes rose up a huge pink ant only a little smaller than its foes. But that wasn't all. Delicate transparent wings now fluttered on its back. It flew up into the air and crashed down on its enemy, crushing its carapace.

"Goddamn it!" was all I had time to say before I was back in the fight again.

The three of us got it done a lot faster this time. I looked sadly at my signet ring, red again. And moved my eyes to the man of the hour, Pinky. Although I was already starting to have some vague doubts on that front.

"Wings? Pinky..." I said guardedly. "Own up — are you a chick?"

Suddenly, Shnoop appeared nearby and started rolling around on the ground and laughing, repeating over and over:

"Shhnooop knew! Shhnooop knew! Big dumb human!"

"Everyone's a comedian." I scratched the back of my head. "Fine, I dub you Lady Pinky. Deal?"

Something at the edge of consciousness touched my brain, but I couldn't quite make it out. Sure, I'd heard that ant mothers are smarter than the rest. Only this one had to be still a baby, and couldn't talk yet. Well, before you knew it, I'd know how to talk Antish.

The path to the inner Rift was open. Shnoop headed in to scout out the situation and I saw a wasteland, in the literal sense of the word. Just dead, barren earth. Not so much as a shoot or sapling or blade of grass. Those beetles must have eaten it all up. Now I could understand why they were so aggressive. They were just dying of hunger, and here they ran right into some free food.

I didn't hurry. The Rift was orange, bordering on yellow. Having seen those insects, I wasn't surprised. But what exactly was waiting for me inside? Shnoop searched while I pondered. Had the whole lot of them crawled out of there already? No way...

Then Shnoop showed me some kind of swamp where the disgusting spawn of the beetles seethed under the watchful eyes of four full-grown bugs. Looked like only the kindergarten had been left behind.

I had another choice again — call myself reinforcements, or go in with my current team. But I was afraid my energy reserves were running low, and there was the risk that I could fall into a stupor at any moment.

We dove inside and walked to the bog. I really didn't want to, but I ate another jelly. Two pets and my own armor took a lot of energy to maintain!

Now we had another problem — the moms started spitting at us. I'd been ready for almost anything, sure. But somehow these bugs seemed to have some signs of intellect. After I dodged the first glob of spit and then the second, the next two hit me at once. What, did they know the word 'warning'?

My armor hissed, instantly dropping.

The weave on my arm partially failed. I hissed in pain as the acid started to eat through my arm. Several more droplets landed all over my body, burning through my clothes and putting me in a world of hurt.

Another red jelly went down the hatch. A whole firework display started playing in my vision. I was right on the edge. But my pets weren't slouching.

Lady Pinky was already tearing apart one of the nannies. Mel ripped into another. It seemed their acid was their main weapon. Unlike their comrades, the shells on these ones were far less durable. And their bellies were actually soft.

I pulled my smoking clothes off me, now in nothing but my white boxer shorts decorated with red hearts. Yeah, I had plenty of them now! And I bought them because I liked the material, I didn't give a damn about the design. But when I had only one pair left after my apartment exploded, Anna took on the responsibility of dressing me and bought a whole box just like them, apparently deciding that the design was important too. Well, the hell with it, it really was a great material!

I sat down on my ass and sighed heavily, trying to cleanse my energy channels. Felt like I was on the verge of exploding from the inside. Energy overload making itself known.

I smiled sadly. Well, Xander, you never thought you'd see the day — your pets doing your job for you.

"Wwwwaaaant?" Shnoop asked, appearing before me and dropping four orange jellies.

I scratched him on his furry head.

"Thanks, little guy!" I said sincerely, knowing how he disliked digging around in corpses. Even the little terror himself seemed to realize that his master was on the brink.

I listened closely to my feelings. The Rift was still open, and I moved my eyes to the teeming little critters before me.

"Come on, time to finish the job!" I shouted at my pets.

Pinky looked at me doubtfully.

"Yeah, yeah, I know you're a nanny too. And these are larvae. But these little things will turn into those monsters that ate your eggs."

The ant squeaked and immediately made its decision. I gathered up that part of my energy that I needed to get rid of. Forming it into a ball of fire, I threw it right at the center of the bog, which instantly burst up in flames. The little larvae started crawling out to the bank in terror, where they ran into Mel and the ant.

Another wave of energy swallowed me up. But it was healing energy, expanding my channels, which were just about to snap with the strain. I looked down at my hand again. There, back to orange! Well done, Slayer Fourth Class Galaxius!"

There were no jellies in the little ones, so we quietly walked to the exit from the Rift. Shnoop quickly ran through the Rift, but unsurprisingly, found nothing valuable.

In the Anthill more bugs began to appear in our path, but they looked lost. The fact that the Rift was closed seemed to have reached their tiny little brains. They stopped working in groups and just cast at us separately, which we could handle easily.

"Dangerrrr!" Shnoop shrieked, appearing before us.

I immediately looked to the right. A dozen soldier ants were running straight at us, formed up into ranks like armored infantry. They tore two inattentive beetles apart in front of us. But now we were all that was in their path.

"Damn, I'd really rather not do this," I said to myself with a grimace, carefully feeling out a powerful soul inside me.

I had to go all-in. The Magma Elemental would do it. But would I be able to deal with it after it was done? Oh, the hell with it! There was still energy in my ring. Alright, time to work!

I summoned the illusion of a big red smudge that looked like a chunk of rock split with veins of lava. It was actually made of rock, with lava seething within it. Taking that bastard down had been a hell of a quest. It had been defending a certain interesting vein of ore that I'd received an order for. I was young and inexperienced back then, and nearly died. So this creature was a kind of keepsake, a memory and a warning to me. But right then I was ready to say good-bye to it.

Just as I was about to drive the spirit into the illusion, Pinky darted forward and stood in the path of the soldiers, spreading her wings and chittering wildly. Damn, they were about to tear her to shreds! She was still smaller than any one of them. But then something amazing happened! They stopped, then started walking around to the right and left of her, trying carefully not to hit her.

Pinky hissed, then stepped backwards to us. Then she looked at me as if challenging me.

"Mel, heel." I nodded at the panther.

Then I stepped closer to Pinky. The illusion still hung in the air. I was ready to put the soul into it at any time. But the ants walked around us as if we were some untouchable island, and then they galloped off through the tunnel about their antly business.

Lady Pinky folded up her wings and fixed me again with her unblinking black eyes. I sighed and relaxed, dispelling the illusion.

"Goddamn, good job! Sorry I called you a chick! You're a goddamn Valkyrie! A pink one!" I smiled.

"Well, now it's time to get out of here. I'm exhausted. As my new Japanese friends would say — sayonara, suckers!"

CHAPTER 13

IT TOOK US A WHILE to reach the exit, but there wasn't much incident either.

After Pinky's matronly transformation, the ants avoided us. On the way we ran into a couple of still walking beetles, which we put down right away. We also saw three Slayer corpses, torn up and with broken weapons, but with Slayer rings and tokens intact. I shook my head as I stripped the dead men of their accessories. I had already personally gathered thirteen rings. Four more bodies were missing the hands their rings would have been on. Seventeen Slayers lost, and that was just on my fairly direct path to the Rift. How many people had lost their lives in this place today?

I started to understand Khrulyov for sticking to me like a tick. I guessed the guy was sick of always losing people. And again, I started to feel sympathy for the very idea of the Center itself, which had its own training department. People had to be trained. And trained well.

I sighed, and gave Shnoop the order to go looking for rings. The little guy hissed his agreement and disappeared. Then the sad accessories started to fall into my palm one after another. Eighteen, nineteen, twenty... Twenty-three... Twenty-eight... Thirty-two... Forty-five... By the time we got to the Rift exit, I had sixty-two Slayer rings in my hands. They had turned transparent after their owners' deaths. No way to know their owners' power, but one thing was sure — they were all heroes. Minus sixty-two Slayers in just one day, in the Anthill alone. Today would be a day of mourning for the Center.

I also asked Shnoop to pick up the remaining weaponry. But even with so many dead, there were few weapons. It was the weak Slayers who died there, with all due respect to them, and their weapons were just as weak. Shnoop pulled out two clubs, three swords and four axes, which just barely fit into the bags of the overgrown Pinky, who carried the whole pile of loot along without a hint of strain. We also found thirty-two knives, which, I suspect, the poor bastards didn't even have time to pull out.

As I walked up to the exit I looked again at Pinky, who stopped like a pack animal when I stopped and rapped on her pink head.

"I hope you'll stay with us," I said.

The ant squeaked in answer, and I released

her soul. It took a lot of energy to sustain it, and I had little enough of it left for myself. Damn shame if she flew off to ant heaven after I poured all that power into her.

Yes, fine! It wasn't the energy that bothered me, it was the prospect of losing our nanny ant and her fighting spirit. But the strengthened creature just went back into my soul vault, seating herself right by the exit as if hinting that she was always there if I needed her. There was a ritual for reviving pets, I knew it. Only... There were too many complexities involved. And it wasn't just a matter of energy alone.

I scratched the back of my head, staring at the pile of junk left behind after Pinky disappeared. Well, you'll have to do something with it, Xander. As it turned out, lady ants are great helpers. I looked thoughtfully at Mel, who looked as exhausted as I felt. She widened her eyes and backed away from me slowly.

I'm no stinking pack ant! she scoffed in my head.

"Yeah, yeah, I know." I smiled at her. "Too proud to help your master, huh?"

The cat thought for a moment, then her gaze darkened. She made a deep sigh and walked up to me, offering me her back.

Sorry. I'm ashamed, I heard in my head.

"It's alright," I said, scratching her behind the ear. "It happens. You know, I think I can handle it this time on my own."

The exit from the Rift was mere yards away,

so I dug my feet into the floor and dragged the heap of metal forward. Caramel carefully walked to the side of me, grabbed the load with her teeth and then, backing up, helped me drag it.

I fell out of the Rift ass-first, in my big white underpants covered in hearts, dragging a whole heap of loot behind me.

"Hold! Hold your fire!" I heard from the side.

I turned my eyes that way. There were far more army men here now than when I left. It looked like there were new groups of freshly arrived Slayers forming up in the trailer park.

Wolf ran up to me with a worried look on his face and a huge RPG launcher on his shoulder.

"Commander, you're alive!"

I stood up and wiped the sweat from my brow.

"Trust, my friend, trust! Where'd you get that, and why'd you bring it here?" I asked, nodding at the grenade launcher.

The bald man reddened.

"Uh, you know, some boys lent it to me."

Those very same boys ran up to us.

"Give it back to them! It's probably worth all they have." I gestured at Wolf.

But he silently stared at the launcher like a little kid at a toy. An old sergeant laughed nearby.

"Let him keep it... We'll write it off as a loss. Where'd you find this badass, Your Lordship?" The man nodded towards Wolf. He can fire that grenade launcher as accurately as a sniper rifle. He took down half the bugs from the last wave all on his own."

"Actually, this 'badass' is a retired captain of the Imperial Special Forces." I smiled. "So yeah, he knows what he's doing."

The army men were stretched out in a line and staring in amazement at Potapov. I guess they saw Slayers all the time, but this was something new to them. Another senior sergeant whispered something to the first, then walked forward. The man, around forty years old, took two measured steps and gave a military salute.

"Your lordship! God as witness, I have wanted to do this for a long time. Thank you, sir, on behalf of me and all my boys."

"What are you talking about, Staff Sergeant?" Andrei asked with a frown.

"Well, you're Wolf! Commander of the Wolfpack!" the fighter said excitedly.

Potapov's face darkened.

"Former commander..." He hesitated. "Of the former Wolfpack."

"I heard, and I sympathize. I truly sympathize! Just two years ago, you covered us from the steppe peoples when they had our convoy backed into a canyon."

Wolf chuckled.

"Which canyon exactly?"

Now it was my turn to chuckle.

"What, were there many?"

That got me a raised eyebrow.

"Enough."

"At Elyn-An, Your Lordship."

For a second, Wolf's face took on a dreamy

expression.

"Yeah, that was some damn job." He reached out a hand. "Good luck, soldier! Look after yourself!"

"And you, Your Lordship!"

"Only I'm not 'Your Lordship'." Wolf chuckled.

"Nonsense!" I objected. "You will be one day, my bald-headed friend! I promise you'll like it..."

I clapped him on the shoulder. And then the pile of loot pulled my gaze back. I moved my eyes back to the army men.

"Well, boys, if you're so impressed with my heroic comrade, would you be so kind as to help us carry all this to our car?"

"Of course, no problem."

The men started picking up the goods. I grabbed my backpack.

"I think I'll just take this one myself."

The pack was full of jellies, and the rings of the dead Slayers.

"Want a hand?" Wolf suggested.

I smiled.

"I can manage," I said, and tried to stand up straighter. "What, do I look that bad?"

Wolf looked me up and down.

"I wouldn't say bad exactly. Just — weird."

I chuckled. Right — heart underpants, boots, scorched all over and splattered with blood from head to toe. A sight for sore eyes!

As we walked to the car, three Slayers intercepted me. One of them I recognized. Some deputy of Khrulyov's. Slayer Third Class ring on his finger, in full battle gear. And two underlings by his sides.

"A moment, Slayer Fifth Class Galaxius!" I shouted to me.

I stopped, wrinkling my nose and scratching it.

"Oh, forgive me! Slayer Fourth Class Galaxius."

I smirked.

"At your service."

"What happened in there?" The man nodded at the Rift. "I have orders to clear it. But we're waiting. By my predictions, after eight hours the flow of beasts should dissipate. But it's easier to take them out from the outside. So we were planning on going in later. But..." Here he looked at me strangely. "It's been an hour now, and nothing has come out. That is quite... unusual."

"The inner Rift is closed," I said with a smile, and reached for his tablet. "You're the big fish here. Put a check mark next to Galaxius. Let Vasily Petrovich know that I'm not just sitting on my ass, I'm getting it done."

"Are you sure?" The deputy commander frowned.

"About what?" I grimaced at him. "That the Rift is closed? Absolutely. Although..." I nodded to the side. "You can always check for yourselves. You need to go in there anyway. Sure, you could sit here on the outside for eight more hours, or you could take me at my word and go in now. Just be careful. The ants are all worked up. And their soldiers have come up from the lower tiers."

The Slayer nodded sagely. "Thank you for the information!"

"By all means. Can I go?"

"Yes! And thank you for your service, Slayer!"

At that I couldn't hold back a laugh.

"You're welcome again. Time to go... buy new pants, I guess."

When I reached the car, everything was already unloaded. I opened the door and looked thoughtfully at the gleaming black leather of the upholstery. Strange to see leather seats in the law-enforcement edition. But I guess the police on the Japanese islands were fashionable types. Or it was the Petersburg crew that decided to swap the hardy and durable cloth for leather that could easily be torn by any sharp object.

Wolf had already climbed into the driver's seat, and at the sight of me he nodded in understanding.

"Just get in, the both of you. Something will tear it sooner or later and you'll have to get it changed anyway. Caramel already did some damage in the back there with her claws on some tight turns."

I looked. Right — already a tear in the back. Her ears burning, Caramel pulled her claws in as far as she could and turned away to look out the window, as if she saw something fascinating there in the trees.

"I see," I said, and just climbed in as I was.

"To the Center?" Wolf asked.

"Nah... Let's go see Arkhip first, at Arkhip's Legendary Armory."

"Isn't it a little late?" Andrei frowned.

"He'll open up for me. And I don't like to leave business unfinished."

Wolf gave a strange chuckle.

"Don't you chuckle at me. If necessary, I could have closed another couple of Rifts like that one."

Wolf looked at me again. His mouth stretched in a crooked grin. He was about to laugh at my funny joke. But then, seeing the look in my eye, he changed his mind for some reason. Then muttered:

"Are you serious..?"

My turn to grin.

"Never been more serious. But I'm not saying I'd have wanted to. As a rule, I try to fit some margin for error into all my work. So it should be pretty hard to die on my team."

Wolf gave me another strange look.

"Come on, out with it. What?"

"With all due respect, Commander, but given your age and biography, you have a very strange skillset indeed."

I looked searchingly into his eyes.

"One day you may learn a lot more about me."

"I get it," Potapov nodded. "Trust."

"Exactly right. Now let's go."

We rolled out in the direction of Irkutsk. Out of habit, Shnoop investigated the road ahead, but there wasn't a single wild beast in the area. They were either scared of the sudden influx of army forces or just hiding. The road was clear.

After stopping at the checkpoint, and slightly frightening the corporal there when he saw my bloody face as I lowered the tinted window, we moved on. But after little more than a mile, I spoke up:

"Stop here. Park up on the roadside."

Wolf obeyed and brought us to a stop.

"Keep the lights on."

It was getting dark already. I pulled my underpants up and stepped out onto the road.

The bald man stood silently next to me with his Whirlwind assault rifle, looking around and keeping an eye on our surroundings. He looked at me in confusion, but asked no questions.

I was waiting for the cavalcade that Shnoop had noticed — armored cars with the Androsov family crest on the side, and a couple of unmarked ones from the Center. When they showed up, I raised a hand and waved, jumping up and down.

The cars stopped. Androsov, Helga, Smolin and Schrader came running from the first one. From the others came a multitude of guards — the Androsov family guard, which, with all due respect to the Imperial Army, was far better equipped than it.

"Alex, you're alive!" Andrei ran up to me and took me by the shoulders, concern clear on his face.

"As you can see," I said with a grin. "You guys off to start a war?" I nodded at the sheer number of people.

"Yeah, we were coming to save you."

"Dumb idea, I agree," Helga said, walking up to us. "I was against it. And that Anna of yours just told us not to worry, said you'd manage on your own. That girl has incredible faith in you, Galaxius."

"As you can see, 'that girl' turned out to be right," I said, shrugging. "Mind if I drive on?"

"Stop!" the duke snapped, unusually sharply for him.

He was still holding me by the shoulders.

"How are you even still standing?"

"I'm standing just fine," I said with a shrug.

Helga stepped closer.

"What is it, Andrei?"

"He has an extreme degree of..." He hesitated. "I can't even explain it. Usually there's either exhaustion or energy overload. But here I have the feeling that over the past few hours, Alex has experienced both. Several times. I'm surprised he's still breathing at all."

Andrei's speech was so concerning that I even paid close attention to my own feelings for a minute. No... I was just fine. Didn't feel about to keel over and die. Aloud, I just said:

"I think you're exaggerating a little."

"Exaggerating? Sit down there!" He unceremoniously sat me down on the roadside, on the wet grass covered with evening dew.

"Andy, it's wet here! And I'm cold!" I said. "Do you guys not have a spare jumpsuit lying around?"

Helga nodded to one of the soldiers. Androsov just said:

"You'll survive, you won't melt."

Barely noticeably, he started to reach out for my energy centers. I begrudgingly admired his work. We Hunters knew where things were and could work with energy contours. But in this world, only the Healers knew how to do that. And Andrei had a wonderful mastery of the craft.

"I don't understand." Androsov shook his head. "I'm still just doing my diagnostics, but your channels are healing right before my eyes. What the hell is this, Galaxius?"

Oops! I thought to myself, and slowed my regeneration a little, which was working at full steam.

"Hell if I know, Andrei. I mean, I'm a healthy guy. There's also such a thing as Family heredity."

That phrase should mean a lot to him, and he himself knew that marriages between the bearers of strong blood could sometimes work wonders.

"Well, I've seen healthier," Andrei said with narrowed eyes. "But I've never seen this before."

"Come on, buddy, I'm sick of this already. Either you let me go or do what you want to do. I need to make it to Arkhip. And I wouldn't mind getting a wash. And some sleep, while I'm at it."

"Arkhip, wash, sleep?" Androsov kept looking at me with confusion. "You need to go straight to the hospital!"

"I don't want to go to the hospital," I said, annoyed. "Listen, I'm out of here."

"Wait," Andrei asked. "Give me five minutes."

A yellow glow shot from his fingers. I felt a freshening effect similar to my own regeneration, only several times stronger. Andrei was redirecting his own energy into my system, tending to the damage.

"Two days of rest at least. And another couple of healing sessions." He shot me a stern look. "If I find out that you're headed to another Rift, rest assured, I'll do all in my power to make you..." He faltered, trying to think of what he had to frighten the mighty Slayer Galaxius. "I'll stop talking to you, that's what!"

"Alright, mommy, I won't," I said with a smile, and wasn't even lying.

Actually, a couple of days of rest wouldn't hurt at all. I had earned some money. Wolf needed to recover too, and I could sure use a rest.

"Right, can I go now?"

"Sure!" Androsov said, and shook his phone. "I have Anna's number, I'll check up on you."

I chuckled. "Anna won't rat me out."

"Damn!" Androsov swore. "You're right. Well, never mind, there are cameras all over the place."

"That's the Center network," I reminded him.

"So what?" Androsov winked to me, then, satisfied with himself, headed for his car.

Helga lingered a moment.

"How is it?" She nodded in the direction of the Rift. "Do you need our help?"

"I don't think so," I said honestly.

"Managed to weasel your way out again?" The

girl smiled sadly.

"I don't do it deliberately." I shrugged again.

Helga smiled strangely at me again.

"Galaxius, you're just so..." She thought for a moment. "Not special..."

Turning sharply on her heel, she walked back to the car. I watched her go in amazement. What did she want from me?

A guardsman ran up and handed me a uniform — a jumpsuit with the Androsov crest emblazoned on it. I chuckled. My hand reached up right away to tear off the emblem, but then I hesitated. Whatever — I could put up with it. I'd almost done something stupid in front of Andrei. Right away I pulled off my boots, pulled on the jumpsuit in the lamplight and gave a thumbs up to Androsov, now sitting out of sight in his car. The leading car honked twice as if it had been waiting for me to get dressed, and the convoy started to move out.

I nodded. "And now to Arkhip's place!"

The old storekeep was waiting for me. The lights in the store were still on. I asked Wolf to park at the back entrance, where it'd be easier to unload the goods.

"Ha-ha, quite the outfit you have there," the old man said by way of greeting. "Nice to see you alive and well. How was it?"

"Fine!" I shrugged. "Just like we suspected, it was an ambush. But I handled it!"

"That's not what I meant." Arkhip grimaced. "How was it at the Anthill?"

I frowned. "It was rough. I have sixty-two rings to take back to the Center."

Arkhip darkened. He couldn't keep the pain from showing on his face.

He nodded. "May they rest in peace."

"Right," I said. "Now let's get down to the haggling. I badly need some sleep. By the way, I didn't get paid for the bait Rift."

Arkhip nodded.

"No pay, huh..." He frowned, opened up his tablet and jabbed at something.

My phone pinged. I took it out and saw a transfer — fifteen thousand.

"Nice magic trick." I raised an eyebrow at Arkhip. "What did you tell them?"

"Put it this way — I vouched for you."

"You're a big fish in the Free Slayer pond, huh?" I smiled, catching myself thinking that I'd had no time to find out about his past, despite all the business we did together. An oversight, as Anna would put it. I'd have to ask her for more details.

"Right! Let's go check out the swag!"

We stepped out, where Wolf, at my order, had already sorted the weapons into 'sell' and 'keep.' One pile was big and one small. Actually: One huge and one tiny.

"Take a look!" I said, nodding Arkhip toward the big pile.

"Um... Commander!" Potapov piped up sheepishly.

"What?"

"Wrong way round! That one's the keep pile!"

I burst out laughing.

"Tell me, my bald friend, did you guys have a limited budget in the Wolfpack?"

"No," Andrei said, shaking his head with a frown. "How'd you guess?"

"Not hard!" I said, still laughing. "Choose the two best daggers for yourself."

Wolf dug around for so long that even Arkhip couldn't take it. After a quick glance, he pulled two short blades in scabbards out of the pile and handed them to Potapov.

Wolf stared at him in wonderment.

"Yeah, looks like you're right!"

"Doesn't just look like it — I am!" The old storekeep smiled.

I sighed and sat down to go through the pile myself, mercilessly casting away anything I didn't need. Sighs of lament came from the direction of Potapov every now and again, but he didn't dare object.

I nodded to Arkhip. "Now take a look."

He cast a quick glance across it: two swords, six axes, forty knives and four clubs. For myself, I kept a backup supply of one sword, both explosive spears and the two decent knives that Arkhip chose for Wolf. As it happened, they were the very same ones I would have chosen.

"That makes thirteen thousand and four hundred in total!" Arkhip said.

I nodded.

"There's more... Let's go inside, it's cold out

here."

"Wolf, do me a favor and bring all this stuff into the store, would ya? All my helpers are asleep already."

Wolf looked at me.

"Please," I smiled.

"No problem!" the big man nodded and energetically took up the task while we went inside.

"Jellies," I said, plunking two sacks down on the table.

Arkhip looked into them and whistled quietly.

"Holy..!"

He started to count them out loud.

"Fifty-four white at forty-nine each — that's two hundred and sixty-five, and forty-two red at three hundred and eighty each — call that sixteen, making eighteen thousand six hundred and fifty. Is that all?"

"No." I shook my head at him and pulled out some carrier bags full of the garbage that Shnoop had pulled out of the old temple. As it happened, I kept twenty red and four orange jellies just for me. There were also some of King's jellies in the stash, and a few left back at the Center too. Pretty decent haul!

Arkhip poured everything out onto the counter and started digging through the pile thoughtfully.

"Holy..!" he said again.

"You're repeating yourself!" I smiled.

"For good reason!" He shook his head slowly.

"That was an Itanian Rift. A rare find. Our scientists have decoded their writing system. What a civilization it was... or still is, who knows! Point is, these trinkets are all the rage among young European fashionistas, and their value... I don't even want to say it out loud." He grinned.

"Well, how much, roughly?" My ears pricked up like a dog scenting a rabbit.

"Put it like this — it's in the tens of thousands. But it's all kind of dirty, so we'll need an expert appraisal. They'll clean it all up, take a proper look. You know how it goes!"

"Fine! I'll leave it all with you. Can you sort it out?"

Arkhip laughed.

"Yeah, no problem. That means I owe you fifty-two thousand, six hundred and fifty rubles. Not bad for one day! Hell! Some people don't earn that much in a whole lifetime! Transfer or cash?"

"Transfer..." I said, but then remembered something. "No, wait. Give me ten thousand in cash."

Arkhip reached under his counter and tossed a roll of fifties onto the table, and a notification came to my phone. Nice... **57,650 rubles.** Not bad at all!

"What do you like to drink?" I asked him.

"Vodka, usually," the old man said.

"What about whiskey or a good cognac?"

Arkhip shrugged. "Well, if it's good, then sure."

"It's on me!"

"How come?" The old man raised a brow. "I already got my fee for the Rift."

"For everything!" I waved a hand at him. "We Hunters... Ahem... I mean there's a rule that I have. A good lead begets a drink. Keeps the good luck flowing!"

"Well, alright." Arkhip nodded.

"Great, that's all. Thanks! I'm off to sleep!"

After I climbed back into the car, I handed a wad of cash to Wolf.

He frowned. "What's this?"

"Your first month's paycheck. I'm giving it to you in advance. That reminds me — we should get you a bank account."

Potapov hefted the roll of cash in his hand, opened his mouth, then closed it and just said:

"Thanks!"

Another bonus for my new fighter's moneybox. Yeah, I know it's the income of a weak aristocratic family or a top mercenary, but... That's just what I decided!

The car shifted into motion and I leaned back in my seat and started to drift off.

That was a fun day today. Just like the good old days!

CHAPTER 14

I SPENT A COUPLE OF DAYS resting, eating and sleeping, and then suddenly got a call from Androsov.

"You at home?"

"Where else would I be, mommy?" I smiled.

"Don't call me that!" Androsov hissed.

To tell you the truth, I had gotten on his nerves for the last few days as his patient.

"Looks like our dates have already come to an end," I said with a chuckle.

"Oh, shove it up your ass, Galaxius! I'm calling about something else. I'll repeat my question — are you at home?"

"Yes, I'm at home. Well, just by the barracks, anyway. Caramel just saw a stray squirrel that happened to walk into the Center grounds. God knows where she's chased it off to."

"Alright, I'll be there in a minute!"

The armored car of the Androsov family guard rolled up ten minutes later. They were using a Tiger, as it happens. I don't know if it was a Center modification, but the very fact showed again that the Androsovs were very close to the Empire.

I scratched the back of my head. The thought came to me that if I'd have asked, they'd have given me one just like that. But asking for little favors like that just wasn't how I did things. If you ask for favors, then ask them rarely, and only for something serious, and always repay them. Preferably in double. And then fortune will smile on you.

Androsov stepped out holding a jacket in a cover and walked up to me.

"Let's go! We need to go into your room and try something on."

"But Caramel..." I said in surprise.

"What about Caramel? Your cat is smarter than most people I know. She knows the way home just fine."

"Well, you're right about that," I said. "What's in the bag, anyway?"

"Come on, you're about to find out!"

"Your Eminence!" Wolf jumped up from the bed he'd been laying on while scrolling on his tablet.

"Oh, lie back down. How many times have I told you that you don't have to call me that?"

"Well, uh..." Wolf snapped his mouth closed, looking at me.

And then Andrei burst out laughing.

"I understand, it's one thing to be on first-name terms with a baron, but another thing for it to be a prince's son. But you better get used to it, buddy."

The man nodded.

"Actually, I'm not here for you. I've come to stress out your boss."

Gesturing like a magician, he pulled the zipper down on the jacket cover and then pulled it off the jacket.

"Voila! Well, what do you think?"

I looked at the tux rocking in the air on the hanger.

"Looks great. And I can tell by the cloth that it's expensive. But this isn't armor. It's a tuxedo!"

Androsov frowned, looking at my disinterested face.

"I see no excitement..."

I scratched the back of my head.

"Well, I'll get you some, one sec!"

I stepped out and knocked on the door of the neighboring room. When Wolf had moved in, I decided to put him in the second room instead of Anna. Better for men to live in the same quarters, after all. For Anna, I managed to get us a separate deluxe suite next door. Weirdly, the girl had been upset when she swapped places with Wolf, but said nothing aloud about it.

"Mind if I borrow you for a minute, Anna?"

The girl stuck her head out the door. She was in that kimono that I brought back from Tokyo for her. Seemed like it was her favorite outfit now.

"Are we going out anywhere?" she asked.

"No, just to my room."

"Then I'll come like this."

She stepped out and followed me toward my room. Anna flew in and I heard a cry of excitement.

"Oh my God! Is that a Haretsky?"

"Exactly right..." Andrei's face split in a grin.

Finally, someone who could properly appreciate his efforts.

"I have two questions. Who is Haretsky? And how much does this piece of... ahem... clothing cost?"

"Haretsky is the tailor of the Imperial Palace. Come on, Alex!" Anna put her hands on her hips, but then softened. "Of course, that makes sense. You are Galaxius, after all!"

"And as for the second question..." Andrei grinned. "It costs nothing. It's a gift."

"A very expensive gift, I guess?" I looked gave Androsov a hard look, then Anna.

Anna rolled her eyes silently. I quickly put two and two together in my head and figured I could accept the tux as a gift. In the end, it wasn't armor or weaponry. Androsov's own choice to spend his money on this crap. Fine.

He'd decided to give me a little gift, and I figured I'd probably find some way to repay him for it. By saving his life, for example, or helping him some other way.

"Come on, time to get changed! There's a shirt under the tux too."

Five minutes later, I looked at myself in the

mirror. Credit where credit is due — it fit me like a glove.

I stepped back into the room. Anna clapped her hands in glee. Androsov smiled widely. And even Wolf gave me a reserved thumbs-up.

"Like a glove!" I looked at Andrei in amazement. "How did you know my size?"

"I'm a Healer, Alex," Androsov said with a roll of his eyes. "I've studied your body down to the last inch by now."

He broke out laughing.

"Although I don't know what the hell I need that kind of information for!"

"Thanks, you know," I said gruffly. "Anyway, I suspect you didn't do all this just for fun."

"Nah... We're going to visit someone tonight."

"Who?"

"It's a surprise!" Androsov burst out laughing and ran out onto the street like a kid.

I looked at Anna.

"Don't get me wrong, you look great in that kimono. But considering my outfit, I think we'll need to find something for you too."

"Oh, I have something already," the girl said, blushing.

"No, no. 'Something' won't cut it." I'd learned a thing or two about women in my time. "How long have you been with me? And I haven't given you a single bonus yet. How about this — you go pick any dress you want. Well, out of those that work for tonight's engagement."

The girl smiled sneakily.

"You might regret saying that."

I gulped and pushed down my inner miser, realizing that I'd maybe expressed myself a little carelessly. But a man has to keep his word.

"Surprise me!" Suddenly, I started to get excited about what she might pick.

"Just remember! You said it, not me!" Anna smiled cunningly again, and was about to step out the door, but stopped. "Are you planning to go out again today? Maybe I could take Wolf with me?"

I chuckled and glanced at the bodyguard.

"Sure, take him, if he doesn't have any more important jobs to do."

I hadn't given him anything to do for today, but he and I had previously agreed on a few responsibilities for him, and they were pretty important to me.

Potapov jumped up from the bed.

"I'm ready! I'll be waiting for you in the car in two minutes!" Damn, the man really didn't like to stay in one place.

He ran off to get changed.

Anna didn't show up again until the evening. Wolf had already come back, and so had Mel, although she brought an unlucky rodent back with her.

When it was time for us to go, Potapov went to the car and I knocked on the girl's door. It swung open...

"You look amazing!" I said in absolute honesty. She wore a long blue dress with open shoulders and a deep swooping neckline. She looked great.

"Thanks!" Anna batted her eyelashes at me and stepped grandly in front of me to the car, where Andrei opened the back door for her with a flourish. Out of habit, I just plunked myself down in the front seat, earning another frown of displeasure from Potapov.

"Permit me a comment, Your Lordship," Wolf said as soon as we got moving.

I grimaced.

"Come on, Andrei, drop all that stuff... I'm sick of it! Call me Alexander, Alex, Xander, Commander if you really must. Leave all that 'Your Lordship' stuff back in the army you'll never join again."

Wolf frowned.

"Hey, hey, I didn't mean to offend you. If you want to go back there after our contract is done, then maybe I could help you out."

Surprise flashed in the old operator's eyes.

"Seriously?"

"As serious as it gets," I said with a smile. "You could help, right Anna?"

"I'm sure I could think of something!" the girl said thoughtfully from the back seat while examining herself closely in a small mirror.

I watched for Wolf's reaction. He thought for a moment, or maybe listened to his gut.

"No, I don't think I'll ever want that again. Memories of that time still cause me a certain... discomfort. It wasn't long ago that I was thrown out of there like a mangy dog abandoned by its master. And I spent more than fifteen years of my life there, starting from cadet's school, serving the Empire faithfully and truly. No — I'm not planning on going back to the army."

"Well, I'm glad to hear it. "So, are we agreed on the forms of address?"

"We're agreed... Alex. Is Xander your callsign?" Careful interest entered Wolf's voice. "Forgive me, but... Did you serve too?"

I laughed grimly.

"Well, it's something like that. But no, I didn't serve. And don't forget, we agreed to drop the formalities. Just ask if you have a question. All that 'forgive me' stuff wastes time."

Wolf nodded again.

"Well, what I wanted to say is... One man, even such an experienced fighter as me..." He smiled slightly at that, and I nodded.

A person without ambition is lost. So I approved of his description. Actually, he was being pretty humble. Wolf went on:

"One man isn't enough for a proper bodyguard detail. Ideally, I'd like to form a group of twelve operators again. I know better than anyone what a dozen good fighters are capable of. Again, the scope of our missions and your... assignments is likely to expand. We don't just have to be your bodyguards — we could also cause your enemies plenty of trouble, believe me. Even Gifted enemies."

I nodded.

"I believe you, Wolf, no doubt about that. And

although I'm completely sure that you're more than competent enough to hire some good fighters, there's one other thing that isn't just important to me, but critical. I have to be sure of the loyalty of every last one of those people. Their personal loyalty to me. You understand?"

I looked him straight in the eye. Without a hint of unease, he nodded his understanding.

"I understand you just fine. And the final choice will be yours, of course. But I have at least one person that I'm sure will meet all your requirements."

"Who?"

"My lieutenant, Sarambaikin, the sniper in my squad."

"The sole survivor of your last raid mission? The one you carried home on your back for over twenty miles?"

Wolf was already starting to get used to how well informed I was, so he just chuckled.

"Exactly, him. I trust him as much as I trust myself. And right now he's practically disabled, discharged from the army with a pathetic pension. With respect, I'd like to ask you a favor. If he agrees to work for you, then please ask His Highness Duke Androsov to help. His skill and knowledge might be enough to heal Misha. Ordinary medicine has done nothing."

I scratched my head thoughtfully. Usually, the most loyal people are those who owe you something — especially their life and health. I looked at Wolf. Or freedom. Nobody is immune to treachery, but this was at least something.

"Alright, we can try," I said. "I'll meet with him and talk to him."

"Thank you, Your..." Potapov caught himself in time. "Commander."

He smiled again. I had already learned the entire range of the former operator's smiles. Some promised a torturous death to his enemies. Some meant he was happy in the moment. But the smile he gave me just then was the grin of a happy man, transforming him from a rabid wolf into a healthy young man.

"Let's get going!" I said with a nod.

Androsov had cunningly given us just an address without telling us what exactly we were in for. That would have worked on me, but no way on Anna, who was always a few steps ahead. I liked that a lot. Just like how I acted in battle, but she acted that way in civilian life.

"That's the Morozov manor in Irkutsk," she said as soon as she heard the address.

I chuckled.

"I think Androsov has something fun planned for us. Or at least he thinks so."

While we drove, Anna read me a short dossier on the Morozovs, and, surprisingly, Potapov had something to add. He said that the Morozovs had an extremely powerful battle Gift. Even Svetlana had superpowers compared to most Gifted. Not to mention her brothers! All four of her brothers were spread out across the Empire, carrying out orders of utmost responsibility, and occupying some most interesting roles.

Wolf noted with a certain unease that Morozova's eldest brother Igor used to be the commander of Eastern Group Imperial Special Forces. Potapov, normally so sparing with praise, said that it had been a pleasure serving under his leadership. But as soon as Morozov got transferred somewhere — Wolf didn't know where, since it was top-secret, — the new commander had led to the catastrophe that had landed him in a special cell and nearly killed him as man and Gifted both.

Basically, if the Goldsmiths hired guards for protection, the Morozovs didn't bother — they hired managers and handled the protection themselves. Their main interests were in St. Petersburg, and they were all connected with the Empire's military industrial complex one way or another. But Irkutsk was too important a city — right on the border of two enemy states — to not invest a certain amount of influence there.

Accordingly, the manor wasn't too ostentatious. It wasn't even walled off. Just a big three-story house in the city center.

Androsov met us in the entrance with a smile, holding his bride Svetlana by the arm, who greeted us first, as the hostess. And somehow she managed to surprise me after all.

"Ah, the cause of our celebration appears!" she said.

"Cause..?" I frowned.

"Well, yes. This is a party in your honor, after all. Or rather, in honor of your new class." She nodded at my finger, my Slayer signet ring burning with orange light.

"Thanks," I muttered, a little embarrassed, and, to be honest, pleasantly surprised.

"Mind if Alex and I have a word?" Androsov asked "We'll come find you after."

"By all means!"

Svetlana took Anna by the arm and the girls walked inside.

"Alright, Galaxius, listen to me carefully!" Androsov began in an unusually serious tone. "This party... I know you don't think much of aristocratic customs, and you tend to do everything your own way. But my fiancée, who, I must note, you personally invited to Irkutsk, is very nervous and wants very much for tonight to work out well. So be a friend and behave yourself properly." To my silent question, he added: "And not like a total asshole. Please don't forget that there are some very influential people here, and you can't just talk to them like you would anyone else."

"Why not?" I widened my eyes in mock surprise.

"No offense, Alex. You know you're my best friend. I'd get into any scrape with you, but you have to know that for the majority of these people, you're a baron. A jumped-up baron. And that same 'majority' has no idea why you have counts and dukes flocking around you. Don't interrupt!" Androsov wagged a finger at me as I opened my mouth to object. "Yes, your feats of combat are impressive. But that just isn't the way things are done in high society. Any more or less wealthy family can hire itself fighters. Good fighters! Excellent fighters! Look no further than that Wolf of yours. Remember, military achievement is great, honorable. But for that alone to get you accepted in high society, you'd have to beat up the Khan of the steppes himself at least." He smiled widely, pleased with his joke.

"Well, where do I find him?" I asked with a shrug.

Androsov laughed at my joke this time, but fell silent at my serious look.

"What, are you serious?"

Now it was my turn to crack a smile.

Andrei looked at me uncertainly, then waved a hand and went on.

"Anyway, formally, you're the head of the Galaxius family now. You can be invited to people's houses without scandal, but such invitations will be made carefully. Ideally, your path to high society should have begun with some baron or other. A viscount at the most. Here, you're being introduced by a duchess!"

"Andy," I said with a sigh. "I get that it's a great honor for me and all that. Honestly, all jokes aside, I'm really grateful. But what is it you want from me?"

"Alex, I'm begging you!" Andrei joined his hands in a gesture of supplication, eyes wide. "Please just don't do anything..." He trailed off.

"Anything what?" I cocked my head.

"Damn it, Galaxius!" my comrade burst out again. "You know damn well what I'm talking about. No killings, no beatings, no debauchery! Best behavior."

"Well, just as long as nobody offends my honor…" I began sullenly. When Andrei put his head in his hands, I laughed and stopped. "I'm kidding, chill out! I'm just trying to think like an aristocrat, like you say."

Androsov lifted his head from his hands and stared at me.

"I'm already starting to think this was a bad idea."

"It was a great idea, Andy! Don't sweat it!" I clapped him on the shoulder again. "Come on, let's get our drink on. To friendship between barons and dukes. Ha-ha!"

Having come to an agreement, we went off to find the girls. I didn't know what serious-mode Androsov was thinking, but I was wondering how many khans there were and how far away the closest was.

The party was… boring. At the start, Svetlana announced the reason for the celebration, i.e. me and my new ring. All the attendees drank to me. Most of them, like Andrei warned me, didn't show even the slightest enthusiasm about it. I even saw some grimacing. Although all their eyes were glued to me for the whole night. Honestly, I never much liked feeling like an animal in a zoo. But, as Androsov said, "it's how things are done."

We drank and chatted. Andrei pointed out

some important people with whom it wouldn't hurt to form a closer relationship. But I just wasn't in the mood today. Today, all I wanted was to get drunk.

The last two days of doing nothing had been exhausting. And the scene of handing over the empty Slayer rings to Duke Khrulyov still replayed itself in my head. It was like the old man lost a few years in a few seconds when I dropped those sixty-two rings on his desk, and he didn't have all that much life left in him as it was. He cared all too much for his own.

Far too much, the way I saw it. A Slayer's work is dangerous, after all. Being that close to it… But, on the other hand, Khrulyov's underlings loved him for it.

There wasn't really a conversation about it as such. He officially invited me go and pick up the money for bringing in the rings. I refused, as is tradition. To which he just nodded and muttered his thanks. After that I bowed, watching out of the corner of my eye as Khrulyov reached with slightly trembling hands beneath his desk. Something tinkled and splashed. I suspected that his famous beat-up cup held something far stronger than tea that day.

All in all, I avoided the nobles. I exchanged a couple of words with Smolin and Schrader, and a few other acquaintances. After a while, an older man came up to me.

"Please allow me to introduce myself," he said. "I am Viscount Alexei Smorodin."

Without thinking, I offered him a hand, which the man shook in faint surprise.

"Baron Galaxius," I said, stopping a waiter and picking up another glass of whiskey. "A drink, Viscount?"

"Certainly," he said, and picked up a glass of his own. "I would like to talk to you. Just five minutes of your time, if you don't mind. Out in the fresh air."

I shrugged, and we stepped out onto the terrace. It was a classic autumn day in Irkutsk outside. Rain drizzled down above us, but the terrace had a roof and it wasn't cold.

"Thank you for saving my nephew and his troops," the viscount began, but at my blank look added: "Viscount Smorodin, Commander of Response Team Two, in the Anthill."

It came back to me. Right, the big guy with the beard. I saw the resemblance as I looked into his uncle's face, although this man was smaller. Either his brother was built bigger or the brawn was on the mom's side.

"You're welcome!" I said with a shrug. "Although... Your nephew is a strong Slayer. I'm sure they had could have handled it on their own."

The viscount nodded. "Could have, I agree. Sergei really has made a good career for himself. But far more people from his group may have died. And he is very attached to his people."

I shrugged again. "What can I say? Good man, your Serge. Respect where it's due."

"In any case, his father is currently on a trip

for some business of our company, so I have been authorized to negotiate with you."

He took out his card and offered it to me.

The card was expensive, printed on fine paper. Considering that I could clearly see the letters in the dark, it was lit by something magical. An expensive detail. Especially for a viscount. On the card it said: *Smorodin Brothers Building Company.*

"The thing is, Alexander, we don't just operate a building company. We provide construction and reconstruction services with the use of magic and artifacts. Incidentally, we also have several enchanters. We build, among many other things, facilities for the Imperial Army. But most importantly — our company is one of just three in the whole Empire..." He swelled with pride. "...to have an Imperial Security Certificate. Do you know what that is?"

"How?" I said with a chuckle, but then caught myself. "No, I don't know, actually."

"Due to the fact that we work with high-ranking officials and secret facilities, our company is extended a guarantee of Imperial Security. If anybody tries to poach one of our employees to find out the weaknesses in their competitors' structures, he is automatically a criminal in the Empire. And the consequences are serious."

I shrugged blankly. "Cool!"

"And here is why I approached you... Well, except to thank you, of course. I heard that you won back your family manor. In our circles, legends are told of the Galaxius manor. It was not our family who built it. But it is a unique object, believe me. I happen to know that much there was made with the use of Gifts and magic. However, no imperial Families or even foreign ones took part in its construction. Yes, yes, we talk to all our friends and competitors. And although it was several hundred years ago, I can tell you with total confidence that it is as I say."

"Interesting." I smiled. It really was pretty curious.

"Usually, it is our policy not to give anyone a discount. We are already booked for several years' worth of work." The viscount wasn't bragging. Judging by his face, he was just informing me. "But if you need anything, then we will be sure to find a way to move you to the head of the queue. And we can even promise you a discount of twenty-five percent. Believe me, that is a very good offer indeed!"

"Thanks, Viscount. From the heart, thanks," I said. "I'll get to the manor and see what kind of condition it's in, then get back to you."

"I won't dare take up a moment more of your time, Baron. Good evening to you!"

I nodded. "And you!"

Just as the viscount and I walked back in, I heard a deep bass voice behind me.

"Don't move, you bastard! I challenge you to a duel!"

What the hell was this..?! Damn, I promised Androsov I wouldn't make any trouble!

CHAPTER 15

I TURNED, AUTOMATICALLY FEELING for my sword at my belt — a regular common sword of Karsk steel.

Fyodorov's sword was actually pretty good. I had found time to inspect it carefully in my time of forced idleness. There was no family sigil on it, only a quote engraved on the pommel: *Honor and Glory!*

I had a moment's doubt there. The steel was great, blue adamantium, a quality sword with plenty of use left in it. Only I had to know what family it had belonged to. Putting aside all the hangups of the aristocrats, I had superstitions of my own.

At my request, Anna got me the info I wanted. It had turned out to be pretty interesting after all. Slayer Fifth Class Semyon Fyodorov was the sole breadwinner of his family, which consisted of his beloved wife and two children — a boy and a girl. Semyon was a strong Slayer, but not the sharpest knife in the drawer. By age thirty he was hanging firmly onto class five, planning to reach class four over the next few years. But the bugs that killed him had no idea about all that.

His son dreamed of his father's profession — he wanted to become a Slayer too. These Fyodorovs weren't even aristocrats. They were just strongly Gifted enough to be Slayers. And the traditions of the Slayers went back generations in their family. The sword wasn't a family weapon in the usual understanding of the word for aristocrats, but it was still an heirloom, handed down from father to son.

Considering that the young mother with her small children would now be living off the small pension of a Slayer, the chance that his son would be able to get any decent weapon by the time he reached adulthood was close to zero. So I packaged up the sword and sent it to the family's address with a note.

To Anton Fyodorov. Your father was a great Slayer! And he died a hero, protecting people. Always be proud of him!

Anna had also used her unusual methods to find out their bank account. And five thousand rubles got sent to it, an amount which an ordinary family could live off for some time and which I wouldn't even notice.

There was a tradition among Hunters — to give a fallen Hunter's weapon to his student. That was if he had a student, of course. I never had one. Nobody really wanted to be my student, since I had, uh, a difficult character. I wasn't really ready for that kind of responsibility anyway. I tended to work alone. Although Grand Master Wulf had given me whole lectures about it.

I smiled, seeing his resemblance with Duke Khrulyov. Anyway, I never did give in. Maybe I should have. There'd be one more good Hunter in my old world if I had.

Anyway, I turned around, already mentally asking Androsov and Morozova forgiveness, and saw two drunken louts jumping at each other like two puffed-up cockerels.

"Who do you think you're calling a bastard, Kalinin?"

"You, Vereshchak! I don't see any other bastards around here!"

"A duel? Fine! You'll regret it soon enough!" The shorter man backed off, placing a hand on his sword.

It's hard to describe in words the kind of rock that fell from my soul then. Actually, rock isn't the word... A mountain fell into an abyss, letting my spirit soar.

I had been totally sure that the man was shouting at me, but it turned out he wasn't... What a relief... Not least for Androsov, who had paled and looked ready to kill someone who he thought had challenged me to a duel and ruined the whole night for his beautiful bride.

Now there was no more need to kill him, all that had to be done was organize the duel.

The party goers quickly formed a gawping crowd, done with their bread and eager for the circus. Androsov stepped forward, holding his fiancée back with a firm hand.

The terrace was small, so everybody stepped out onto the street. The gentlemen held umbrellas for the ladies, so orderly, so noble, so aristocratic! The combatants received final instructions from their seconds as they warmed up their muscles.

I started to get bored watching it all, and even whiskey didn't inflame my excitement, and so, to make things more interesting...

"I'll bet on the viscount!" I shouted. "A thousand rubles!"

Total silence descended. Even the would-be duelers stopped their warmup. Dozens of pairs of eyes looked at me strangely.

God damn it, Xander! At the prospect of a good show, all my instincts and habits from my old world had reemerged. What was a mere decade in this world, especially in a young body full of furious hormones, against my long stint back there? All the veneer of the civilized world fell from me, and out from under it peeked the predatory grin of a professional who had spent his whole life risking it.

There had been no 'duels' in my past world, of course, let alone to the death, but competition matches were a frequent and necessary ritual. Actually, that wasn't quite right. There were duels, but they were rare, and never brother against brother.

Hunters were always learning new things, and since they sometimes met up only once every few years, they never missed the chance to fight in search of the answer to the eternal question: which Hunter is worthy of the title of First? That might be called sparring, but not dueling.

Androsov quickly made his way through the crowd to me. "Damn it, Alex!" he hissed.

"What's the problem?" I wasn't planning on backing out. There was no direct rule against betting, probably because a noble aristocrat would never make a bet at such a serious and responsible event in a million years! Ha-ha!

The people came alive, and there were cries of scandal and accusations of unbecoming behavior — careful and indirect ones, but still.

"Ladies and gentlemen! This is just a misunderstanding! Baron Galaxius has spent his entire life far away from his homeland!" Androsov said, trying to smooth the situation over.

Now the nodding heads turned merciful, even sympathetic. What did they think of me..? That I grew up in Africa?!

Something snapped inside me. I laughed, took out my wallet and counted out ten hundred notes, raised my arm high with the bills clutched in my fist, and waved them around.

"Bets are on! A thousand on the viscount!"

Oh, gods! The look I got from that old woman in the strict dress with carefully coiffed hair. I didn't know who she was or who her husband was, a podgy old man with his mustache ends twirled up, but I could tell I'd fallen in her estimation to the level of the lowest riff-raff. Even her husband shook his head as he looked at me. But when the woman sniffed and walked away, the old man sighed and winked at me!

The bet was taken!

The two fighters collided like flea-bitten lions. They fought furiously and without mercy, but not for long.

In the end I lost my thousand, but was still happy with the show I got. In fact, I'd placed the right bet on the stronger fighter, I could tell that for sure. The only thing I didn't consider was that he was much drunker than his opponent. The moron slipped and fell on his ass at the most crucial moment! The underdog took the victory...

As for why they didn't charge their bodies with energy to drive out the alcohol, only they knew.

The duel was to first blood, and regardless of their furious fighting, after the very first wound they calmed down and it was like nothing had happened between them.

No attempts to finish each other off, no insults. The viscount accepted his defeat and apologized, to which his opponent answered that he respected his strength, and wouldn't take his family weapon away.

Hmm... Me, on the other hand, I worked over that asshole in Japan so hard that I didn't even know if all the healers and surgeons of the Empire of the Rising Sun could put him back together.

After the duel, I spent some time with Androsov and Morozova. I made like I was having fun, and that I was happy. I listened attentively as various people praised Morozova for such a well organized evening.

Incidentally, I wasn't ignored either. It was really something when young ladies kept coming up to me and asking me to dance.

Normally I would have been only too happy to, but there was something too predatory about the looks in their eyes. They were looking at me as a potential husband, not as a person.

Anna mingled nearby, helping me identify who was who.

All the minor aristocrat girls who were out to find themselves the best possible husband were focusing their attentions on me. Now that was a road I didn't want to go down. After all, they were the ones doing the looking here. A Hunter takes what he wants, he doesn't wait to be chosen.

The night was saved only thanks to Anna, who stated outright that she didn't want to dance with other aristocrats or listen to their compliments. So she kept dragging me away to dance herself.

Just as I thought all the fun was over, life reminded me who I was and tossed an adventure my way. Thank goodness, just like usual!

"We've picked up a tail," Wolf said calmly at the wheel, and took out his gun.

"Got it..." I answered just as calmly.

"Ugh, I'm so tired," Anna said with a yawn. She must have a lot of trust in me by now, since she didn't seem worried.

We had only just left the Morozov manor. Androsov, as if sensing something, had offered the services of his family guard as an escort, but I refused. Why ruin my reputation? People would start saying Galaxius couldn't take a single step without help from Androsov.

I sent Shnoop out to scout and discovered that there were a whole seven cars packed full of fighters tailing us, including a real-life Master. They clearly weren't local — they had to be mercenaries hired by King. Either he'd run out of his own men or had none stupid enough left. As it happens, he hadn't shown any sign of himself for a while, which was why I assumed it was him.

Now the question was, what to do with them? If I reached the Center, they wouldn't be able to move against us, but would that be any fun? And it wasn't just about fun, either. Since they had a job to do, they might kidnap Wolf or Anna alone later.

"Mel, would you mind jumping out the window and going and biting their faces off?" I asked my cat, petting her on the head. She had eaten so much at the party that she was hiccuping all the way home.

"Burp..." she grunted, and tried to get up, but

slumped back down again.

"Gotcha," I said with a smile, stroking against her fur. "Too fat to work. Fine, stay there."

Five more minutes passed, and I thought maybe they'd fall back unprompted. They didn't. And most importantly, did they know that we knew about them, and was this their way of hinting that it was time for a fight?

I tracked them through Shnoop to make sure I'd know if they were about to start shooting. Well, I say Shnoop tracked them. Actually, he'd already swiped a couple of their guns and magazines that weren't nailed down properly.

And on top of that he was very bored, and decided to dispel his boredom at the expense of the men.

He tied a few of their shoelaces together, cackling all the while.

"You really want to sleep?" I asked Anna.

"Uh-huh," she said, shifting to get more comfortable on my shoulder. "Can you just make them leave us alone today?" she asked, looking up at me hopefully.

"Of course!" I said. No need to disappoint her. "Watch and learn." I raised my arm theatrically, and clicked my fingers.

The cars behind us suddenly swerved off the road, crashing into the ditches either side. You'd have thought they just saw a wall of lava raging toward them. Were they really that easy to scare?

Hell, two of their cars crashed into each other, and one swerved so hard that it flipped over.

I had seen that ability online, the lava wall. A certain High Mage from Brazil had used the skill on a city during a war with another country. Practically a quarter of the city had been destroyed, and the technique was caught on video.

Shame mine was only an illusion, but it did its job well enough.

"Thanks!" Anna whispered gratefully, settling down.

Poor thing, she was exhausted... I'd have to give her a day off — she was working round the clock for me these days.

Everything was fine at home, and I had to carry Anna to her room, already deep asleep.

Wolf didn't want to sleep, and I didn't care what he did, that was his business. But I sure went to bed... Important day tomorrow — I was going to finally visit my mansion.

* * *

After the ball
The Morozov Manor
Irkutsk

Svetlana and Andrei were seated comfortably upstairs on a soft couch in the duchess's bedroom, lazily sipping chilled champagne more out of habit than thirst or a desire to get drunk.

"Alexander isn't quite as wild a character as you say," Svetlana said with a smile, now away from prying eyes and curled into a ball with her head on her lover's knee.

"You just don't know him well enough yet!" Androsov said, waving a hand. "Why are you defending him anyway?"

"Because you had him so scared that he was afraid to do anything, and he kept glancing our way almost all night long!"

"Scared!?" Androsov burst out laughing. Of me?! Galaxius?! Like I said — you just don't know him well enough! Maybe he'd be scared by..." Andrei thought for a moment. "Actually, I can't think of anything or anyone... Well, I don't think I can, anyway!"

"You're wrong, my sweet." Duchess Morozova smiled down at him. "You just don't know people... Or rather, men! You're like little children! Maybe you can't be scared, but you're easy to embarrass or offend!"

"Offend?" Andrei frowned. "But Alex isn't someone who gets offended easily — he's more the type to offend others!" Andrei grimaced, remembering something. "Actually, he's always offending people!"

"Calm down, dear!" Svetlana gently took her betrothed by the arm. "It's just..." She paused. "This is, as far as I can remember, your first real friend. Really, a true friend, I can see that as a woman! Try to be a little kinder to him — he's hard on the outside, but inside, who knows what's going on?"

"I definitely agree with you there." Andrei brought the duchess's hand to his lips and gently kissed it. "I have absolutely no idea what's going on inside him. And what little of it I've caught sight of... Lana, it scares the hell out of me!"

* * *

Early in the morning, while Wolf was readying the car for our trip, I stopped in to see the Center commander. If I disappeared again without warning, Gramps might think I forgot, or worse — broke the deal.

"May I, Sir?" I called out, knocking on Khrulyov's door.

"Ah, Galaxius, come in! Take a seat, I'm just about to pour some tea."

I smiled. Tradition is tradition. Silently, I waited for the end of the mandatory ritual with the steaming samovar and the bowl of honey, which he moved closer to me. Gramps watched closely as I added the first spoonful and sipped the tea.

"Good?"

"As always, Sir."

"Mixed herbs today, the last I have left. Won't be any more until the next season."

I smiled, and sipped more.

"Well, all rested up?" the old Slayer asked, getting straight down to business.

"Sure have, all good."

The old man sharply turned his big monitor toward me, showing a map of the Rifts.

"Which one will you go to first?"

"This one here." I pointed. "At the edge of the

Perimeter."

The old man scratched his head thoughtfully.

"Have you read the profile?"

"Yeah, I've studied everything on the site. Do you have anything to say about it? That's why I stopped by."

Khrulyov quickly retold what I already knew, except that I was surprised at how many attempts there'd been to close it. Fifteen, but for some reason only nine logged on the site. There had been some 'experts' invited in from the outside who also didn't make it.

I nodded. "Got it."

"Doesn't give you any pause?"

"None at all," I said, then corrected myself: "I mean, the Rifts don't. But I do wonder who you'll have me take along."

The old man smiled, tapped something on his keyboard and gestured to the monitor again.

"Here, look."

I looked. There was a long list of twenty-five names on the screen. One name was highlighted green — Helga. Right, she was mandatory.

My eyebrows shot up. "Why so many?"

"Many?" The Center raised an eyebrow right back at me. "Were you listening carefully when I told you about these Rifts?"

"Extremely," I said.

"Well, if you were, then I'm sure you understand that a couple of dozen people is just right for a Rift like this."

I smiled.

"May I ask you a question, Sir?"

"Go ahead," the old Slayer nodded.

"What made you recruit me for this job? I mean, apart from as a way to pay for my stay here, which you could have just taken in cash."

Gramps looked at me thoughtfully, but said nothing, leaning back in his chair and scratching his beard.

"Let me guess. You think there's something in me that allows me to close Rifts. The ones that your regular troops can't close. And that I can help remove three — excuse the expression — pains in your ass."

"You guess right," Gramps praised me.

"In that case, don't you think I know best how many people I need?"

At first Khrulyov frowned, but then a smile shone through his beard.

"Forgive an old man his hangups. Fine, how many will you take and whom?"

I started jabbing my finger at the screen.

"Helga, Androsov. I've worked with Smolin, I'll take him too. I also need three elementalists, ideally ones who have worked with each other before, who know what they're doing and who won't launch any fire balls into my back."

Khrulyov thought for a moment.

"We have some suitable." He told me three surnames which meant nothing to me. "Anyone else?"

I shook my head. "That's enough."

"Seven people, are you serious?" The old

Slayer gave me a dubious look.

"But we already..."

"Alright, alright." He raised his hands in a gesture of surrender. "You drink your tea. Oh, and I have to ask you. Have you changed your mind about joining us more permanently?"

"Will this ever end?" I smiled.

"Oh, believe me, it'll never end." Khrulyov laughed, and picked up his own big cup with its chipped rim.

"By the way, Sir. I nearly forgot," I said. "There's something I need. Am I right in thinking that in cases of need, the Center gives out weapons and equipment?"

Gramps narrowed his eyes.

"To Slayers on the payroll, yeah."

When he saw my scowl, he hurried to add:

"Just tell me what you need. Maybe I'll give it to you, ha-ha, who knows."

I smiled. Judging by his bookshelves, he wasn't just one of the most experienced Slayers, as confirmed by his current position, but also one of the most well-read. I had no idea why he was talking to me like we were old pals. Although, there was a reason the nickname Gramps had stuck. Every Slayer knew their Gramps would take care of them to the end. It was probably part of his image as a caring grandpa.

"I need a magical bomb."

"Holy shit!" The old Slayer laughed. "You know how much one of those costs?" He sighed. "I'm asking you to close the Rift, not blow it to kingdom come. The beasts will still come out of there sooner or later."

"Well, I'm not planning on blowing it up! And I don't need a really powerful bomb. A second-degree charge should do it."

"Second-degree?" Khrulyov frowned. "Hm, still no toy. But fine, we can do that."

"First I want to swing by my manor today and see what's going on over there. And then I'll be straight to the Rift!"

The old duke nodded his head. "The family stronghold is an important matter. And I'm not your boss, anyway. So yes, I understand and approve! They'll all be ready when you get back!"

I jumped up. "Thanks, Sir!"

"Wait! What about your tea?!"

I smiled, and downed the full cup of burning hot liquid in a single gulp. That was nothing! In my time I'd eaten hell's burdock, at a time when food was hard to come by, and drunk water from the Cursed Swamps too.

Anyway, time to go!

CHAPTER 16

Elite Golf Club 'Legend'
Outskirts of St. Petersburg

THE ELDERLY MAN TOOK A BIG SWING and hit the ball with his club. It flew along an unpredictable trajectory before plopping into a carefully manicured pond on the golf course.

The man swore under his breath.

"Shitty game! Idiotic traditions!"

For some time now he had been trying to get to grips with this fashionable new game of golf. Well, new wasn't quite right... It was new in the Eastern Empire. Westerners had been playing it for quite a long time. And for some god-awful reason it was considered a game of aristocrats. Every time he went to any negotiations in Europe, he had to think of excuses for why he couldn't have a meeting over a game of golf. Strange, these westerners. Everybody knows that proper business is done in the restaurant.

His young assistant teed up a new ball and raised his eyes.

"Allow me to suggest another club. This one isn't suitable for that kind of swing."

"Oh, teach me more, smartass!" the man snapped in annoyance, but then took a deep to breath to calm himself and reached out a hand. "Give it here then. Which one is right for this shot?"

His attention was drawn to a golf car quickly approaching. It stopped and a young man climbed out of it, smiling.

"Still won't stop trying, eh?"

"Speak, don't beat around the bush!" the old man grumbled. "I can tell by your face that you bring bad news."

The smile dropped from the young man's face. "Galaxius..."

"What, again?!"

"Eliminated all our assassins, and stole their car too."

The old man burst out laughing.

"I'm starting to respect that boy. And as my respect for him goes up, my respect for you and your skills goes down."

The young man tensed, pursing his lips.

"This was bad luck."

"Again?" The old man burst out laughing again. "Once is chance, twice is coincidence, but three times is a pattern! Don't you think the people who came up with that saying were smarter than you?"

The young man stiffened even more. Everything had been going just fine for him until Galaxius showed up. He had risen quickly up his career ladder, and in the estimation of his lord too. Until that kid came along.

"In addition, there has been a hearing, and his manor and signet ring have been returned to him."

"What an unpleasant... stroke of bad luck." The old man kept on laughing, nervously now. "Let me guess... It was the Dolgorukovs who returned his ring to him?"

"How did you know?" The young man looked surprised.

"It's obvious how! Actually, it was your pauper ancestors who sold the ring to the Dolgorukov collection. Stupid decision! And I told your father that he was making a big mistake. But he was more interested in gambling and womanizing. Far more than power and money."

The young man's hands clenched into fists. His aura of power visibly hummed.

"Settle down!" the older man snapped. "You may be a promising Magister, but you can't stand up to me. And I hate when a pet bites the hand that feeds it."

"Pet?" The young man failed to hold back his scowl.

The old man laughed mockingly. "Oh, sorry. I meant... Junior partner, of course! It's just that the title of 'partner' next to your name is becoming more and more illusory. A few more failures, and I'll count my debt to your father paid off. And you will continue your career... somewhere else."

The younger man squeezed his fist hard to keep himself in check. "Should I continue to work on Galaxius?"

"What do you think? Of course! I need his manor."

"But what for?" The young man cocked his head. "I know it's your business. But this isn't just a matter of principle, is it?"

"Let me put it this way, although it's none of your business. Of course the principle is important. But I need that manor in particular. For reasons that you do not need to know."

"It will be done!" was all the young man had to say, nodding.

"Yes, do try," the old man said, and turned away as if the other had ceased to exist. "What did you say this club is called?" he asked the youth acting as his golf coach.

* * *

Two hours of travel passed to the tune of a boring seminar by Wolf, who had decided that at that moment I needed a complete education in how the special forces operate in the field. I'd already realized that I'd need more than one fighter. But hiring new people took money, lots of money.

We finally drove up to Lake Baikal. The road

ran along the southern part of the lake, and before me opened up a view of the vast glimmering surface of the largest body of fresh water on the planet.

Since the edge of the Epicenter covered the northern part of the lake, the Slayers kept a small fleet here. The situation wasn't quite as bad as with the deep-water Rifts off the coast of Japan, but surprises could still happen here when Rifts opened up under the water and started spitting out all kinds of beasts.

The southern part was more or less calm. Baikal was famous for its fishing reserves. Some species of fish had successfully multiplied with Rift beasts and started attacking fishermen. Others, on the other hand, were sought-after in the catch due to their unique culinary value and matching price tag, which didn't put off the gourmands in the capital at all.

The family manor happened to be on the southwestern shore. And as it turned out, the chunk of land that I'd won back from that idiot count who wanted to destroy me was also on the shoreline. Almost as soon as we turned off the imperial highway, we were in my lawful territory.

Actually, to officially register my claim, I had to go to the settlement Galaxiton, where an imperial administrator was waiting for me. He had been appointed by the government to keep an eye on my lands and people in the absence of a lawful master.

I hadn't really wanted to bring Anna with me,

but was unable to resist her pushing. She certainly knew more than me about managing an estate, but King's people weren't snoozing.

All the same, we got there without incident, and just now we were driving into the small town. In its heyday almost fifty thousand people had lived there. Now that the Galaxius name had fallen, the people had slowly started to leave. There were only hunters and fishermen left. The surrounding land itself was considered not only unpromising, but even dangerous, given that the border with the Khanate of the Grand Steppe was less than two hundred miles to the south.

As we drove slowly through the streets, I saw that most of the houses were still solid. Since the taiga was so close, the overwhelming majority of them were built as log cabins. But many of the houses had shutters nailed closed and bars across the doors.

When we drove into the small square next to the town's administration building, I tensed a little. There were a couple of hundred people hanging around in the square as if waiting for something. I mean, not just something. They had to be waiting for me. The local governor must have warned the people of my visit.

The car stopped. I reached for the door, but Wolf shouted sharply, then climbed out first, grumbling. He silently inspected the crowd for a while. Only then did he open the doors for me and Anna, one hand kept meaningfully on his Whirlwind.

I stepped out and looked around. The crowd immediately started up. I heard hushed conversation. Most of them were — 'He's so young!', 'He's just a boy!', and 'Looks like our hopes were in vain...' Damn, who were they hoping to see? An imperial cortege with an entourage and guards?

I smiled and walked up to the town hall, where a short and fat man with clever-looking eyes stood on the threshold.

"My respects, Sir Galaxius!" He hopped down the stairs to meet me, reaching out a large and soft palm for a handshake. "I am Counselor Third Class Arcadius Vysotsky, at your service."

I shook the fat man's hand and introduced myself.

The administrator smiled. "Want to give me a speech? Or will we get right down to business?"

"A speech?" I frowned.

"Well, yes, all these people are gathered here for you. Life has not been sweet for them recently. You understand, people always hope for the best."

I looked up at the sky. It didn't look like rain, the weather was nice.

"Let's take care of the papers first. And then I'll think of what to tell them," I answered.

"Of course, of course, as you say," the fat man simpered. "But it might take a while. Quite a lot of business has piled up."

"Talk to the people, Alex," Anna said quietly. "They deserve it."

I frowned. If there was any Gift that Hunters

weren't renowned for, it was public speaking. I never did like crowds. Hell, I didn't even like people that much. All my socializing in my past world had consisted of talking to the elder to get my orders. Well, and waiters and ladies of easy virtue after a hard day's work.

Still, I stepped forward and raised a hand. The sun suddenly came out from behind the clouds, and a single beam of light lit up the ring on my finger, which flickered with an unnaturally blinding light. The people immediately fell silent, staring at my raised hand. Wolf chuckled in understanding nearby.

"Look at that, a sign."

I clucked at him and put my hand in my pocket. "That's all I need, signs!"

"Hello..." I faltered.

How to address them? 'Ladies and gentlemen'? 'Good townsfolk'? Serfdom had been abolished in the Empire quite a long time ago. All people lived in family lands voluntarily. Although some agreements for 'voluntary' service were little different from slavery in some Families. Commoners signing those agreements was a headache for the imperial security services. Personally, I didn't plan on forcing anyone.

"Hello!" I said, deciding in the end to just start. "My name is Alexander Galaxius. I am the lawful ruler of these lands, and the head of the Galaxius family. I do not promise that Galaxiton and the surrounding lands will turn into a paradise overnight. But I will go to every effort to improve your lives here. The only thing I can tell you straight is that while you're on my land, I will stand up for your rights and promise you my protection so far as my power extends."

I wanted to say that I'd protect them, but I didn't like to make promises I couldn't keep. I had no idea what might happen here, and even now I couldn't be totally sure that I'd always be there. And I had no family guard just yet. I'd need to make one... I wondered, would dragons make for good guards?

Beyond that my enthusiasm and imagination ran dry. I glanced sidelong at Anna, who gave me a smile and a thumbs-up.

"Dear villagers!" the fat administrator spoke up. "Do you have any questions for our young baron?"

Damn, I wasn't going to get out of this that easily.

An elderly man stepped forward, took his hat off and bowed.

"Your Lordship! My name is Vasily..." A stout woman standing next to him, apparently his wife, elbowed him in the ribs. "Vasily Petrovich, I mean... I have a contract for some land, signed for fifteen years with your, ahem, family. Trouble is, some of the land is in the chunk that the Ignatovs possess. They took the land away. What can we do?"

"Yes, yes," the people hummed.

Some spoke about relatives living in other lands. Some spoke about land and properties currently expropriated. From what I learned from talking to Anna, life under imperial oversight was quite lax, so many had moved into the central estate.

And the excesses of the local landlords was widely known to all.

"All the lands of the Galaxius family will be returned to its old borders! That I promise you. I am already working and thinking on it. I hope the solution will be peaceful."

More chuckles from the crowd, sounding very sarcastic. I guess things weren't done that way here.

"Forgive us, Your Lordship," a big man in the front row said. "We doubt that you will be able to resolve all this peacefully. And we also don't see your guards anywhere."

I got an amused look from Wolf as if to say 'I told you so.'

"In the case of necessity or military conflict, believe me, I have more than enough power," I said with a smile.

They all started grumbling again, but the ones who caught my amused glance lowered their eyes to the floor for some reason, and fell silent.

I raised my hand again, this time making do without special effects — the sun was back behind the clouds.

"Thank you for your attention, dear people! That is all. I must get on with business. And while I'm not planning on moving here just yet, I'll be visiting often. Sooner or later we'll bring a steward here who I'll be sure to introduce to you."

The people went off on their business, muttering to each other. It seemed they had cause for gossip and rumor today.

"Come on, Arcadius," I said, with a nod to the fat man. "Let's go discuss our business."

When I entered the building I expected to see tables piled high with papers, but the place was actually pretty orderly and comfortable. Three assistants sat at computers. Although there was a paper filing system, it only contained important original documents of rights. Documents that had to be on paper, with signatures and seals.

"Arcadius, this is Anna, my trusted representative. For everything that concerns the economy, be so kind as to discuss it with her. My comrade and I are going to ride around a little longer.

"Might I ask where you're going?" Arcadius pricked up his ears.

"Well, where do you think? To check out the family manor. The family nest, I might even say. Why else did I come here? And by the way, why are you stationed down here at the town hall instead of in the castle? Judging by the photos, it's a lot comfier up there."

"Please wait a moment, Sir Galaxius," the administrator said, holding up his hands. "There are some difficulties there."

I pursed my lips. "What difficulties?"

"With your visiting the manor."

"Is there some problem? They seem to have

emailed me all the deeds and so on. And Anna has the originals in one of her folders."

"No, no... It isn't that!" The fat man waved his hands nervously. "Your claim is all in order. You just can't get there physically."

"I don't get it. Explain..." I narrowed my eyes.

"You do know what Gift your family had... I mean, has?" The administrator grinned anxiously.

"Well, um... yeah." I smiled.

"The fact is that the servants of the Empire were unable to reach the manor." He paused again for a moment, choosing his words carefully. "It was too dangerous there."

I raised a brow. "Dangerous?"

"Rift beasts, Your Lordship. Whether the remnants of the Galaxius menagerie or something new, we don't know. In the end, the imperial mages decided to just put up a force field."

Surprising. "Why didn't they call the Slayers?" I asked.

"There are nuances involved. It is still private property, after all. And they would have called them, if the force field failed to hold up. But it did hold up. However..." He faltered again.

"Spit it out already!" I said, losing my cool. "What else?"

"The problem is that maintaining the force field costs energy every day. And you were possibly not warned that a certain amount has been added to your debt, the amount spent by the Empire to hold back the beasts and maintain the force field."

"A certain amount?" My voice deadened.

"Yes, I have it all accounted for here." He took out another folder. "Here is the cost in jellies, and here are the visits from the imperial mages to renew the shield. The total amount is here."

Anna grabbed the folder from his hand first. Her eyes widened, and she whistled.

"God damn!"

She silently handed the papers to me. I looked inside them myself.

"Whoa!"

Suddenly, the Galaxius manor had become a very expensive asset.

"I still want to go take a look at the force field. But we'll need a guide."

"Yes, of course. Lex, help him." The administrator nodded to a young man, who instantly jumped up from his computer. "This is Alexei Trotsky, my assistant. He will show you the way there."

"If you need anything, call," I said with a nod to Anna, who took a seat in the administrator's chair, causing his eye to twitch slightly, and pulled a folder of prepared documents toward her with an air of ownership.

We drove out of Galaxiton and drove toward the manor. Helpfully, it was only a couple of miles away. And soon I started to see the shimmer above the ground, which formed into a dome around the Galaxius manor.

I tried to remember everything I knew about it. Magic domes had been used since the old days. Mostly in battle, to cover armies or cities under siege. They were created by Gifted specialists, or powerful artifacts which were created by those same Gifted, but with the help of Artificers. They were an entirely ordinary item, although expensive. Their cost grew depending on the power of the barrier and the area it covered.

From what I saw of the bill, the area covered was a single hectare. Judging by the plan, it protected the main building of the manor and a couple of outbuildings marked on the map as 'stables.'

We drove right up and stopped outside a tidy log cabin emitting light smoke from its chimney.

"Petrovich!" Alexei shouted as he stepped out of the car.

'Petrovich' appeared from the outpost — a middle-aged, practically old man with a Slayer fifth-class ring.

Right, I remembered the name 'Petrovich' in a statement of expenses too.

"Hey there, Lex! Who's this you've brought?"

"The new owner."

"Oops!" The retired Slayer looked anxiously down at his rough shirt and trousers, far from freshly washed. He was chewing something too, and now he hurriedly wiped his hands on his shirt. "I wish you good health, Your Lordship!"

He stood to attention.

I walked forward and offered him a hand, which he shook slowly.

"Nice to meet you, Petrovich!"

Of course, the old Slayer noticed my ring. His

face split in a happy grin.

"Nice to see that the new lord is one of us."

"One of us, that's right." I nodded. "Come on, Petrovich, tell me how your watch is going."

"Well... Hard to say it's going at all really." He shook his head. "Pretty quiet place. Except that the wildlife's getting frisky, mating season's started. But they don't have a lot of space anyway, so they regulate their own population — by eating one another. Once every six months, an imperial mage comes and renews the dome. And I guess I'm here as the boiler man." He chuckled.

"Boiler man?"

"You know... I keep the power on."

I followed him into a small shed, where there was a weakly humming cube and chests on shelves at the sides.

"I throw in jellies to keep the energy from dropping." He pointed to a gage inset right into the cube. "Right now it's in the yellow zone. When it falls to the red, I'll need to put a fresh one in."

"How much energy does the dome spend?"

"It doesn't take much as long as it isn't overloaded, Your Lordship. Two white jellies, morning and night, that's more than enough."

I scratched my head and roughly estimated the cost. It all seemed to match up. The main expenses were in erecting the dome in the first place. That was far more than the ongoing costs. Supporting the dome really didn't take much energy. But the amount required increased sharply if something started hitting it. That, from what I understood, was pretty simple.

"Look there, Your Lordship!" He pointed a finger at the veil of the dome, where some subspecies of wolf was running toward us, four others chasing behind it. "They're hunting a wounded brother." Petrovich said.

Without seeing it, the first wolf ran headlong into the force field, which erupted in sparks. Howling, the wolf fell back in a state of shock. His brothers following him ran into him and tore him to shreds before our eyes.

"And that's how they have to feed," the old man said. "That's why there aren't a whole bunch of 'em."

"Well, if there aren't a 'whole bunch of 'em,'" I said, scratching my head, "then why weren't they all killed in the beginning?"

"I mean, there aren't a bunch roaming free. But I wasn't here in the beginning. The old doorman who served here after the field was first put up told me it was total chaos inside the castle itself. They said the army even considered dropping a bomb on the place. But then either someone intervened or they decided it wasn't worth the bomb."

I looked out at the castle itself. Of course, it wasn't really a castle. I had seen real castles in Europe. It was, unusually for the locality, a stone three-story structure made of huge blocks. The wings stood out for their height. Roofed with large tiles, the house looked imposing. And the total area, according to those documents, was over ten thousand square feet. Although, my old family the Goddards had a manor five times the size.

"What do we have to do to bring down the force field?"

"Uh, just don't feed the machinery for three days," Petrovich answered readily. "And the field will fall on its own." He narrowed his eyes and looked at me carefully. "What, can we bring it down?"

"No, no, not so fast," I said. "First I need to prepare. Sit here with Andrei a while. I'm going to take a look around, get some fresh air."

"Unwise," Wolf said, shaking his head.

"I'll take Caramel with me," I said, petting my loyal animal on her big head. "It's all just meadows and fields... Oh, and the woods over there, but I won't go in them, I promise. What could happen to me here?"

The bald man grimaced. "Stuff always happens after words like those, in my experience."

"Oh, don't be superstitious!" I said. "Alright, I'm off!"

Of course, I was headed out with a specific goal in mind. And Shnoop was already getting ready to scout ahead for me.

CHAPTER 17

IT ALL WENT JUST LIKE ANNA told me it would.

My manor, by happy coincidence, had been under an impenetrable defense all this time, so it hadn't been looted. Although she hadn't known anything about the beasts inside. Her hands couldn't reach everywhere, it seemed, or her curious little nose.

I knew that there was no reason not to take her at her word, but for some reason I just hadn't imagined how well protected the place was. Or just how it was protected. I thought they'd just set up a light outpost and maybe once a week someone would check to make sure the house wasn't being carried off brick by brick. And maybe if something happened to the house, then raise the alarm.

But as it happened, nobody had even been inside, which had to be good news.

The first thing I did was take a look around. I walked back and forth and realized that there had been people walking around here; there were tracks all around me. And Shnoop found hidden caches in the woods. At least twenty supply crates, which we'd loot and hand over to Wolf for safekeeping. There were sleeping bags, tents, observation equipment and radios. The place had clearly been closely watched, along with the people who came to it. But that wasn't the work of the army, but of whoever wanted my mansion. And they'd been at it for a long time. Some of the supply caches were so old that a lot of stuff had just rotted away. Like the food supplies, for example. Although the military rations were hermetically sealed, the wild beasts that lived here in the forest had no respect for packaging. They just wanted to eat.

There were plenty of critters around too, including squirrels.

When Shnoop appeared on Caramel's shoulder instead of mine, I immediately got the picture. My cat tore off from where she stood and raced away.

Doomsday for the squirrels! And anyone who got in her way. I hoped there was no squirrel king there, because he was about to be uncrowned.

After examining everything I could, I went back satisfied. I basically knew what I needed to do here, I just had to figure out the boring formalities. That meant filling out a few forms for missing property deeds, but they weren't kept here.

"We need to go back to City Hall in Irkutsk," I said to Wolf when he came back.

"Anna, how much time will it take to fill out the forms?"

"Mmm..." the girl answered, studying the papers that the workers of the military administration were obliged to keep. "I think we can have it done in two hours. This is too important a matter, high-priority. No queues for us."

Great! That suited me. We quickly jumped into the car and headed back to Irkutsk. Incidentally, that was a problem too. The manor was nearly two hundred miles from the city, and living there permanently would be tough. Considering my family's Gift, I would have built the manor a long way from the big city too — you never know what might happen.

But if I was there and my enemies here, then I'd need to think of a system of defense. That meant more and more money, but more importantly — loyal people!

The formalities at City Hall went even faster than I thought.

The Empire was well and truly sick of my manor, which required an enormous amount of money and constant attention. And if something suddenly happened to it, then heads would roll. Which was why they'd protected it like the apple of their eye.

"You are now the full-fledged owner!" After I

signed on the line, the official did the same. "My congratulations and sympathies!"

On that note, we said good-bye to him and headed back. Another couple of hundred miles on the odometer.

Some military men and one Slayer were waiting when we arrived. They checked all my papers, then got straight out of there. They were glad to have that boring job behind them too.

I could imagine how happy King and his goons must have been then. Now I had to protect this place all on my own. On the other hand, I didn't think that'd be such a big problem. I did want to move here after all. But how?

First I had to fix up at least one wing, so that I could live in some kind of comfort, and at the same time move my people in here. Then I'd have to hire a work crew.

I had other thoughts too, but all in good time.

"Can we go in?" Wolf asked in his usual manner.

"Who knows?" I shrugged, stuck my hands in my pockets and walked up to the barrier.

Anna paid no attention to me at all. She was staring at her phone, reading something. She was often doing that, since she had to know everything and stay aware of what was going on.

So as not to shock my people, I approached from the other side of the manor, to check things out without prying eyes. Shnoop had already run around the whole place by then.

I walked up to the barrier and placed a hand

on it. I needed to feel it out, sense it. I stood there like an idiot, eyes closed and arm raised before me. The barrier was high quality, triple-layered. Whoever put it up was no amateur. Clearly the work of a learned master who knew how to do the job properly.

Good thing I didn't need to break the barrier, or wait three days. It was currently powered by jellies, and clearly weakened. I started firing off needling blows of aggressive energy, hitting it right where the weave was weakest. The first layer fell within a minute, then the second. Now there was only one left, the last.

The third was harder to remove, because when it fell, the barrier would sound the alarm. That wouldn't bother me, but as soon as it happened, there'd be an Imperial Fast Response Unit on the way here. Every town had one. And I'd have to waste a couple of hours on them, and they'd find out that I'd destroyed the barrier. I knew how the bureaucracy worked, and I doubted they'd be quick to confirm my ownership or disconnect the alarm system. So I spent ten more minutes carefully removing the alarm weave, then destroyed the final layer of the barrier.

Anna walked up and cocked her head at me. "I didn't know you knew anything about artificing and constructs."

Shnoop had told me that she was coming, but I decided not to stop working.

"Didn't I tell you that I'm a man of many talents?" I turned to her with a smile.

But the smile quickly fell from my face along with the barrier.

My agent Shnoop had quickly darted inside and was transmitting his view of the place.

The sight I didn't like was the bones of creatures in the manor. They were fresh.

"Move!" I said sharply to Anna and got moving myself.

"Danger?" She was quick on the uptake.

Danger, yes. Only I couldn't understand what was happening. Shnoop was showing me a great many strange sights that I hadn't had time to process yet.

I led Anna to Wolf and left her with him.

"Wolf, you stay here and keep an eye on Anna, make sure not so much as a hair on her head is harmed." The man listened to me carefully.

"Big trouble, huh?" was all he asked.

"At least medium, let's say, but I don't know for sure yet."

"Alright." He nodded calmly, with no sign of any nerves, and went to open the trunk where he kept the weapons.

I didn't bother waiting for Wolf to get all his combat gear on. Instead I summoned Caramel and walked toward the entrance to the main building.

As I walked up the old steps leading through the overgrown wintry garden, I suddenly got the shivers. This place was incredible. The railings I felt beneath my fingers were the products of a stone-carving art that sculptors had used two hundred years ago, but they still looked brand-new, with no scars or cracks.

The manor itself was huge, but at the same time looked compact. Without putting it too grandly, it was obvious at a glance how old this place was, how rich a history it had.

Of course, I had learned all that was available on the history of my Family, but there was a lot I couldn't find. Although I hadn't really tried all that hard yet.

The manor... How long had I been working towards it? Yeah, yeah, alright, for me a couple of weeks is a long time. I was used to just going and getting what I wanted, but here... The rules were just different in this world. There was plenty about me that seemed savage to the people here, but I wasn't about to change. Completely changing myself for others wasn't something I could ever do. I would make my own rules, and others would either respect them or die if they opposed them. That said, they could kill me too — I didn't count that out. If they could succeed. At that last thought my lips twisted into a grin. And I pushed open the closed door.

It wasn't locked. When I entered the large hall, the raw and musty scent of age struck my nostrils along with the stench of corpses. The stench of death.

Why should this shuttered place be stinking of death after all this time? And where had all these skeletons come from? I could tell for certain that they were skeletons from various beasts.

"House ishhh cllleaaar!" Shnoop crooned,

popping up on my shoulder.

He had checked all three floors.

"Good beast!" I stroked him on the ear for a job well done. "Now go and check out beneath the house. We either have a Rift or a rat colony in our basement. No other way I can explain where all this came from."

I had no idea what to expect, so I even drew my sword. These beasts had to have done some damage.

My deepest fears were confirmed when Shnoop appeared on my shoulder, trembling with fear and pointing the way with his paw. Since he hadn't transmitted to me what he'd seen, it was something he wanted me to see for myself.

No sense putting it off. I ran that way. Maybe I shouldn't have left Mel with Anna? Although, no. What could be so dangerous here?

But all my Hunter's instincts were on guard, ready for anything. Except what I saw next. There wasn't far to run, just to the stairs to the basement. I ran along bones and didn't even notice them, but in the cellar, it was... I was struck dumb.

The whole place was filled with bones practically to the ceiling, and I had just one question.

"What the hell is going on here?"

"Don't knowwww..." Shnoop said, covering his face with his paws.

"Well, go find out!"

I had expected a battle, but found a hoard of

bones to clean up. There was more than one room in the cellar. There were other doors leading away, but we'd have to remove a lot of bones before we could get to them. I should have gotten myself a dog — Mel doesn't much like bones.

I summoned a slime, but I think even it was surprised, and burbled something uncertainly. When I told it to eat *only* the bones and nothing else, it brightened right up.

Judging by the bones, their owners had been gnawed and chewed by something not very large, but both voracious and powerful.

Shnoop ran ahead. I sensed him hitting some impenetrable force, and then starting to leech energy out of me like a pump. I automatically cut the supply in shock. The enraged little guy popped up right in front of my nose.

"Nn-n-neeeed!" he spat in annoyance.

Well, need means need, I guess. If there was anyone I trusted, it was that little punk.

He disappeared again, and started to drain energy from me in uneven bursts again. The last surge nearly fully exhausted me. The shock had me sitting down and seeing rainbows. What the hell did he run into?

I was in hostile territory, so I quickly took out a red jelly and started to chew it. After a second I realized that wasn't enough and immediately bit into another.

Shnoop had poked his way into a strange room. I got a feeling that the walls of this dungeon were older than the structure above, far older. The place reeked of eternity, and on top of that a kind of hopelessness.

The room wasn't all that large — maybe a thousand square feet, with very high ceilings. The walls had niches, and there were stone pedestals in the corners covered with unusual symbols. There were also shelves that were almost empty, but here and there I made out an old tome and scrolls, some of which had been thrown onto the floor where they lay under a thick layer of dust mixed with a large number of human bones, rusty weapons and armor.

It seemed there had been a serious battle here, just as there had been all over the castle. Judging by the fact that some of the skeletons bore the family's signet rings, the enemy that had put them down must have been powerful beyond belief.

Shnoop dove back, looking thinner and shivering. He must have spent a lot of his own energy too, getting inside there. But I could see the way now.

Swearing and sweeping aside heaps of bones that my slime had yet to eat, I walked on further and leaned against a large stone door. On the right was a precise groove in the wood, the face of a honey badger grinning happily above it.

The way it worked seemed pretty obvious. The lock could be opened with a signet ring. I placed my fist on the wall to insert the ring into the groove. The heavy door shook, and slowly began to move aside. But the barrier, which had completely exhausted me when Shnoop phased through the door, hadn't gone anywhere. It shimmered with sickening green light, blocking the way.

I closed my eyes and started to work on the barrier. *Holy hell, now that's what I'm talking about!* I'd definitely never seen anything like this in this world, although I could remember something like it from my past one. It took a lot of people a lot of effort to crack a lock like this, specially trained people. No way did I have the energy to remove it now. But the barrier was blocking a room in my family mansion. That meant there had to be some other way to open it, without brute force.

I scratched my head in thought.

"What do you need from me..?" I mused aloud.

Then, heeding my intuition and using all the common sense I had, I simply placed my open palm on the barrier. I felt an almost imperceptible pinprick. Reflexively, I pulled my hand away. There was a small bleeding cut on it. And then the superpowerful barrier, strong enough to protect even the treasures of the Emperor himself, emitted a loud cracking noise and disappeared without a trace.

Automatically raising my hand to my mouth and licking off the blood, I shook my head. I'll be damned!

One careful step, then another. I scanned the air. No mistake — the barrier was gone. So as not to 'overwork' poor Shnoop, I switched on an ordinary flashlight and started carefully looking around the room. What the hell had happened here?

I sensed power behind me. I turned around sharply, pulling out my sword and powering my armor.

"Finally, you have come!"

Opposite me stood an actual skeleton in scraps of clothing. It held an unusual sword without a speck of rust on it. The sword shone quietly, and I couldn't tell by the look of it what metal the blade was made of.

"What the hell do you think you are?" I blurted out in surprise.

"My name is Darkest, last of the Family of the Immortals. I am sworn in service to your family, young man. To serve and protect it until death itself. Unfortunately, I failed. Enemies destroyed your Family. All I do was spend my immortal soul to erect a force field around the family vault, and use the last of my strength to ensure that these bones awaited the return of the one true heir — you. I have little time. In a few minutes, I will finally depart for oblivion. I hope that I have at least somehow helped my sovereigns."

"A few minutes?" My mind geared up to the speed of a supercomputer. I thought feverishly over what questions to ask this thing in just a few minutes. "Who destroyed my family?"

"You can figure that out easily enough yourself." If the skeleton could smile, he'd have smiled then. "The corpses bear signet rings. It is not hard to find out so long as you have a little of the common sense that always was given to your family."

So this dusty old guy was mocking me now. Fine, maybe it was a dumb question.

I thought for a moment. "Alright. Tell me everything you consider necessary, then."

"This is the vault of the Galaxius family." He waved a bone arm through the air. "The assassins managed to carry some things away before I put up the Shield of Rot, but most of the family heirlooms were not in the vault at that time."

His dry joints squeaking, he walked over to some pedestals in the corner, waving for me to follow him. He pointed a bleached finger at twelve cubes standing in a square.

"These are the pedestals of your family swords. For hundreds of years, the Galaxius family mined and purchased rare Rift materials, to forge the most perfect weapons in this reality." He reached out a hand as he lectured, pointing.

"Here was the sword Ursa. The head of the family guard, Anton Galaxius, took it with him along with a squad of guardsmen not long before the catastrophe in the north, on orders from the Emperor, when the snow beasts invaded from the polar circle.

Here was the sword Hydra, belonging to the eldest daughter and strongest beast fighter in the family, Alena Galaxius. She always worked alone, and was abroad helping her Japanese friends at their request, who were hunting a gigantic beast in a Rift on their islands.

Here is the pedestal for the sword that I hold in my hands, but have no right to. Its name is Aquila, the youngest of the family swords. It was waiting for the youngest heir of the family to grow up. The sword never got to meet him; the heir was killed in an attack. I was forced to take it, for I had too little of my own strength left.

Each of the twelve swords is unique in its own way, each with unusual properties. I think you can figure them out yourself. But that is not the most important thing."

The skeleton reeled, breaking off for a moment, but went on.

"The power of the Galaxius clan, a power which all the rulers of this world have envied, was in the synergy of all its swords. When all twelve of the swords are held by people of a single blood, their power is greatly multiplied!"

He pointed again at the first pedestal.

"Here was where the collapse began," Darkest pronounced, shaking his head. "Anton did not return from his campaign. He simply disappeared after completing the mission he had been set. I suspect that he was betrayed. But the Galaxiuses could not prove it. That is where the family's fall began. Without the twelfth sword, matters worsened. The owners of the remaining swords began to fall one after another, in similarly unclear circumstances. Only three swords remained in the manor.

This one here..." He pointed at his own. "Was

in the stone. Two more, by the name of Scorpius and Lynx, third and second swords, were in the hands of the young heirs of the Galaxiuses, who defended their manor to their dying breaths. Their swords were most likely carried off by the attackers."

He turned to me.

"My time runs short. One more thing... I see the signet ring on your hand. But it is a ring of a vassal of the Galaxiuses, just like the one upon my finger." He span the ring with the honey badger on it on his bone finger.

"Just as there existed the twelve swords, there existed also three rings. One worn by the head of the family, the second by the chief of the guards, and the third by the head of the family's wife. They, too..." The skeleton shivered again. His bones trembled as if about to collapse, but then seemed to gather themselves again. "They also have their purpose, which you will have to discover on your own. That is all, young Galaxius. My time has come."

He fell silent for a second, but couldn't take it any longer, and shook his head. This corpse must have been a real shithead in life.

"Good luck to you, young honey badger! You will need it. What I see here now would make me grieve for the final fall of the family, if only my soul had remained immortal. You are weak. Very weak. I hope you do not die too soon."

The bones began to collapse into dust, and suddenly I surprised myself by shouting:

"Wait!"

* * *

The Galaxius Manor
Lake Baikal, southeastern shore

Darkest Gardius Euclidius, last of the family of the Immortals, had already made peace with the thought that he would not be revived. He had served the Galaxius family for hundreds of years. Faithfully and truthfully, trying to somehow atone for the sin and the pain that his own family had inflicted on humanity. After all, they had obtained terrible knowledge. Knowledge which should never have come to light. But his family thirsted for power. Power over the world. And it would have gotten it if not for the Galaxius line. After learning the secret of Necromancy, the family altered their bodies and changed their name to Immortal. Then they built huge armies that they planned to use to take over the whole world.

Their campaign for power had begun from this very place. It was here where they found the crypt outside of time and space, the one that gave them their inhuman knowledge. They broke the Ruthenian army, the southern nomad army, the Dragon Dynasty army. Japan was next, and all that separated them was a strait.

At that moment the first and still young Emperor of the future Eastern Empire, while holding back the undead hordes surging westwards, sent a group of his best fighters led by his best friend — the future founder of the Galaxius line.

Though suffering heavy losses, the group was able to take the stronghold of the Necromancers. In the end, it came down to one man left on each side. Incredibly after such a battle, the young Galaxius still stood solidly on two feet, and so did he, Darkest, youngest son of a now practically dead family.

The Necromancers had gained knowledge of that which was most sacred all over the world — the human soul itself. And thanks to that, Darkest was able to sense the soul of the young fighter standing against him. And it was the strongest and most unusual soul he'd ever seen. Something made him drop to one knee and swear an undying vow of loyalty, half expecting that the young warrior would still send him after his brethren all the same. But, to his surprise, the first Galaxius accepted him into service. The now headless hordes of the undead partly collapsed on their own and were finished off by the allied armies.

Returning after some time, Galaxius, with the humble title of Baron, tore down the gloomy citadel of the Necromancers, then built his own mansion on the foundations. Once again using his body and the bodies of his family to cover a terrible threat to all humanity. His friend became Emperor, and founded the Imperial Family. And as for Galaxius... He just settled down and started producing heirs, laying the foundations of a strong family.

Then followed many years of fighting and treachery leading to the downfall of that family, which, in principle, had made the rise of the Empire and the Emperor possible.

Most of Darkest's power had been spent on the barrier years ago, so he could not sense or see the human soul so clearly anymore. But what he did see, he didn't like. Too weak was this heir to a great family. It seemed that the blood of the Galaxiuses had thinned, and would soon disappear completely from the world. What a shame.

The last energy left his bones, and he started to fall apart, never to rise again, his last duty to his sovereign fulfilled.

"Wait!" the young man shouted, barely not a boy.

And Darkest felt enormous power in his voice. Power comparable with the founding father of the family. As his consciousness faded away, suddenly, one after another, the souls of monstrous beings started to hook into his own soul, beings that had never before existed in this world.

His departure stalled, and the last thing he saw were the young man's eyes burning with inhuman light, and his spirit vision showed a whole host of animals and beasts behind the man's back, all appearing for a moment in this world. Every last one of them staring at him with their thousands of eyes. He sensed his soul taking on form again. And that his departure of today would not be final. His soul would return to the endless cycle of rebirth in which all humans were trapped, even those as bad as him.

"In the name of the family, I thank you for your service, Darkest. You served your own family with loyalty, and now it's time to rest," the young man pronounced firmly.

Although no, Darkest's now non-existent tongue balked at calling this man that. Before him was the worthy head of a family, one of the Great Families.

Darkest smiled mentally. It seemed the planet would again tremble before the might of the Galaxius Guard, which had for years stood in the defense of humanity with a hot heart and cold head and was populated by man and beast alike. And the ancient Necromancer, with a conscious clearer than it had been for years, departed to be reborn.

CHAPTER 18

I LOOKED AROUND. My attention was draw to a text engraved in the stone right above the pedestals for the swords, carved into the head of a honey badger. I started to read it and immediately felt an otherworldly chill, along with amazement and a little excitement.

Let's start with the fact that it was called the Galaxius Family Code. What I was reading reminded me of something familiar and close to my heart in my past world.

I shook my head, driving away a strange feeling. It wasn't the Hunter's Code. Hunters were individualists. But what I saw here was something more... human, maybe. That said, the style of storytelling and the content evoked endless respect in me. After reading it to the end, I could say for the first time that *this* was exactly the family I wanted to restore. The family whose heir's soul had been replaced by mine in his body, thanks to whatever dumb chance or whim of fate.

How fascinating... I slowly ran my hand over the engraved words. An old message to the young generation. There were some very good tips in there, but also crazy ones unsuitable for modern aristocrats.

For example, 'Family is above all' matched pretty well with modernity, but not 'Follow only your own wishes.'

What have you gotten yourself mixed up in, Xander? What is this family with its strange swords and history?

The Hunters had a technique that allowed them to use souls to empower their weapons, and the highest technique was to seal those souls into the weapons themselves. Now that was hard to do, and dangerous. In this world I had seen something like that in Japan, but the masters there were only experimenting, and the results were often unpredictable. Like, for example, with that loaned sword that Nakamuro gave me to 'test out.'

What were the chances that the 'Hydra' sword had contained an actual Hydra? Or was it just a name?

He had also said something about synergy. I was already used to the fact that the people in this world knew many things, but didn't understand them.

For now, the only thought that came to my mind was of how ancient the weapon was, which was why it was so powerful too. It was a well-known fact in my world that the older the weapon, the more surprises it can carry. When a weapon kills, when it kills a great many — it absorbs tiny particles of the souls of the fallen, making it stronger. But the trouble is...

I remembered that Don Sharpeye had a pike that was over six hundred years old, and one time it started to weep. Really — a green poison started to seep out of it. And none of us knew why it had happened. There were many possibilities. Sometimes Rhunology, Ritualistics, Alchemy and Artificing all together gave new and unexpected results.

There was also another option. That pike could have been enchanted and even more ancient than we all thought, with hidden charms that activated over time.

Anyway, enough reminiscing.

I looked closely over the sword that had come into my possession, the youngest of the Galaxius family swords. The metal shone brightly. And the glow was maintained by the soul within it. I delved deeper, trying to feel out the entity. There — an eagle nestled within the sword by the name of Aquila. Not an ordinary earthly eagle, but an altered one from a Rift.

In living form, it would have been a ferocious opponent with a fifteen-foot wingspan. However strange it might sound, this soul was 'excellent-grade,' I could tell that right away. Some unknown craftsman had found a way to convince the soul of the proud bird to climb into the sword of its own will, and that was most of the battle won for creating a good weapon.

Souls driven into weapons by force often serve poorly, sometimes even do the owner harm. With this one, the job had been done properly. No doubt the weapon had some other unusual properties too, but I'd have to figure them out later. For now, only one thing was clear to me — it was doubtful that this sword would break any time soon. And the grinning face of the honey badger, which also served as a counterweight on the pommel, would announce that Baron Galaxius had his own family weapon now. However, unlike so many useless but very expensive toys, this blade was fit for real combat!

What else was waiting for me here? There were dozens of different rooms, but seemed to be under some kind of protection. Well, I was in no hurry, so better to start with the first.

Even Shnoop couldn't get in there, the room was so well sealed. I suspected the walls contained built-in strips of kordelium, a metal which prevents shades from entering. Or something equivalent to it.

As I approached the correct wall, which served the function of a door, and pressed my ring into the niche, I started to laugh.

"You gotta be kidding me! No fair!" I blurted out.

Energy! Opening this door would take a whole ocean of it. But what was the point of putting up such strong protection, which demanded such a colossal cost of energy in addition to family blood? Only one option occurred to me.

All the Galaxius vaults had been in siege mode all this time. A useful option to have, and we used it in my past world too. When the owners don't show up for too long, the defense systems kick in and start to assume they're dead. Either that or the mode is activated manually during an attack.

That was the main idea — to make sure enemies didn't use children, bastards and other bearers of family blood who could be lured in with power and money, or just plainly intimidated. And then unwittingly used. That was what this mode was for.

A kid simply wouldn't have the energy to open it. Training him up and endowing him with the necessary skills might take fifty years, through which he might become wiser and more independent as he gained in strength. Adult members of the family were less likely to betray it. So I guessed, anyway...

Ugh... I hated to admit it, but there was no point in me even trying to open these rooms. It'd cost too much energy. I'd have to close over fifty Rifts just to get started with the first room.

And what would come next? There might be many more of those rooms, and each might need more and more energy to unlock, although there was no way to know yet.

Whatever; time to forget it for now and move

on, but first...

"Shnoop!" I called out to the critter.

"Whaaaat?" he drawled, still thinner than usual and glancing sidelong at me with a certain trepidation.

"I'll feed you and boost the energy stream later, don't worry! And I owe you an ice cream!" I smiled at him disarmingly. "In the meantime, gather up all the signet rings that are lying around here, and anything else that might come in handy to us, and hide it all somewhere safe. You heard the bag of bones."

"I heaaarrrd!" he sighed, and disappeared.

Then I started to look around to see what else I might find.

In the time that I'd been here, I already had one thing figured out. I should have given this manor to the people who wanted to get their hands on it, and then laughed at them while they tried to deal with it.

As I turned down a passageway where the door hung broken beneath years of dust, I stopped in my tracks. My entire path was littered with skeletons, and more than just that. There were fresh corpses which had only recently begun to decompose. I summoned my little scout again and sent him ahead. It looked like this depopulated mansion may actually be home to several forms of life. And they were very close.

Armadillos. That's what they call those little dinosaurish critters. Quick little beasts with a club on the tail and a thick shell covering the whole back. They could grow up to three feet long, and had a hell of an appetite. They could eat for days on end and still be hungry, and that made them very angry. And one tier below us was their lair.

I didn't know where they came from, but there was no end of them. And not far from them, just a couple of hundred yards away, there were goblins settled in separate quarters. At this point I started to doubt the clarity of my own mind. How could that be?

The armadillos sniffed me out almost right away as soon as I got close enough. I wasn't really trying to hide anyway. When Shnoop showed me them, I was taken aback, but still headed off to deal with them.

And I wasn't alone. Next to me was Pinky, clearly hungry, and another two dozen different ants. I had also summoned flying creatures to distract attention from the air. And, as a cherry on top, two snakes that I sent straight to the goblins. Their strength and venom would be too much for the little green thugs.

Worst of all, Shnoop hadn't yet shown me the entirety of my underground domain. And I had a fear that there was a lot more down there than I first thought.

And that gave rise to another question. How was I supposed to move people in here with all this mess?

I met the first armadillos personally. They were dumb and angry, but my sword was sharp and my hands experienced. I charged the sword with power and aimed for their heads. That'll teach the little bastards to stick them out of their shells. Curiosity killed the cat, as they say. Or the armadillo, I guess!

I had killed ten of them already when I suddenly nearly lost my heel. A tail ending with something like a spiky ball of bone, a kind of club, struck me on the back of the foot. Good thing my armor held up, but it buckled hard. Still, I managed to finish off the rest. They were pretty weak enemies.

I scratched the back of my head in confusion. There really was something strange going on here.

Shnoop had begun to draw me a complex map of the dungeon, all the parts of it he could reach. That is, the parts that let him in. The dungeon was part natural, part man-made.

I walked forward, absent-mindedly eating jellies and fighting off enemies that attacked me. I didn't process what my pet was showing me right away, but then it all slowly began to order itself into a kind of elusive, but seemingly clear picture. My intel was too poor, but it seemed like all this had been done as part of some clever plan.

I tried to walk through the broad corridors, not wandering too close to where the largest hordes of enemies were gathered. It wasn't time; I needed to figure this place out before fighting. Still, I walked in the direction of the armadillo nest. I had seen something through Shnoop's eyes. And it was so incredible that I wanted to see it with my own. And as always, Shnoop hadn't let me down or twisted his intel.

My flashlight fell on the old shell of a long dead armadillo with the bones of a skeleton inside an empty bone 'house.' And upon its shell was the crest of the Galaxius family. So that was what this was. These beasts had been bred specially here. And, judging by the fact that they bore the crest, they must have lived alongside the family. But most of them had died off over the past centuries.

I sent Shnoop to the nest, asking him not to get too close. Judging by the particularly large size of the beasts with their cracked shells, they were already very old. Maybe some of them even remembered their old owners. But that was all for later. The wild young ones wouldn't let me by so easily. First I'd have to make some careful preparations.

I kept looking through Shnoop's eyes, and another thing drew my attention. Can I walked forwards and stopped before a huge thick door made of a metal I didn't recognize. The door was ajar, as if someone had unlocked it and it had swung open under its own weight. And then the beasts had tried to open it further, striving to get out. I sent Shnoop in there and he was nearly eaten by a huge toad that shot out its long tongue at the little guy when he appeared in our reality.

"Ssshhhhon of a BITCH!" Shnoop shrieked in fear, reappearing beside me.

But he'd had enough time to look around. And I didn't like what he showed me one bit. I'd figured out already that all the beasts I'd found so far were former pets of the Galaxiuses. But beyond that door were wild Rifts full of wild beasts, and I had no idea how many.

Shnoop went off once more and barely dodged a stream of fire launched by some unknown beast that he didn't see. I decided not to risk it a third time. I'd seen enough to know it was going to be tough in there.

Now I understood why the Galaxiuses, according to legend, were head and shoulders above the other Families. They just had their own personal place to train right at home. They'd made it by hand, or maybe always had it — who knows. But the fact remained.

I walked up to a familiar bas-relief of a honey badger with a niche beneath it for a ring. I stuck my ring in there and the bas-relief flashed green at first, but then changed to red. I chuckled and stuck the ring in it again. The light show repeated. And this time I felt an electric shock, which told me that the first time wasn't a mistake — it wasn't going to let me in.

I scratched my head and looked closer. Honey badger — check, slot for the ring — check, Galaxius — check. What else did they need? And then I remembered the three rings held by the head of the family, his wife and the chief guard. I'd call them the High Rings, to differentiate them from the other family rings. Intuition told me that only one of the three rings would work here. Which meant I wouldn't be able to seal up this dangerous zone for now. Oh, well — something to come back to in better times.

After weighing all the pros and cons, I decided to risk sending Shnoop in a third time after all, asking him to move in short leaps so as not to make himself a target. Through his eyes, I saw a real war raging inside. A war between beasts from different Rifts. If any of them made it out through the half-open door, they'd run into the former pets of the Galaxius household. A kind of buffer zone. And then further into the house. But who had put down all those beasts that had been in the main part of the house itself? I scratched my head in thought, and headed back.

Shnoop deftly gathered up twenty jellies. The snakes had furiously bitten the goblins. But once I realized that the poor things could serve me for good, I unsummoned the beasts, or rather let their souls go. Then I cast a sad glance at the magic-sealed vaults of the Galaxius family and headed to the exit.

As I neared the stone steps heading up from the cellar, I heard gunfire, then loud growling from Mel. Someone must have gotten into a fight. My heart sped up and I started running up the stairs in huge leaps, my new sword in hand.

I jumped out and ran up to the exit, and there I saw something strange — Caramel was fighting with a semi-transparent creature, and I was surprised to see that it was smaller than she was. Wolf provided covering fire with his Whirlwind. Most of the bullets flew through the creature, since it spent most of its time immaterial. Caramel's sharp claws flew straight through it too. But at some point the shadow turned material, and at that moment it struck Mel hard, so hard that I felt her armor cracking and immediately demanding more of my energy.

I charged my sword with power and rushed to attack. Only as I ran closer did I see that the semi-transparent creature was a real-life honey badger. Black fur, long thick tail, white back and head. And a huge mouth full of teeth. The beast was as if smiling happily, basking in the glory of battle.

"Mel, get back! Now, back to Wolf!" I barked at her.

The panther snorted, but jumped back. In that short burst of battle, I noticed that the transparent honey badger was refusing to cross a seemingly invisible border that began at the bottom stone step of the manor.

Holding my sword before me, I started carefully approaching. The honey badger growled at the sight of a new enemy, and, in an ungainly gallop, rushed to attack me. But the closer it got, the less sure it became. Within a yard of me it skidded to a halt and stuck its huge black nose into the air as if scenting something.

I crouched down on my heels and offered it my hand, knowing that its jaw could engulf all my fingers. My arm even, right to the shoulder. But my intuition had its own opinion! The honey badger walked up and sniffed me, materialized for a moment and licked my hand with its sandpaper tongue. Then it looked at Mel and Wolf standing there in confusion and sniffed in annoyance. It turned away and, with a parting look into my eyes that said something like 'you're on your own now,' it lumbered off into the manor.

"Hold on! Wait!" I shouted.

The hell with that! I tried to reach for his soul, but ran into trouble. The soul was neither living nor dead. That is, the body was somehow both bound with the soul and not. Honestly, I'd never seen anything like it before even in my past life. Although I had heard about it from old Hunters. It was a Legendary Immortal Soul. Its owner could not be killed, only exiled from reality for a very short time. Where on God's green earth had the Galaxiuses found such a creature?!

The beast ignored my summons and kept just ambling away, then disappeared into thin air.

"Ssshhhorrry, he chashed me awwayy!" Shnoop said, appearing on my shoulder and drooping.

"No wonder," I said, shaking my head. "That thing could chase anyone away. One minute!" I shouted to the others, and went back into the house to examine the heaps of bones. "So that little monster eat all those beasts that escaped from the cellar?"

"Looksshhh that way," Shnoop said on my shoulder with a shrug.

I smiled.

"It was a rhetorical question. But I'm glad we agree. Let's go back."

I walked down the stairs and called out:

"Wolf, Mel, come over here. But be careful. Stop at the bottom of the steps first."

As soon as Wolf placed a careful foot on the first step, the transparent honey badger suddenly appeared out of nowhere and started snapping its jaws. The elite soldier reacted well. He jumped back in a flash and brought up his Whirlwind.

"Hold your fire!" I shouted.

The honey badger stared balefully at the outsiders, scraping a clawed foot on the ground. It paid absolutely no mind to me at all.

"Looks like we have a problem," I said. "Back off."

The pair stepped away, and the honey badger, turning its ass to the repelled invaders, kicked its back legs a couple of times like a dog trying to bury its shit, then proudly marched back into his territory.

I stepped down and walked to the others.

"What are you two doing here anyway?"

"Decided to have a little Safari," Potapov said. "The grounds aren't large, so Mel and I shot some game. None of it got away. But that strange beast gave us trouble." Andrei frowned, looking toward the mansion. He had the soul of a warrior, and he wasn't used to losing. "But I'll get to him in time!"

"I doubt that." I smiled. "Anyway, you don't need to. It looks like he's on our side. Well, on the family's side, anyway. I just have no idea how to explain to him who's who yet, and make him obey."

Andrei narrowed his eyes at the manor. "Well, what's in there, anyway?"

"Honestly, a dump that needs cleaning up. There's only one thing I know for sure — nobody but me will be able to live in this manor for now. On the other hand, at least we can be sure no more beasts will crawl out."

"No more beasts? Are there many in there?"

"Oh yeah, enough, believe me!"

"And you think that little critter can put down all of them?"

That made me laugh.

"Wolf! It's a honey badger. Of course he'll take 'em all down. And if he gets knocked out, he'll take a rest and come back and put them down again. That's what these critters are like." I scratched my head. "They remind me of Hunters."

Wolf's eyes widened. "Of who?"

"Oh, uh, nothing! Let's go. Anna must be sick of waiting. It's just..." I sighed heavily.

Wolf shot me a tense look. "What now?"

"Oh, just my greed taking hold and choking me! Tell me, how many beasts did you two kill and tear apart in your 'Safari'?"

"Um, maybe forty," Wolf said, scratching his temple. "Not counting the pups. Caramel is a great partner!"

The panther snorted in derision, but I could tell by her face that she was pleased with the praise.

"Exactly!" I said, waving a hand sadly. The imperials really screwed us with... I mean, they really overdid it with the barrier, and now I have to pay for it!"

"Well, no offense, Commander, but if I ran into that honey badger unawares, I'd be the first to want to put up a force field!"

"That's for sure," I agreed. "Come on, let's go."

Petrovich was standing by the gatehouse, somewhat absently rumpling the hem of his shirt and shifting from foot to foot. He stood next to the car.

"Your Lordship," the old man began awkwardly.

"Yes?"

"What about me, sir?"

"What do you mean?"

"Well, the Empire paid me to look after things, and now it looks like the dome is gone, and I'm no longer needed."

I smiled at him. "You a local man, Petrovich?"

"Well, I'm not from Galaxiton, I'm from Crow's Nest, which is currently in Ignatiev territory. But yeah, I'm from the same area."

"Can you make it a month without pay?"

"A month? Hell, longer than that. I have my Slayer pension too, and my pay was good. I just..." He hesitated. "I can't just sit around and do nothing."

"That's a good trait. Stay here for now, Petrovich. Wolf seems to have shot all the dangerous wildlife, but other stuff might show up. Do you have anything to fight with?"

"Of course!" The old Slayer smiled, ran off to one side and came back with a weighty double-barreled shotgun.

I grimaced.

"What the hell is that piece of crap?"

Petrovich's face fell.

"Wolf, can you give him something from our supplies?" I asked, turning to Andrei.

Potapov just laughed right in my face.

"Hell, boy, I'd trade some of our guns for that 'piece of crap.' It only looks bad. They're well-made machines. But it's been around a hundred years since they were made. A very individual gun, no doubt."

"Hey, you know your weapons!" the old man said with a smile.

"What do you mean?" I frowned.

Wolf explained. The thing was, that shotgun was an artifact itself. Unlike those magic rounds that we got from the would-be assassins, this shotgun was itself a reservoir of magical energy. It was loaded with ordinary rounds, but also had a container for jellies. And when it fired, some of that energy flowed into the shot or slug, significantly increasing its stopping power. Yes, they were still less lethal than special modern antimagic rounds. But nonetheless, in a pinch, the shotgun could be used against Gifted or beasts. Outside of Rifts, of course.

"May I?" I took the gun and looked at it curiously.

I'd never liked firearms. Never used them in my old world. Just couldn't trust that powder to work when I needed it to. But I could appreciate the craftsmanship.

"How come they stopped making them?"

"How can I put it..." Wolf scratched his bald head. Unlike me, he was an expert and enthusiast of firearms. I suspected he knew all there was to know about every weapon on Earth. "It's like when the crossbow replaced the bow," Potapov said. "Any farmer can fire a crossbow bolt and impale a knight in plate armor, trained for decades and equipped for a small fortune. Same situation here. Charge the shot and it doesn't matter how bad your aim is. One, two, three rifles, sure, they won't pierce your armor." Here he thought for a second. "Actually, I don't know about your armor at all. But I'm talking about your average Gifted here. Anyway, if fifteen fire at once, the average Gifted will have a tough time. That's why they switched to magical rounds, which..." He laughed grimly. "Which supposedly aren't available to just anyone, according to the officials. In any case, they cost so much money that the average farmer can't buy one. And he'd have to train his sharpshooting skills just to use it anyway, not like this shotgun."

"But!" Petrovich piped up, "I do know how to shoot! It's just that Sir Baron asked me to show him what I'd use against the beasts. So I did. But I have other guns too."

"Can you show me?" Wolf said, his ears pricking up.

"Not today," I said with a smile. "Let's go. And Petrovich! Do me a favor! Don't tell anyone the barrier is down. I'll tell the authorities that we've cut the power to it. Let them all think it's still up for three more days."

* * *

By law, government administrator Arcadius was to remain at his post for two more weeks with full pay, which I, of course, would be required to pay to him, in order to officiate the transfer of the manor into the new owner's hands. I instructed him to keep running things as normal. I would stop by, and two weeks later I would free him from his honored obligation.

That last didn't seem to make him happy. Judging by the reports, he had been living here for ten years, and had a house and two wives in the town. Liked to go fishing in his spare time. And he liked the life just fine. Anna somehow found all that out.

The cheerful fat man gave me the impression of an intelligent person. At least, my famed intuition had no objections to him. There was just one thing left — for Anna to check the accounts and make sure they all added up. I hate thieves. But if it worked out, we could consider taking him into service with the Galaxius family in his retirement from duties of the state. That was if no better candidate came along.

We drove along in the car and Anna bombarded me with questions, to all of which I answered the same.

"I'm handling. I'll tell you later."

She pouted, offended. But when I took a little

bag out of my backpack and offered it to her, she couldn't help but ask:

"What's this?" She smiled shyly.

"Family signet rings. I need to know which Families they belonged to."

Anna frowned.

"Is this what I think it is?"

"I don't know what you think it is," I said, my turn to frown. "But these people destroyed the entire Galaxius family."

Carefully, as if into the mouth of a snake, Anna put her hand in and took out a few time-darkened rings.

She immediately screwed up her eyes in concentration, then took out her tablet and typed on it, apparently comparing family crests.

"This is the Syominy family. The line officially died out around thirty years ago. This is the Kondratov family, stopped existing even earlier, almost forty years ago."

A few more rings.

"This is from the Stolypins, who fled the Empire almost a hundred years ago after being sentenced for treason. They live in the Dragon Empire now. Same again... Syominy... Another one... Kondratov again..."

The next ring she took out she brought closer to her eyes, chuckling as she looked at the crest without even glancing at her tablet.

"Let me guess. Another dead family?"

"Oh, no. Not at all. The Rasputin clan, one of the strongest Families in the Empire. Along with the Stolypins, they caused a revolution, but also had to flee seventy years ago. And they were sentenced to death for treason. Strange — they were already out of the country when the attack happened. And they were forbidden from setting foot in the Empire again! How did they end up here?" She raised her eyes to me. "And while the Stolypins may have been a weak family, the Rasputins were pure monsters! They almost did it! Alex, these are dangerous people to mess with. Very dangerous!"

A smile spread across my face.

"Keep on going, I want to know more."

But, after going through all my bags, she discovered no more families involved.

"There were seven families, I know that for sure," I said with a frown.

"Well, the simplest assumption is that they weren't involved in the fighting. Or they were the weakest." She looked at me meaningfully.

"Or the most cunning," I said, continuing her thought. "Who managed to either clean up after themselves or just avoid the fight in the first place."

"Your assumption rings truer," Anna said, nodding. "I did try to find information from public sources. Of course, it's been a few decades now, but still, there should have been some information left somewhere. There just isn't any. A short note — seven Families eliminated some rebels. That's all. Everything else written on it has been thoroughly scrubbed. I couldn't find anything."

"Sucks." I scratched my head.

"Sure does," Anna nodded.

"Well, at least I know two of the culprits," I said, leaning back in my seat and smiling in satisfaction.

I felt a pleasant warmth spreading through my body. This was one of those perfect moments in life — when the Hunter caught a trail. And if the Hunter catches a trail, then he reaches and kills whatever beast is at the other end of it, that is, of course, if he's a good Hunter. And I'm not just a good Hunter — I'm a damn good Hunter!

*   *   *

One of King's numerous hideouts
Somewhere on the outskirts of Irkutsk

There was a commotion outside the doors. Two guards jumped out of hidden niches, charged with energy and ready for battle.

King charged his armor and pushed the two maidens he had just been enjoying in front of him.

The noise subsided, and a guard poked his head inside.

"Sorry, sir! We're having a little trouble."

"What is it?" King backed away.

He very much liked living. He had no desire whatsoever to die.

"We've driven them off. I think it was snakes."

"You think?!"

"Four guards are dead. I saw with my own

eyes, they were fighting snakes from the Rifts. But as soon as they killed the things, their bodies disappeared right before our eyes!"

The head mob boss of Irkutsk grimaced. "Who died?"

"Four inner circle guards, sir."

"The hell with them!" The gang leader waved a careless hand. "Strengthen the guard. Quadruple its strength! Hire mercenaries, pay them any money! I need to be better guarded, more guards! Stronger!" At the last word he broke into a hysterical shriek. His eye even started to twitch.

In the meantime, a young man sat nearby in a black car, digging into a burger with gusto. He swapped jokes with his bald driver, and at the same time watched what was happening with the help of his invisible pet. When the show was over, the boy smiled widely and said:

"Always keep your enemies on guard!" — which earned him a confused look from the driver.

After that, he just waved a hand and kept on chattering about nothing.

INTERLUDE: SHNOOP

Past life

"HOW DO YOU PUT UP with that asshole?" Old Mac mumbled, trying to pull some eggshell out of his thick beard.

"Takeshhh one to know one!" came a hiss from above, and another egg fell down on his head.

This time the old Hunter was expecting it. He caught the egg in midair and launched it deftly at the happily giggling shnark in the distance. Unsurprisingly, the egg disappeared again and then suddenly reappeared, heading straight back toward the Hunter. Mac caught it again and fired it back at the cocky critter.

I smiled as I watched the spectacle. For all his grumbling, Mac loved me like a son, and that extended to my little pet Shnoop too. But they never missed a chance to needle each other. I watched the inhuman reactions of the old Hunter against the shadow-walking little shnark. I'd long ago stopped keeping score, but I'd say Shnoop was in the lead with that egg in the beard.

I sipped my warm spiced ale brewed by Mother Talga, the hospitable hostess of a large inn called Hunter's Joy. Mother Talga was not unfamiliar with marketing — the inn was on the outskirts of the city, almost beneath the walls of the Hunters' fortress. By virtue of our profession, we were rarely home. But when we were back, we tended to have pockets full of gold yearning to be spent. And then the very best casks of ale were heaved up from the establishment's famous cellar, the kind the ordinary citizenry couldn't buy. Mother Talga demanded a king's ransom for them, but nobody objected. Nobody was forced to buy it. Have normal beer if you want, or pay for something nicer. Anyway, it was no secret that successful Hunters (and most Hunters were either successful or dead) could afford it.

Right then there were just five Hunters in the fortress, not counting the mandatory 'defensive dozen,' or along with the Grand Master — 'devil's dozen.' The defensive dozen was, as a rule, made up of Hunters taking a break for rest and relaxation at home, or young ones who had only just made the rank of Hunter. It's almost impossible to keep a real Hunter in one place for long.

At that moment, all five of us were gathered. Wizened beasts of various ages and appearances, but all united by one thing — each of us was, without exaggeration, worth at least a hundred men in any army in the world. And some of us — I looked at humble Dan, an ageless man who looked like an eternal student and at the same time some sort of bum, — could put down a thousand troops without batting an eye.

But that was all theoretical, of course.

It was due to their strength and abilities that Hunters always remained neutral and avoided fighting ordinary people. Unless, of course, the issue began to concern the Brotherhood of Hunters.

I smiled. Once, the northern wildlings decided for some reason that a lone outpost of Hunters would be easy and rich prey for them. They knew for sure that over ten people were in the camp, with a sizable supply of produce and alcohol. What can you do? Hunters are provident people, and if they decide to keep a supply, they make it a big one.

Trouble was, the wildlings didn't know that one of those people was Dan, who had nearly frozen his ass off chasing a Marble Yeti around snowy mountain slopes, and was now warming up inside and out by the fire. Half-drunk Dan, who the guards almost dragged up onto the walls, couldn't even figure out which direction his enemies were coming from. As he told me later, he wasn't just seeing double, but quadruple. In the end he came up with nothing smarter than to start swinging wildly, attacking in an area. Since then, only one road has led to the far outpost. The second is now blocked with tons of boulders, tombs for the unfortunate morons who wanted to drink on our tab.

Mac swore again, and went back to his pride and joy — his thick beard, strangely at contrast with his smooth bald head. At the same time, he was still looking from side to side in search of my pet. Old Mac was a legend. Grand Master Wulf himself treated him with respect. One could only guess at his real age. Direct questions on the subject got you only a middle finger, and veiled hints were ignored with a smirk.

"Shhhhurrrprishhe!" Shnoop said, appearing with a basket of what must have been hundreds of eggs pouring out over the sides.

Mac just blinked, and the entire waterfall of eggs disappeared in a blue flash.

"Bashhhtarrd!" Shnoop wailed, reappearing in the distance.

His fur smoked slightly. Guess he got hit too.

I clapped my hands.

"Alright, that's enough! Wrap it up. Mother!" I raised a hand. Of course, the owner of the establishment served the Hunters personally. "One tub of ice cream. You have some, right?"

"For you, kiddo, we always have it." The stout old woman smiled.

At over two hundred and sixty pounds and a height of five feet and five inches, she looked like she should be rolling around. All the same, she was very fast and agile for her weight. Although she gave the impression of a kind grandmother, she was no simple woman. She definitely had a Gift. And considering how she sometimes joked with Old Mac about things the rest of us just didn't understand, she had been alive for quite a long time.

"Nobody eats it except you anyway," Mother said, staring into space. "Except that little critter of yours, I meant."

"Thanks, Mother," I said with a noble nod. "Take it, Shnoop."

My unhappy, but no longer smoking pet appeared for an instant and grabbed the bowl in his two paws, stuck his tongue out at Old Mac and then disappeared back into the shadows.

"Bring the bowl back!" the innkeeper shouted strictly.

"Sshhhhure will!" came the answer from somewhere in the ether.

Shnoop had enough trouble with pronunciation as it was, but now he was talking with his mouth full.

I smiled warmly.

Many people were still shocked by my pet. Practically everyone considered him useless. Or worse — a pest. But I just couldn't imagine what life had been like without him anymore.

It was so long ago...

* * *

The first time I met the cheeky little shnark was when I received an order to tear down a nest of rock gargoyles in the ruins of an old temple after they started carrying off cattle and people from a nearby village.

That was many, many years ago.

I already had a reputation in certain circles for breaking all my weapons, but that time I set my own personal record. Three broken swords against four enemies — that was a lot, even for me. But they were damn strong monsters! That meant I wasn't going to make a profit on the job. Oh, well — at least I'd earned some rep!

However, when I saw the stone egg laid by the monsters, I brightened up a little. Those beasts reproduce very, very rarely and are almost impossible to tame alive, but if you raise one from the shell, you can train it to guard your house. They were dumb as a post, but rich rulers paid big money for them. After all, it's very hard, practically impossible, for an ordinary person to deal with an invulnerable beast like that.

I could already taste my profits as I climbed the column up to the half-destroyed roof. But as I reached out my hands, the egg suddenly disappeared. From the side I heard a hiss of glee. And, out of the corner of my eye, I saw a shnark. It darted out of the way of my throwing knife. Two spells also failed to hit it. Then his happy cackling faded into the distance, carrying away the only thing that would have kept my account in the black.

Shnarks had a reputation a practically harmless, but very pesky creatures. Precious little was known about them. It was believed that they were the inhabitants of another dimension or world. No scientific explanation had been found for their ability to teleport through the shadows. They hadn't been studied much at all, for the simple reason that most living shnarks were only seen from behind and afar while they carried something away, cackling with glee.

I learned all I could about them in the Fortress library when the stubborn little bastard started to follow me around for some reason, and behaving based on some strange code all of his own. He didn't take valuable things from me like money, weapons or equipment. But a pint of ale, a chunk of meat straight from my plate, or my potential loot, which by his logic wasn't mine yet — he saw that as his god-given right.

On some missions, he took the loot from under my nose at the worst times. What hadn't I tried to stop him? I'd set traps, placed wards.

Hell! I even went to see that old witch who gave me a repelling charm that she claimed would keep the shnark at a distance. I always suspected witches were fakers, but this time I confirmed it personally when the cocky shnark stole the charm from me and ate it right in front of me, grinning absently all the while. Back then I still entertained the thought that that sort of thing might kill him, but little did I know...

Actually, for a few years he was a malevolent spirit in my life, who caused me occasional but significant trouble. At some point I just started to accept it, only trying to resist out of habit. But he seemed to take that as some kind of game. And all was well, until one night I woke up to something scratching me on the chest with sharp claws, hissing something incomprehensible. My Hunter's reflexes took over — I grabbed the dirty little rat, which turned out to be the shnark. But it didn't do anything, didn't try to run away or disappear.

It just hung there in my tightly clenched fist. In surprise, I loosened my grip. The thing hissed and tried to say something to me. After a couple of minutes I realized what he was trying to say:

"Resssshhhhhcue!"

"Uh, rescue..? Rescue who? Where?" I frowned.

And then the little critter really surprised me. A misty portal suddenly appeared at floor level, a little over a yard tall. The shnark dropped down beside it and waved his little arms, still hissing. He managed to make himself a little clearer, and I made out the words:

"Thissshhh wayyy!"

"Are you sure?" I narrowed my eyes.

The critter kept on hissing and waving his arms. But now he was trembling too. That portal had to be draining a lot of his strength.

I decided not to hold off to put on my gear. It

was all I needed, for that little bastard to croak! For some reason, instead, my mind focused on the thought of helping him. Picking up my sword lying nearby and climbing over the buxom village girl who was sharing the bed with me that night, I dove through the portal into the unknown. As I went, I thought — *where's your common sense now, Xander?*

Around me stretched a gray world bereft of stars and sun. To the left and right lay a gray desert of short, waving grass, but I felt no wind. Boulders large and small were piled up, forming something like houses. And at that moment, amid those little houses, chaos reigned supreme.

A huge gray shadow pursued the little brothers of 'my' shnark. And they could do nothing about it — the monster moved instantly, just like them. Any it reached it simply devoured.

"Reshhhcue!" he whined again at my feet.

Honestly, I don't remember much of the fight. I recall one thing — it took all of my skill and a lot of luck. It was the first time I'd ever fought a semi-corporeal spirit. I had to use everything I knew and all the tricks I'd been saving for a rainy day. I think the battle went on for a long time, too. Felt to me like I lost a few years of life that day, draining myself dry by using spells that I had planned to never use again in my life. I hoped that was the last time.

At the end of the battle I lost consciousness, but later awoke to a multitude of blue eyes staring at me — the surviving shnarks. When they saw I was awake, they beamed. Each of them started to bring me 'gifts.' One brought an old coin, another a shard of bright glass, another a ring with a huge diamond. The biggest diamond I'd ever seen!

It seemed that each of these items had a certain value to the gift-givers. I swept all the riches into a pile, intuitively realizing that it would offend them to refuse. Only I had nowhere to put the stuff. As if understanding the problem, one of them brought an old worn handbag into which I put all the gifts into. At the sight of me accepting their 'gifts,' they hissed with glee. And one of the shnarks, the one that had been following me around, translated the hissing:

"Thhhha-a-annnksshh!"

"No problem," I said, standing up. "Mind if I get back now?"

This time the portal they cast was a little bigger. I climbed through it and came out face-first into a pond, crashing through the ice that had covered the now far from warm autumn water.

There was a self-satisfied giggle above me. I swam out swearing, but took solace in the fact that it woke me up at least. When I reached the shore I looked back and ground my teeth, shouting into the dark:

"You damn prankster! Couldn't you have sent me back to my warm bed? You owe me one, don't you?"

In response came another happy cackle, and no more answer. At least he didn't send me to the other side of the world, I guess. The village and tavern was a few miles' walk away, barefoot through the fine snow and piercing cold wind.

* * *

I smiled again.

Honestly, after all that, I thought the critter would make himself useful. Like hell! I got nothing close to gratitude for him. The 'games' went on for another year and a half, and I accepted them with a certain amount of apathy.

But after that year and a half was when the first serious shift in my life took place.

* * *

Who knew there'd be so many of those monsters?! And all because they'd raised their own King. I told them they had to hurry. But the locals said the Lair had existed for only two years, and that it took more than ten to grow a King. Either they didn't notice it soon enough or this pack had already arrived here with a young King from somewhere else.

Anyway, after putting down the outer guards and the powerful soldiers of the 'inner circle,' we ran into a mighty, almost invulnerable entity that started to force us out of the lair.

Thank the gods that I'd brought Dan with me for some dumb reason. Actually, it was because he'd been drinking for two weeks straight, so I thought he could use some fresh air. As for the job, it was for pure meleers, or 'universals' like me, which Dan wasn't. But right now, it really helped.

It was hard to carry two wounded while running away from an invulnerable monster snapping at my heels. Yeah, maybe Dan couldn't hurt it, but somehow he was able to scare it. Every flash he cast could have burned dozens of people to a crisp, but all it did to this monster was stop it for a moment.

It worked once, twice, three times. But then the enemy realized the flashes weren't harming it, and it charged through the next one with the firm intention of crushing us into paste. At that point, I really thought it was the end. Lowering the boys to the ground, I nodded to Dan and said:

"Get out of here!"

He understood, crossed his arms at his chest in our ritual gesture of farewell and respect, then grabbed the bodies and charged for the exit.

As for me, I stood up, trying to give them time to get away, and promising myself that if I made it out of this, then I would always, I repeat — ALWAYS — trust my gut. If only I'd spent a little more time training. Well, at least Dan now knew for sure what he was dealing with here. And in a maximum of a week, better trained brothers would come and nail this beast to the floor. All I could do now was buy them some time.

Sword gone, axe gone, all my knives gone. All I could do was try to dodge its blows. But my strength wasn't unlimited. And I was still weak then, no denying it. At some point a blow caught my arm and shattered it, hurling away my last short sword and pinning me on my back.

The beast spat, bit, fought. Its saliva melted through the stone around us. This was it — my time to die. But then I saw a tousled shnark appear beside my sword lying on the ground. It hissed: "Xxanderr, Alexshhh!", and disappeared with the sword.

The next moment the monster shook, then fell down dead on top of me.

As it later turned out, the shnark had traveled through its thick skin into its huge body and stabbed the creature in the heart with a surgeon's precision. The trouble was, the little guy hadn't considered that the insides of that bastard were a real-life acid factory.

He died instantly.

I barely managed to make out his tiny little soul against the huge and powerful soul of the King, which was trying to push itself forward. And again, without understanding why, I released the soul of the powerful beast, which could have been a powerful soldier in my army, and grabbed at the little smudge that was the shnark, pulling him into my inner vault.

Then came the first oddity — the shnark didn't dissolve into my ocean of souls, but remained on the surface as if staying at the ready and trying to be close at hand.

* * *

It took me four years and untold money and stress to reincarnate Shnoop in this world. I'm not sure why I felt the need, but I never once regretted it. Once a confirmed lone wolf, now I couldn't imagine life without the little bastard.

"What the hell!?" Old Mac turned up his nose and pulled his foot out from under the table. His boot was splattered with a stinking horse apple.

And another joyful giggle from nowhere.

"And Shnoop takes a clear lead! "You're getting old, buddy!" I laughed.

Mac muttered a curse at me and tramped over to the door to wash the dirt from his boot, and Shnoop appeared in front of me. Carefully, he placed in front of me a plate of half-eaten roast goose and a dead cat, then lovingly looked into my eyes with all four of his big blues and asked rapturously:

"W-w-wwwaaaant?!"

CHAPTER 19

WITH A SILENT CHUCKLE, both hands behind my back like a drill sergeant, I walked back and forth before my lined up raid group and looked into their faces. There was some displeasure on their faces, but no confusion or apathy, at least.

Three mages — two girls and one guy, and they all happened to be viscountesses and a viscount. Of course, they'd all heard of Galaxius. It had been a long time now since I'd heard 'lowly baron.' And these mages were class-five Slayers too, higher-ranking than their more noble brethren and my friends.

"Alright," I said, finally stopping. "Have you all studied the details of the Rift?"

"Yes, sir!" Duke Androsov said, playing his side of the game with a smile.

"What's the main challenge of this Rift?"

Here, Helga spoke up:

"The fact that it starts with a narrow passageway. And whatever the Slayers do, the octopuses manage to meld together and regenerate."

I smiled and nodded.

"Right."

The 'octopuses' were what the Slayers called a species of slime that had, unlike their younger cousins, a hard skin that was practically impenetrable to spells. But inside that skin they could roll around as much as they wanted, and they usually fired long tentacles out of it, which was what made them seem like octopuses.

And they could only be killed by hitting their core inside the jelly-like body. Another trick up their sleeve was the ability to meld. That's right — you cut off the first row of tentacles and the wounded monster backs off, then melds into the body of a comrade. Then there are two cores in one body, and the monster is twice as large and much harder to take down.

And yes, Helga was right — the place did begin with a small room with a single passageway with enough space for only two Slayers to fight shoulder to shoulder. And from the other end of the corridor came the octopuses, like a cork in a bottleneck, sooner or later forcing the Slayers back to the Rift.

"Can I ask a question?" Androsov asked, raising his arm like a school kid.

I nodded.

"Yeah, sure."

"I understand why you brought me along. I'm a Healer, after all. But why do we need mages if their skins are impenetrable to their Gifts?"

"Take out your tablets," I smiled.

They all did as they were told, and I sent them all a video recorded by one of the last Slayer groups to visit this Rift.

"Now watch closely."

The screen showed the scene of a furious bloodbath. This was the moment when the Center had decided firmly that it had to close this 'problematic' Rift, and sent ten class-three Slayers there at once. Real beasts themselves, but still human. The entire video on the site went on for almost eight hours. That was how long the group of Slayers butchered their way through the jelly-like group of monsters until, finally, having taken no losses but completely drained their armor, the Slayers left the Rift. I didn't send them the full video, just a small clip.

"Fifteen second mark, watch."

"I don't see anything!" Androsov said, voicing the confusion of them all.

"Look again."

They watched it again.

"We still don't see anything!" The count frowned.

"Look again!"

Helga sighed. "How long do we have to stare at this thing?"

"As long as it takes," I said, rolling my eyes

and giving them a hint: "Look further back! At the third row of the monsters."

"It can't meld," one of the viscountesses said.

"Your name?" I asked interestedly.

"Irina Troyanskaya."

"Excellent, Irina. And why can't it meld?"

She looked at the screen again. But then the viscount beat her to it.

"It was just burned by a fireball. It's trying to meld with another, but it can't seem to do it."

"And now go to two minutes and thirty-five seconds, please."

Irina answered again, more confidently this time.

"And this time it was hit with an ice spear right after the tentacles were cut off, and the result's the same."

"How did you even spot that?" Androsov asked in wonderment.

"By looking with my eyes, not my bare ass... ahem, forgive me, Your Highness." I chuckled.

No need to explain to them that this was my job. I was sure that the analysts at the Center had studied this video. But how much experience did the analysts have, twenty years? What was that next to my decades of experience as a Hunter? And I had been a damn good Hunter in my day. So I just shrugged.

"Guess I got lucky."

At that, Androsov laughed too loud for comfort.

"Sure, sure, lucky! I believe you."

"Enough talk," I murmured, smiling back at him. "Let's move on. Do you get the idea?"

Now Helga stepped forward, blushing. Apparently she was so used to being first in everything that she was embarrassed to have missed that detail.

"The melee fighters break the skin. The mages cauterize the wound. And we finish them off. Right?"

"Got it, Helga!" I clapped.

At first the girl smiled in satisfaction, but then frowned and crossed her arms at her chest as if suddenly remembering that she had an image to maintain, and was supposed to be treating me with indifference.

"And that's why accuracy is top priority for us. Accuracy, ladies and gentlemen!" I looked thoughtfully at the mages. "Also, if you hit me in the back with a fire ball or ice spear, then I won't die right away, and believe me, I'll make sure you live to regret it too. Got that?"

"Got it," the mages said, suddenly lowering their eyes.

"On the other hand, Khrulyov himself chose you as his best Elementalists out of twenty-five people."

That brought smiles to their faces.

"Pavel, Helga. You know me and I know you. Don't run in front of daddy into the frying pan."

"That makes you daddy, huh?" Smolin asked, laughing good-naturedly.

I looked around.

"Do you see another raid leader here?"

Pavel wiped the grin off his face.

"I do not, Commander!"

Haha, he was still messing with me. I smiled at him.

"What role are you going to play?" Helga asked, crossing her arms.

"Me? Guess you could call me a universal soldier."

Six pairs of eyes swiveled to look at me.

"You'll see it in action soon enough. To the cars!"

*　*　*

The Rift was reinforced. Not to the same extent as the Anthill, of course, but the exits were covered by a full-fledged platoon from the Imperial Army, complete with heavy weapons. As a rule, the local forces had been able to handle the octopuses that broke out so far. The Center didn't forget to periodically send Slayers inside to 'cull' the population, but the Rift was at that moment rated 'currently unclosable,' so eruptions of monsters could occur any time. To prevent them from wandering around the area, the decision had been made to build an outpost here.

We stopped by some mobile rest houses. I climbed out of the car and was greeted by the local lieutenant.

"Good health, Your Lordship!" he said with a swift salute. "Decided to cut down the bastards' numbers, eh?" He smiled.

The young man was just a little older than me. Not long out of the academy, I guessed — eyes gleaming, hands itching to act.

"Hello, soldier!" I nodded at him. "I have an idea for closing the Rift. But we'll see how it goes."

"Closing it?" The fighter's eyes widened. "But I heard..."

"You talk a lot, soldier!" Wolf said suddenly, approaching from the side and earning a look of distrust from the lieutenant. "Slayers have a job to do, and they do it. Your job isn't to think, it's to cover their backs."

The lieutenant looked Wolf up and down, now returned to his previous fitness, and for some reason decided not to object. He just nodded and walked away to his soldiers.

I chuckled, looked at Potapov and shook my head. He suddenly smiled.

"They're bored. So they're dicking around. We went through it a lot, many times. Let 'em get too relaxed and they'll end up sent back to their folks in body bags."

I waited for my group to assemble around me. Gave brief instructions. Mostly just to make sure they knew the score.

Then we walked into the Rift.

The entrance cavern was empty. Before us yawned a single dark passageway. This particular cave had no gleaming moss or other sources of light. We all had flashlights, just in case. The main lighting was provided by Viscount Matochkin, bearer of a fiery Gift, who cast a lit orb above our heads that provided surprisingly good light.

"Wait!" I shouted, and sent Shnoop forward.

They shot sidelong glances at me, but said nothing. For the look of it, I closed my eyes and sat down on the floor in a meditative pose.

There was an annoyed hiss on one side. I'd bet my family ring it was Helga. I suppressed a smile and kept on watching.

No labyrinth of caves in here. Actually, this was one of the simplest Rifts I'd ever seen. It was the shape of a dumbbell, or more a club. The farthest cave opened up a little, and the spot we were in now was like the counterweight at the end of the pommel. And the wood between it, a single broad corridor that our enemies were already crawling through towards us.

* * *

As for how those same enemies came to be — that was a fascinating sight. There was a huge amorphous mass in the large cave at the end, and right before my eyes — well, before Shnoop's, really, — it began to belch out more and more new enemies, which immediately went crawling into the passageway toward us.

It seemed that in their usual state, all these monsters just chilled out in the same body, crawling out and taking on separate forms only in times of need. And when the main mass got too large, it divulged individuals to go raiding outside the Rift. Interesting creatures. I'd seen something like them in my past world too.

I nearly groaned in disappointment. Shame I had all my raid to worry about. As if it weren't enough to just have to think of a way to kill our enemies, now I had to think of a way that wouldn't look too strange to witnesses. Not my thing. But what can you do..?

The goal of the battle was simple — break through into the main cave and put down the big bad boss.

"Contact!" I barked, jumping to my feet and baring my sword. "Get ready!"

Androsov whistled. Helga muttered something with a shake of her head. These rich trust-fund babies had decided I needed a better weapon, and had tried to give me all manner of gifts. Helga even brought me a sword of Balean steel. Nothing unusual. Although no, that's not true. Its white gleaming steel could have easily held all my energy. But the price tag bothered me — a hundred thousand. It was one thing to accept a tux, but quite another to accept a weapon like that. So I refused. I tried to be gentle about it. But it seemed to have upset Helga anyway, although she tried to show no sign of it. I could get my hands on my own weapons.

So I just brought Aquila with me, trying not to reveal it until the battle started. I got some more throwing knives from Arkhip too, the ones I'd learned to use as a kind of grenade.

The blade of the sword, already gleaming with the souls overflowing it, which I still hadn't taken full account of, shone even brighter when I charged it with energy.

"Whoa!" I heard from behind me.

"What kind of steel is that?"

The mages discussed my weapon in a whisper, and I smiled, pleased with the effect it had. I do like to surprise people!

Shnoop watched, and I counted. The first 'wave' of octopuses was already streaming through the tunnel. At a glance it looked like there were more than twenty — twenty to hold us in the narrow tunnel and still replace front-line wounded, letting them slink away and merge back into the collective to recover.

But we didn't walk into the tunnel. Why would we? The monsters would reach us eventually. We spread out in a semicircle and waited for them to get to us. I stood in the middle, Helga and Smolin to my right and left, the mages behind us, Androsov behind me and ready to heal.

The beasts squeezed out of the narrow tunnel like toothpaste out of the tube. I nearly lost my cool — would the others be able to hold them back and keep them from reaching the casters? I moved forward to take the first blow on myself.

Damn, these beasts were quick! Tentacles flew to the left and right. Caramel darted around nearby, cleaning up after me. The mages totally missed the first one we wounded. It darted between its comrades and disappeared behind them, no doubt merging with one of its comrades.

"Shit!" I shouted, not searching too long for a

suitable expression. "Don't mess up! Pay attention, God damn it!"

"Sorry," came a woman's voice from behind me.

I didn't have time to do more — I was fighting and still watching the inactive mothermass in the corner of my eye.

We managed to take down the next one we wounded. It pushed out a little to the side, attacking Helga, who dodged and cut off its tentacles.

And then it headed toward the passageway. But I stood in its path, sweeping my sword and depriving it of a couple more tentacles.

I shouted:

"Hit it!"

And hit it they did, hard. Good thing they missed me. The beast span, disoriented. I drove my sword into its core. The creature screeched and died.

"Just like that. Keep it up, guys."

The mothermass still did nothing, but a tremble passed over its surface like a nervous tremor.

When we finished off another two more octopuses the same way, one after another, the mass livened up and started spitting out new creatures — exactly three. This thing could do math. Alright, the picture was looking clear.

I squeezed a red jelly in my hand, although I still had plenty of my own energy left, and summoned half a dozen bugs at the other end of the corridor. The distance was great and the souls were strong, so I was knocked off balance for a second.

* * *

"Alex!" Androsov shouted in alarm from behind me.

Within a flash the Healer's energy surged into me, instantly restoring my power. I chuckled and cut off two more tentacles of the enemy attacking me. I barked again:

"Hit it!"

Two fire balls slammed into the beast, and I finished it off like before. One of them had hit me, but I felt just fine.

Healers are damn handy to have around! I thought to myself.

"Stop!" I shouted to Androsov, who was still pouring energy into me. "That's enough."

He nodded, looking at me strangely, tensely. Like he always did, actually. I suspected that the far too attentive young man had noticed some inconsistencies in our energy levels, but now wasn't the time.

My bugs attacked the flank. I'd chosen the right critters for the job. Their mandibles deftly bit through the tentacles reaching toward them, and the octopuses themselves didn't seem capable of changing their strategy. They first tried to use their tentacles to sweep their victim off its feet, and then somehow sharpened the end of a tentacle and tried to stab through their prey. But the big beetles didn't knock down easy, and from what I could see it was a struggle to get through their shells too.

The enemies opposite us seemed to get second thoughts, and backed away slightly. Helga wiped sweat from her forehead and shifted a lock of white hair out of her face. Her blue eyes gleamed.

"Do you hear that? Something's happening over there!"

"I don't hear anything," I said as convincingly as I could, watching the mothermass again.

It looked as if in a stupor. Waves began to pass across the body, but it did nothing. The bugs pressed on, but it still did nothing. I waited to see what it would do.

In the end, the beast made a decision. It started to haphazardly spit out new 'spawn,' shrinking itself at a rapid pace.

"Now," I whispered only to Shnoop, and a heavy weight suddenly lifted from my backpack.

The bomb was like a kettlebell, and no wonder — it weighed fifty-five pounds. For a second Shnoop arose above the mothermass and then, like a dive-bomber, flew in and dropped his bomb with a cackle of glee.

"Take that, sshhhithead!"

The shockwave shouldn't hit us, but I didn't want to take the risk. So I barked:

"Everyone out of the Rift!"

The others obeyed — good thing I made it very clear to them that any order I gave had to be followed right away. They all jumped out without question. Then one of the viscountesses tripped over a rock. I grabbed her by the collar of her jacket and threw her out. Then, like a true captain, I left the ship last. The Rift, I mean.

Once I got outside, I ran almost head-first into the barrel of a high-caliber machine gun, which Wolf was holding up with a slight effort. I raised my head and smiled:

"You like big cannons."

"Of course." The bald man grinned. "Are you finished, Commander?"

"We've only just started." I smiled and looked at my watch, waiting just fifteen seconds. In that time, the shock wave should have passed through the whole tunnel. I just hoped I hadn't collapsed the whole thing like a house of cards.

My fighters said nothing, just stared at me dumbly, trying to figure out what was going on in my head, their eyes full of so many questions. But none of them said a thing — smart cookies. Maybe they'd be some use yet.

After counting out the fifteen seconds, I nodded.

"If I don't come out after ten seconds, come in after me. Is that clear?"

They all nodded. I jumped in.

There were some whole, some wounded beasts wandering around in the entrance cavern, but every last one was at least scorched and disoriented. I had ten seconds to take them out without witnesses seeing it, and I used that time to the full. Generously expending energy from my stores, I started throwing knives at the speed of a machine gun, aiming at weak spots.

When, after ten seconds, Helga jumped through first — of course, — there were only three healthy enemies left in the entrance cave and one wounded. Mel caught up to the wounded one and held it, slashing with a paw inside it and scraping its core, killing it.

Then the others came in too. Distracted for a second, I let them finish off the two beasts themselves. Then I went back to watching my movie by director Shnoop, famous in certain exclusive circles. The monster looked bad — it was twisting, bulging, several blobs falling off it. Only it looked like the blobs had no inner cores, so they just fell to the floor as scraps of inanimate flesh. The explosion hadn't destroyed all the living enemies that had already separated. Even a couple of the beetles were still alive, snapping their mandibles and still chasing after wounded octopuses.

"Forward!" I shouted, and ran into the corridor, knowing that there were still five octopuses left in there.

We worked our way through them slowly but surely. By then one beetle had been taken down and the other I released by hand, mentally thanking it for its service.

"Attention! Prep artillery!" I shouted, which brought an unexpected laugh from Androsov. "Fire at the spot I hit!"

I took my knives in both hands and sent them flying into the monster one after another. I threw just as well with both hands. The others weren't sleeping, and a second later two fiery swords at once were driven into the gap I'd opened up in the mothermass, followed by a spear of flame.

"Again!" I shouted, and threw two more knives.

The others fired again. After the third volley I saw that the beast's skin was starting to melt, failing to hold its form.

"Now light it up with everything you have!" I shouted in satisfaction, moving aside out of the firing line.

They really did light it up. The onslaught of casting went on for five minutes, transforming the creature into a part burned, part frozen lump, something like a heart still beating weakly inside it.

"Ladies first..." I said, gesturing gallantly to Helga.

"What do you mean?" she asked with a frown.

I let the smile slip from my face and barked at her:

"Finish it off!"

With no more delay, Helga jumped forward, raising her magnificent sword. I appreciated the girl's potential once again. And once again found myself asking the question — who was she, anyway?

The beast's heart literally exploded into pieces. A fresh breeze of energy flowed into us, telling us the Rift was closed.

Then Helga looked in surprise at her hand. Her ring had changed, burning bright red. Nice! Just what I wanted!

CHAPTER 20

IT HAD BEEN THREE DAYS ALREADY since I removed the barrier from my mansion. If I understood how things were done in this world correctly, that meant the trouble was about to start.

Before now, my property had been under the stewardship of the Emperor, but now an heir had appeared, me, and claimed his rights, and that... really sucked for him, in a way.

My property could now be taken away, plain and simple, and the thieves might be considered in the right if they could cook up a decent excuse. Nobody cared about weak aristocrats. If you can't defend what you have, then you shouldn't have it. There's nobody to do your job for you. That was why Wolf brought me here, and then went back to the Center himself, annoyed and offended by my refusal to let him take part in the upcoming slaughterfest.

Ugh. He really gave me an earful, he wanted to stay that badly. He even went so far as to say that it was his job and he didn't give a damn about the danger. But unlike him, I gave a shit about his life. After all, I didn't have all that many loyal people. In the end I managed to stick to my guns and stay in my manor alone.

Now I was walking through it and wondering if I did the right thing. What was the chance that there'd be an attack today? It would make sense for them to attack, but I had no way to know for sure.

King, that bastard, had managed to hide himself better since the attack from my snakes, and they couldn't reach him again. And I wasn't even trying to kill him then, just scare him and remind him who he was dealing with. He was turning out to be a bigger coward than I suspected. Hmm.

Damn, it really would suck if nobody turned up today. I couldn't wander around here much longer, and I'd given my bodyguard only today off. I suggested a week, but he refused.

In the meantime I tried to make friends with the honey badger, and learned one thing for sure — he was a total asshole. He just ignored me and kept roaming around the house. Sometimes he went down into the dungeons to kill something tasty and top up his energy.

As it happens, I'd studied him and found out

how he'd even managed to go on existing in this situation. There was no big secret to it, just a link to a very old and interesting artifact. So old that it had outlived its intended lifespan and broken. And now it was only performing at ten percent of its old power.

The artifact had been set into the wall in the master bedroom on the second floor, so that it was always kept safe, but it seemed time hadn't been kind to it. Or maybe somebody had just damaged it. No way to find out now.

If the honey badger didn't find another reliable energy source, then it was done for, there were no other options. Half a year more at the most and it'd be gone. The artifact would stop working entirely.

Alas, I was no artificer, and couldn't fix it. Even if I was one, there was no guarantee it could be fixed. It might have taken a couple of years just to research and study it. Different technologies, in the end. The only thing I was sure it used were runes, as Shnoop had shown me. Runes that were entirely unknown to me. There was only one way the creature could survive — by attaching itself to me, but the dumb cretin didn't seem to understand that. I mulled all this over as I sat in my living room, on a rather large and elegant sofa marred with blotches of mold and rot.

After figuring out this honey badger, I'd bring in a whole brigade of cleaners. Expensive ones. I really wasn't used to this kind of filth.

"Shhhhon of a bitchhh!" Shnoop groaned,

appearing on my shoulder and starting to swear profusely about a certain transparent beast.

"He found you?" I asked sympathetically, stroking him to calm him down.

The honey badger burst into the room in pursuit of his rival, or whatever he thought Shnoop was. When he saw the little guy sitting on my shoulder, he immediately lost interest in him. Although he didn't go far and kept casting angry looks back at Shnoop from time to time. Or he just wanted us to think so — he kept looking strangely toward me.

A real weird cat, but we'd seen weirder.

The honey badger didn't have free reign for long. After just a couple of minutes, Caramel burst into the room and flew at him. The panther was staging a real hunt on the honey badger. Not to kill him, but just to shake him up.

Just in case, I had told the honey badger that if anything happened to her, then I'd force him into service with me and then take him to the vet to be fixed. Shnoop liked that idea, but for the first time the honey badger seemed taken aback, and started to get the picture.

When Caramel arrived, he had to turn transparent again and disappeared into the bowels of the manor.

An angry woman is a terrifying sight! The panther ran after him to pick up the trail. And then Shnoop left to go scouting. He was my eyes today.

As if it weren't enough that I had to keep an

eye on the woods to make sure nobody suddenly came out to give us a nasty surprise, I also had to do the same with the basement. Would it be better to just booby trap it?

Left alone, I stared out through the window in deep thought. Even if nobody showed up today, I could just think of it as a rest day. Sometimes it's nice to just sit and do nothing.

When the day ended, and then the evening, and then night fell, I wondered if I messed up with the timing. Guess I thought too much of myself and my house. Maybe my enemies were coming, but they might not be in such a hurry after all.

Truth be told, I was already getting hungry anyway, and had run out of the supplies I brought with me. I was too bored, and just ate for the hell of it. Plus, I had Caramel here. And Shnoop had somehow managed to get his grubby face into my bag of chips.

* * *

The Galaxius Manor
Lake Baikal

Pops carefully climbed out of the top hatch, sat down on the armored vehicle roof and brought his binoculars to his eyes. Peace and silence reigned around him, violated only by his elite squad.

"All clear, climb out," he said, rapping the grip of his pistol against the armor of his beloved 'Swallow.'

The written-off Dogfish-class APC had come by happy chance into the hands of the commander of King's assault team, Semyon Semyonych Bordunkov, known in the criminal underworld by his nickname, Pops. He had even gone to his master and asked him for a small loan so he could afford to buy the toy.

The normally tight-fisted Ivan Ivanovich gave the man the money this time, reasoning sensibly that it wasn't a bad idea to add to his own car fleet using his underling's money. And Pops blew off every mote of dust that landed on the thing. He overhauled the whole engine and suspension by hand, swapped out all the worn parts, modernized it and even repainted it. You'd never know to look at the imposing vehicle that it was already over thirty years old.

His assistant climbed out of the hatch beside him. The other crew members followed.

"There's one thing I don't get, Pops. Why couldn't we just throw some green at the army? We could have had them bring four SPGs here and blow that manor to hell."

"Are you a moron, Chubs?" The head enforcer of the largest criminal gang of Irkutsk looked glanced sidelong at his assistant. "King said we have to be as careful as possible with the manor. He'll make us account for every broken window."

"Broken window? What, so no grenades, even?"

"What do you think, idiot? Of course not!"

Chubs took out his binoculars and looked

through them.

"Well, all looks quiet. Can't tell who's inside."

"According to our data, only the baron."

"What, he's alone in there?" Chubs frowned mistrustfully.

"So it seems."

"My ass, boss. From what I've seen and heard, he ain't no dumbass."

"Listen, you! What do you think, is King a dumbass?"

"No, of course not! I didn't say that!" His deputy raised his hands, looking scared.

"Well, there you go, he knows better than you what to do! Listen up." He raised his voice. "We go inside, clear the place, load up everything valuable into the cars, then get the hell out of dodge."

"Pops!" Chubs shouted to him, still on top of the car.

"What's up?"

"I just saw some kind of animal on the steps. Huh, no. Guess I just imagined it."

"You need to drink less," Bordunkov said with a grin. "Come on, boys, move out!"

* * *

It all started at night, which I was happy for, actually — it meant I wasn't wrong, and there'd be some prey after all. And I also hoped there'd be some fun.

True, I had my suspicions that my house wouldn't survive it. For that very reason I met our guests in the woods outside the manor instead.

I sent Shnoop out to spy on them right away, since I couldn't really see what was going on myself. I really missed my old Eagle Eye seal, and I never was any good at casting it separately. Yes, there are such spells, but they're hard to master without a hundred years of experience. A seal I could make, but I couldn't keep casting the single-use version over and over. I remembered cases when I'd tried the technique, and then walked around for a whole day blind.

The more Shnoop showed me, the lower my jaw dropped. And that was putting it mildly. Twenty cars? Really? Just for little old me, all alone. And so many people started to pour out of them. They must have brought eighty men!

True, it wasn't like they were all seasoned professionals. And the cars were ordinary civilian models too. Just one military vehicle. I hoped to God it didn't open fire with its twin machine guns on the house. If it did, I'd shove them up the gunner's... Well, he'd find out where.

I thought there was nothing that could surprise me, but these guys managed it. Four semi trucks started to drive up to the house at once, and now my eye started twitching.

Where was I going to bury all these people? If there were more of them in the trucks, then this wasn't funny anymore.

It turned out they were empty, just transport for an ordinary robbery. Eighty people just to rob an old abandoned manor? That was weird.

Oh, there were four snipers at once headed in my direction, probably looking for good positions. Holy shit! They even brought their own air support.

Caramel yawned louder than usual, but then got a warning look from me and quietened down.

I had my armor up and my throwing knives on me, along with the remainder of the kunai that I'd brought back from the Empire of the Rising Sun. I was ready for battle, and now all I had to do was figure out how best to start it.

All my foes carried firearms. Apart from that, at least a quarter of them were Gifted.

* * *

The Androsov Manor
Irkutsk

"Master, I have information for you!" young Androsov's senior guardsman said, walking into his office.

Andrei was sitting and poring over a clan book on Rift beasts with healing properties. He was already feeling shitty, but by the face of his guardsman he could already see that the news was bad.

"Let me guess," he said, rubbing his temples. "My father has come up with something else?"

"No," the guardsman said with a shake of his head.

"My sister?" That wasn't uncommon either.

She had the kind of personality that often got her into trouble.

"Long way off!" The man let a smile touch the edge of his lips.

Androsov thought for a moment. Since he didn't spit it all out at once, that meant it wasn't a catastrophe.

So what could it be, for him to come and say it personally?

He didn't have to think for long. As soon as he remembered his friend he got a look on his face like he'd just fallen into a cold pool. He jumped to his feet.

"Galaxius!" he said, definitely a statement and not a question.

"Right," the man said with a nod.

"Dead?!" the count asked, then smiled crookedly, realizing that was the most terrible option and therefore the least likely.

"Not yet, but can't say either way," the guardsman said honestly. "According to our information he's alone in his manor, and right now there's a convoy of a certain crime lord's cars speeding towards him."

Androsov pursed his lips in thought, then grabbed his phone. After two dozen rings without an answer, he called Anna and asked her how things were going. She confirmed to him that the stubborn bastard had gone there on his own, in the hope that he'd be attacked and gain some riches.

"Idiot!" Androsov cursed.

"Sorry?" The head of his personal guard looked confused.

"Not you. Galaxius is an idiot!" He rapped his fingers nervously on the table. "Right," the heir to the Androsovs said firmly after a moment's thought. "Assemble my guard! We're heading there! Full combat gear!"

"Got it," was all the guardsman said, turning on his heel to carry out the order.

Sure, he might have said that it wasn't their business, that there might even be consequences for the family. But who was he to argue with the son of Prince Androsov?

* * *

Snipers! Men who like to sit as far away as possible and deal death so fast that you don't even get to know what killed you. But today was not their day. I killed them so fast that they barely had time to be afraid, let alone angry. All they could do was die. All I had to do was creep up unnoticed and deliver a couple of rapid attacks with my energy-charged sword. That's where the easy part ended. From there on I had to actually think, to avoid putting myself at risk. I could just attack them head on, sure, but I had no desire to take any risks.

Caramel was walking around on her own, searching out her own victims.

The honey eater watched through a window, whipping its tail back and forth, ready to welcome the guests when they came in.

And they would. The assault group spread out through the grounds of my manor. They seemed afraid that something bad was about to happen, and didn't relax even for a moment.

Only the men in the trucks didn't seem to give a damn. They just sat there smoking.

Time went on, nothing happened and I started to get bored. I decided to add some action. Creating a lightning bolt, I filled it to the maximum with as much power as my low-level magic skills could muster, and fired it at a group of three men with no armor or other protection.

BOOM!

I heard a deafening explosion. My lightning bolt landed where I wanted — right between the people and the earth, hitting them only slightly. You don't always have to kill your enemies. A wounded man causes far more trouble for his comrades than a dead one.

The shooting started. Only not towards me. Someone pointed at some bushes I might have been sitting in, and the whole bunch of them fired at it. True, they didn't keep going for long.

"Find him!" Wait, they wanted to find me? Weren't they afraid I'd come find them?

Although, why would I bother doing it myself?

I created ten wolf illusions and sent souls into them.

The wolves sat to attention and patiently waited for my orders. But Caramel ran over to check what was going on. She ran slowly by the wolves, her head proudly raised, showing with a disdainful luck that she was the boss around here.

Now this was getting more interesting. They didn't give a damn about the lightning bolt, or the fact that I was near them. They just kept moving purposefully further toward my residence, and that started to get on my nerves.

There were dozens of them, and I couldn't be sure that the weakened honey badger could handle them all. What if they tore down my house? Or got so well dug in that it'd take me a week to dig them out again?

Enough! If they didn't come to me, I'd go to them!

I made a grand entrance, of course! Sword in hand, huge angel wings burning with fire on my back. The wings were an illusion, but the point was to draw the attention of every single person there.

"Why'd you bring so few people?" I shouted, loudly enough for them all to hear me. "Do you think I'm an easy mark?"

I stepped out of the woods, my figure now clearly visible.

They all saw me. And sent all manner of spells flying straight at me. Most I took on my armor, the rest I just dodged, running back and forth.

I didn't rush to run at those shooting at me. On the contrary, when the shooting stopped, I stood up straight in a proud posture and showed them what I thought with a gesture of my finger.

I love trolling people! More and more of them

ran toward me. And that was just what I wanted. That said, they didn't all act so directly. There were some who tried to surround me, or move undetected from cover to cover.

Roughly speaking, they were trying to encircle me so I couldn't escape into the woods. Shnoop showed me all of them. And I had Caramel and the wolves waiting in the woods.

The toughest opponents were two Gifted whose rank I couldn't tell at a glance. Somewhere around Veteran, but no way to be sure. They moved with power-strengthened speed and attacked me at once.

And that actually helped me. The enemies instantly stopped firing, afraid to hit their own. They didn't know yet that my flank was covered. Well, three of them already knew... but couldn't tell the others. Too busy being eaten by wolves.

Now shooting and the flashes of techniques began all around me. A few of them hesitated in the hope of figuring out what was going on. They were probably getting all kinds of information through their ear pieces, and now they had to figure out how to regroup.

Poor guys... I'll find a place under the ground for all of you! I won't leave a single one of you alive to tell anyone about those wolves.

While I fought off the two Gifted, I looked over the battlefield and didn't strain myself too much. I just stayed on the defensive, although I could have killed them four times over already. One was a very green young man who should have had a rake in his hands, not a sword. He was holding that thing like it was a saber, damn it.

I couldn't help it. I swung my sword and cut off his hand, then delivered a lightly powered stab into his liver. His armor collapsed in just one hit.

"How did you..." was all his comrade uttered, who didn't like what I'd done.

Damn, now this one was going to go nuts and start pressing harder. He'd find a second wind and fly at me in a furious and righteous rage, so just in case... I summoned an armadillo illusion and sent it right at him to distract his attention. It worked!

Of course, I could have killed him even without that, but this way was more fun.

Right, time for more action. I ran into the woods, where the battle was in full swing. Caramel had already gotten tired of killing them, there were so many.

It took me thirty seconds to create dozens of illusions of Hunters from my past world. Thank the gods and the Code that I didn't have their souls, and they were just simple illusions. Armed and fearsome illusions.

They added another ounce of confusion to the battle and turned it into total chaos, which was just what I wanted. I ran toward them.

Now my work was really cut out for me. I charged my body to the limit with energy, which gave me power and speed. Then I jumped from one to another, killing them, and even then their numbers dropped slowly.

A couple of them even made it into the house and died there, although the honey badger died too. True, it was already staring out the window again and waiting for more victims. An immortal warrior that I didn't even really want to tame. Every incarnation like that one demanded a lot of energy. For now the artifact was paying for it, but later I'd be footing the bill.

For a moment I smiled as I imagined the sight of the dumb honey badger dying all over the place and me sitting there swearing and reviving it over and over again. Nice joke. I'd have to make an anecdote about it.

Minus a head! Look at that! One of the assholes decided to sneak up on me and stab me with a spear. When his dead body fell, I jumped up to it and picked up the spear, then threw it at the nearest machine gunner, who turned out to be a good shot, the bastard, having already dropped my armor by thirty percent. Not all their men were cross-eyed.

Whoa, what was that noise..? With no clue what was happening, I span around, and just in time. The next moment, a military armored car came slamming into me, the one the leader of the group was riding in.

Ugh! Turns out I could fly beautifully.

"Wowwweee, cool!" Shnoop said, appearing beside me in an instant and widening his eyes as we flew.

I landed on both feet and felt an urge to hit that car with something or ask Shnoop to throw something into it. Only — the ride was almost mine already, so why ruin it? After all, hit it hard enough and what would be left inside? Right — corpses! And anyway, it turned out to be harder than I thought.

There happened to be a strong Gifted inside, who waiting specially to catch me while I took a breather. And I didn't see it coming. Through some miracle, he managed to create an icicle that was so huge and powerful that I barely managed to dodge it. The other ten smaller ones I didn't manage to dodge at all. Sure, I parried them with Aquila, but there were other people too. I had to retreat deeper into the forest, waiting for the enemy to reach me.

And he seemed in no hurry. He walked in a stately fashion, like a king, hands in his pockets. Had he come for a battle, or a stroll? He wasn't paying any attention even to my illusions. Unfortunately for him.

I created a snake and stuck a soul into it. It crawled up to him and attacked, and he just laughed at it.

And then I launched an icicle of my own at him. That surprised him. First his armor fell completely, and second — he thought I was a universal. But he was even more surprised when the snake bit him in the face and filled it with venom.

Some others saw that, and now they started to attack every illusion as it appeared, not knowing which were real and which fake.

Oh, now this I didn't like. Shnoop showed me the leader, who was currently trying to control shaking hands to dial a number on his phone.

The very same phone that appeared in my own hand a second later.

"I do goooood job?!" Shnoop hopped up and down on my head after his successful theft.

"Great job!" I praised him.

Everyone likes to be praised.

"Damn, don't you think you got something confused?!" The corpse of a squirrel hung from Caramel's mouth, and now she was playing with it happily. "We're at war here, and she... Ugh, chic-... women," I said, sighing heavily.

Oh! New victims! I mean, ahem. I had some new problems. I had missed someone with a phone after all, and they'd already managed to report how badly they were getting their asses handed to them.

At least thirty cars were barreling down the road toward us. Only this time they were different, but I couldn't see exactly how yet, so I sent Shnoop to get a closer look.

Damn. It was Androsov.

Who the hell ratted me out? How did he find out? And most importantly — why the hell was he headed here to ruin everything personally?

He just couldn't let me have any fun. And now I watched as his people started to jump straight into the battle, and very soon there was nobody left for me to fight. Just a few runaways who decided to get out while they could. As it happened, they put down that strong guy too, and I'd wanted to do that myself. What a shame.

All that was left was to sigh heavily and order my wolves to chase down the runaways. I'd already said that none of them would survive. Maybe I'd wanted to take a prisoner before, but not anymore. After all, there was the risk that Androsov might hear or see something that he didn't need to know yet.

The entire slaughter ended in less than half an hour.

"YOU'RE ALIVE!" Andrei shouted at the sight of me, and rushed up to look me over.

"What, you think they could have done anything to me?" I chuckled self-confidently.

"Looked like there were quite a lot of them here," he noted.

For the next ten minutes, I listened to Androsov lecturing me on my carelessness. Seemed to me he was just mad I didn't ask him for help. But only a little mad, knowing that his status prevented him from doing many things that I could do easily.

"I'd invite you inside, but it's... messy." I said with a vague wave. "Let's go take a seat in that summerhouse, no need to stand around."

He agreed, but only after checking me for wounds. Said he didn't want me to die while we talked. I was fine, not a scratch on me, just didn't have much energy left.

While his people followed his orders to gather all the bodies into a pile, some bad news came in.

Always how it goes. That's why you don't stick your nose in other people's business.

It turned out there had been an aristocrat among the attackers, and Androsov's people had smoked him. We went to see who it was. The aristo turned out to be that guy I wanted to kill. The only powerful Gifted among them.

Truth be told, they'd sent me garbage again. Trying to drown me in numbers, I guess. Or maybe they thought I wouldn't be at home?

Whatever. Back to the dead aristocrat.

"Goddamn..." Androsov groaned. "The Verbitsky family."

"Great." I nodded to him indifferently. "Should I expect a complaint from them, a declaration of war, what..?"

"Not you." I tensed at that. "Since it was my people who killed him, this is a little more complicated."

"Well, when has anything been simple in our lives?" I wanted to say more, but cut myself off in time. Our lives were different.

"The Verbitskys are a princely family," he said by way of clarification when he realized I didn't understand the full tragedy of the situation. "And worst of all, we've been at loggerheads with them for years. An old story, when they wanted a wife with a Healer's Gift for a man of their family. Would have been fine, but the groom was a total asshole, and they got a refusal."

"So what happens now?" Androsov looked seriously upset.

Seemed like it was his own fault, but the problem was that he'd wanted to help me, and had been acting with good intentions. Damn it.

"Lawsuit? Duel? War? Choose the option you like the most." Andrei smiled sadly.

I thought for a moment.

And, after a glance at Androsov's serious face, decided to think a little more.

As it happens, he didn't once say that he was sorry he came. I don't think he even considered that for a second.

"Maybe we could just bury him? Make like he was never even here?" Bury him... That was my nice way of putting it. I'd feed him to a slime and that'd be that.

"That's not how this works," he said, cutting me off. "I assure you, everybody will know by tomorrow. We need to send a message to them first, and advance our own complaint against them. But what complaint?"

"Are you going to get it in the neck from your dad?"

"I don't even know. On the one hand, he doesn't like them either, and has nearly come to blows with them before. On the other hand, this isn't a good enough reason to go to war."

I went back to mulling the matter over, and it occurred to me that I could use Anna's help.

"Alright, how about this?" I thought I'd found the best option. "Decide for yourself what to do, and lump it all on me. I was the defending side, after all. Say that I asked your help for a very important favor. Family business, that kind of thing."

He seemed to like my idea a little, but not a lot.

A long silence, then he said: "There is one option. But you might not like it."

Judging by the look on his face, I figured it couldn't be anything terrible, or else why would he be smiling?

"Just do it!" I said with a shrug. "The last thing I need is to spark a war between two royal Families."

"Are you sure?"

"Yep!" I answered calmly, wondering to myself how much could be looted from that other family if there was a war. Shame when only poor people do the attacking. It was enough to compare the cars that Androsov's guard rolled up in with the ones those pathetic attackers used.

Androsov took out his phone and called his father. I listened with concern, but couldn't seem to hear any shouting yet. He described the situation to him in a few words, then asked him to connect him to the head of the Verbitsky Family. He said he knew what to do.

Hmm. Such faith in his son. The father didn't doubt him for a second, doing what he asked at once. Trust was high in their family!

"Gennady Pavlovich?" Androsov began in a serious, even aggressive tone. "I, Andrei Androsov, wish to officially declare to you that you have gone too far this time." Did he really know what he was doing? "Your kinsman got himself killed by my people tonight. And you won't be getting away with this easily. My father will be contacting you soon, and you and he will discuss the details."

They spoke for ten more minutes, and I have to say, I felt proud of my friend. He should have been a poker player — he was a natural bluffer.

"The REASON?!" Androsov allowed himself to raise his voice. "You think I can stay on the sidelines when my sister's fiancé is under attack?!"

If I had been drinking something at that moment, I would have choked on it. Did he say his sister's fiancé? *Oh, no, you didn't..!*

"Andy!" I said, tearing myself from my seat. "I take back what I said about doing whatever you want!" I whispered to him loudly, nearly right in his ear. "I was hoping for a declaration of war, not that!"

Androsov chuckled, and I realized that this was exactly the outcome he wanted.

END OF BOOK THREE

Want to be the first to know about our latest LitRPG, sci fi and fantasy titles from your favorite authors?

Subscribe to our **New Releases** newsletter:
http://eepurl.com/b7niIL

Thank you for reading *The Hunter's Code!*

If you like what you've read, check out other sci-fi, fantasy and LitRPG novels published by Magic Dome Books:

NEW RELEASES!

Crossroads of Oblivion
a portal progression fantasy adventure series
by Dem Mikhailov

Gakko Academy
a portal progression fantasy adventure series
by Evgeny Alexeev

War Eternal
a military space adventure LitRPG series
by Yuri Vinokuroff

The Hunter's Code
a LitRPG series by Yuri Vinokuroff & Oleg Sapphire

I Will Be Emperor
a space adventure progression fantasy series
by Yuri Vinokuroff & Oleg Sapphire

An Ideal World for a Sociopath
a LitRPG series by Oleg Sapphire

The Healer's Way
a LitRPG series by Oleg Sapphire & Alexey Kovtunov

A Shelter in Spacetime
a LitRPG series by Dmitry Dornichev

Kill or Die
a LitRPG series by Alex Toxic

Living Ice
a portal progression alternative history series
by Dmitry Sheleg

The Bard from Barliona
a LitRPG series
by Eugenia Dmitrieva and Vasily Mahanenko

Condemned
(Lord Valevsky: Last of The Line)
a Progression Fantasy series
by Vasily Mahanenko

Loner
a LitRPG series by Alex Kosh

A Buccaneer's Due
a LitRPG series by Igor Knox

A Student Wants to Live
a LitRPG series by Boris Romanovsky

The Goldenblood Heir
a LitRPG series by Boris Romanovsky

Level Up
a LitRPG series by Dan Sugralinov

Level Up: The Knockout
a LitRPG series by Dan Sugralinov and Max Lagno

Adam Online
a LitRPG Series by Max Lagno

World 99
a LitRPG series by Dan Sugralinov

Disgardium
a LitRPG series by Dan Sugralinov

Nullform
a RealRPG Series by Dem Mikhailov

Clan Dominance: The Sleepless Ones
a LitRPG series by Dem Mikhailov

Moskau
a dystopian thriller by G. Zotov

El Diablo
a supernatural thriller by G.Zotov

Mirror World
a LitRPG series by Alexey Osadchuk

Underdog
a LitRPG series by Alexey Osadchuk

Last Life
a Progression Fantasy series by Alexey Osadchuk

Alpha Rome
a LitRPG series by Ros Per

An NPC's Path
a LitRPG series by Pavel Kornev

Fantasia
a LitRPG series by Simon Vale

The Sublime Electricity
a steampunk series by Pavel Kornev

Small Unit Tactics
a LitRPG series by Alexander Romanov

Black Centurion
a LitRPG standalone by Alexander Romanov

Rorkh
A LitRPG Series by Vova Bo

Thunder Rumbles Twice
A Wuxia Series by V. Kriptonov & M. Bachurova

Citadel World
a sci fi series by Kir Lukovkin

In order to have new books of the series translated faster, we need your help and support! Please consider leaving a review or spread the word by recommending *The Hunter's Code* to your friends and posting the link on social media. The more people buy the book, the sooner we'll be able to make new translations available.

Thank you!

Till next time!

Made in United States
Troutdale, OR
03/28/2024

18796177R00219